# Crosscurrents / Modern Critiques Third Series

## Edited by Jerome Klinkowitz

# Naomi Jacobs

# The Character of Truth

## Historical Figures in Contemporary Fiction

Southern Illinois University Press
CARBONDALE AND EDWARDSVILLE

Printed in the United States of America
Edited by Susan Thornton
Designed by Design for Publishing, Inc.
Production supervised by Linda Jorgensen-Buhman

93   92   91   90      4   3   2   1

**Library of Congress Cataloging-in-Publication Data**

Jacobs, Naomi, 1953–
    The character of truth: historical figures in contemporary
fiction / Naomi Jacobs.
        p.        cm.—(Crosscurrents/modern critiques. Third series )
    Includes bibliographical references.
    1. Fiction—20th century—History and criticism. 2. Historical
fiction—History and criticism. 3. Characters and characteristics
in literature. 4. Literature and history. I. Title. II. Series.
PN3335.J27   1990
809.3′044—dc20                                                          89-39329
    ISBN 0-8093-1607-2                                                  CIP

    "The Photograph Becomes a Mirror: *Coming Through Slaughter*" in
chapter 2 first appeared in *Studies in Canadian Literature* 11.1 (1986): 2–18.
Reprinted with permission.
    Portions of chapter 4 were first published in *Science-Fiction Studies* 14.2
(1987): 230–40. Reprinted with permission.
    "Kathy Acker's Plagiarized Self" in chapter 4 first appeared in *Review of
Contemporary Fiction* fall 1989. Reprinted with permission.
    Portions of chapter 5 were first published in *Missouri Review* 8.2 (1985):
164–178. Reprinted with permission.

    The paper used in this publication meets the minimum requirements of
American National Standard for Information Sciences—Permanence of
Paper for Printed Library Materials, ANSI Z39.48-1984. ∞

*for Alfred and Christabel Jacobs*

# Contents

# Crosscurrents/
# Modern Critiques/
# Third Series

I N THE EARLY 1960s, when the Crosscurrents / Modern
Critiques series was developed by Harry T. Moore, the
contemporary period was still a controversial one for scholarship. Even today the elusive sense of the present dares critics
to rise above mere impressionism and to approach their subject with the same rigors of discipline expected in more traditional areas of study. As the first two series of Crosscurrents
books demonstrated, critiquing contemporary culture often
means that the writer must be historian, philosopher, sociolo-
gist, and bibliographer as well as literary critic, for in many
cases these essential preliminary tasks are yet undone.

To the challenges that faced the initial Crosscurrents project
have been added those unique to the past two decades: the
disruption of conventional techniques by the great surge in
innovative writing in the American 1960s just when social and
political conditions were being radically transformed, the new
worldwide interest in the Magic Realism of South American
novelists, the startling experiments of textual and aural poetry
from Europe, the emergence of Third World authors, the

rising cause of feminism in life and literature, and, most dramatically, the introduction of Continental theory into the previously staid world of Anglo-American literary scholarship. These transformations demand that many traditional treatments be rethought, and part of the new responsibility for Crosscurrents will be to provide such studies.

Contributions to Crosscurrents / Modern Critiques / Third Series will be distinguished by their fresh approaches to established topics and by their opening up of new territories for discourse. When a single author is studied, we hope to present the first book on his or her work or to explore a previously untreated aspect based on new research. Writers who have been critiqued well elsewhere will be studied in comparison with lesser-known figures, sometimes from other cultures, in an effort to broaden our base of understanding. Critical and theoretical works by leading novelists, poets, and dramatists will have a home in Crosscurrents / Modern Critiques / Third Series, as will sampler-introductions to the best in new Americanist criticism written abroad.

The excitement of contemporary studies is that all of its critical practitioners and most of their subjects are alive and working at the same time. One work influences another, bringing to the field a spirit of competition and cooperation that reaches an intensity rarely found in other disciplines. Above all, this third series of Crosscurrents / Modern Critiques will be collegial—a mutual interest in the present moment that can be shared by writer, subject, and reader alike.

Jerome Klinkowitz

# Acknowledgments

A NUMBER OF people and institutions have helped this project come to fruition. At the University of Missouri, Bill Holtz and Speer Morgan deserve special thanks. At the University of Maine, the English Department provided release time as well as less formal kinds of support. Chairs Paul Bauschatz, Burt Hatlen and Pat Burnes were particularly encouraging; I am grateful for their enthusiasm and faith. Many thanks to Marilyn Emerick for her invaluable clerical rescue service; to Paul Grosswiler for his comments on an early version of the manuscript; and to Gertrudes Link and Karl Albrecht, who provided coffee, kuchen, and a room of my own in Germany.

The Women in the Curriculum Program at the University of Maine funded research on Aphra Behn and Kathy Acker. I appreciate the cooperation of those journals where portions of this work first appeared: *The Missouri Review, Studies in Canadian Literature, Science-Fiction Studies,* and *Review of Contemporary Fiction.* At Southern Illinois University Press, Robert Phillips and Jerome Klinkowitz gave valuable advice in the early stages, Susan Thornton provided attentive copyediting, and Susan Wilson efficiently shepherded the manuscript through editing, her graciousness seemingly unflagging despite the vagaries of my itinerary.

Finally, and most of all, I thank Scott Ruffner, whose energy, imagination, and wit have taught me more than I can say.

# Introduction

THERE IS A new cast of characters in fiction these days. No longer are we surprised to see a fictional protagonist chatting with some famous politician, punching out a well-known evangelist, or making love to our favorite newscaster. No longer do publishers puff, "Never before!" or serious critics raise eyebrows when a novel intimately details the life and death of Che Guevara, two crucial years in Eleanor Roosevelt's development, or the psychology of Flaubert. William Styron's *The Confessions of Nat Turner* was one of the first such works to receive critical acclaim; he would use the device once again in *Sophie's Choice*, in which the concentration camp commandant Rudolf Hess figures prominently. Anne Frank may or may not appear in Philip Roth's *The Ghost Writer*. E. L. Doctorow's *Ragtime* featured Harry Houdini, Emma Goldman, Henry Ford, and Evelyn Nesbit. William Burroughs has cut up Dutch Schultz; Kurt Vonnegut's *Mother Night* demystifies a spectrum of Nazi luminaries; T. Coraghessan Boyle follows Mungo Park into the Congo; the Pulitzer recipient William Kennedy explores the moral and cultural significance of Legs Diamond. The phenomenon has permeated short fiction as well, with Donald Barthelme's describing "Robert Kennedy Saved from Drowning," Barry Lopez's analyzing the mystique of Jerzy Kosinski, and Judy Lopatin's following the Raymond Radiguet-Jean Cocteau love affair. Nor is it confined to American writers, though the scope of this study does not include the many fine European and third world novels in this mode, such as Anthony Burgess's *Napoleon Symphony* (1974) and *Abba Abba* (1977), Christa Wolf's *Cassandra* (1983), or Carlos Fuentes's *The Old Gringo* (1986). After centuries of exile, the historical figure has returned to serious fiction.

Contemporary fictional practice is here distinctly at odds with the canon of literary realism, though hardly with the history of narrative or early instances of novel-like narratives in English, in which historical figures were common. Under realism, which assumed that historical materials and characters must be treated with objectivity and accuracy, such figures have been regarded as presenting formidable aesthetic or creative difficulties. But with the weakening of the hegemony of realism in the twentieth century, brought about in part by challenges to the concept of objective representation, writers have increasingly come to believe that whatever problems have been felt in the past evaporate along with the epistemological presuppositions of realism. The writers of these pseudohistorical and antihistorical fictions have been directly and indirectly influenced by theories of history, character, and language that question the existence and even the desirability of factual truth, unified identity, and aesthetic perfection. Freed from the constraints that had limited the use of historical figures under the reign of realism, contemporary writers are using such figures with increasing frequency to serve a variety of fictional aims.

My subject here is not the nonfiction novel or the traditional varieties of what Mas'ud Zavarzadeh has termed the "fact novel": the historical novel, biographical novel, and roman à clef in the realist mode. Such novels are based on an essentially conservative, respectful approach to historical figures and history itself. Zavarzadeh describes their use of facts as "comprehensional" (64): the author, assuming that facts are the primary source of knowledge, searches for facts and seeks to comprehend their meaning. The biographical novelist collects and interprets facts of personal history, the historical novelist facts of social history, the romancier à clef the "real facts" behind the official facts of public lives. Yet all aim to remain faithful to the facts and hesitate to trust more intuitive forms of knowledge; they assume that "fact" is a valid category of knowledge, that facts have discernible meanings, and that the more facts one has, the more valuable one's interpretation of a given historical situation or individual is likely to be. The underlying belief is that historical reality is "knowable, coherent, significant, and inherently moving" (Foley 96), and that history must always take precedence over fiction when the two conflict.

Nonfiction novels differ from these "fact novels" only in that their writers aspire to record without interpreting, to use facts "phenomenalistically" in the construction of an individual, localized version of history rather than a national or epochal one (Zavarzadeh). But the goal is still accurate representation, if not of what really happened, at least of what the writer genuinely believes happened. Norman Mailer, for example, offered *The Armies of the Night* as a completion of history, taking over at "precisely the point where . . . the historian in pursuing the experience would be obliged to quit the clearly demarcated limits of historical inquiry" (255). Yet even while recognizing that all histories are "unfair" (262) and undependable in details, he presents his novel as an accurate historical record of what the March on the Pentagon was like—for him. Similarly, he terms his later *Executioner's Song* a "true life novel," a "factual account" of the Gary Gilmore story. As a journalist, Tom Wolfe maintained a similar purity of intention; for all the audacity of his methods, he has said that he does not claim the "right to make up anything. I think it kind of kills the whole thing. . . . Because part of the impact is the fact that you're telling the reader *this happened.* . . . This is not fiction." As for his practice of inventing interior monologues from the point of view of a subject who might "scream bloody murder" at the portrait, Wolfe justified such hypothetical characterization on the grounds that he felt he was "doing it accurately" (96). Like the fact novels, nonfiction novels are restrained by a "commitment to the facts" in both characterization and plotting (Weber 45).

By contrast, the uses of historical figures in recent decades are often neither factually based nor historically justifiable. These books sometimes have the flavor of a roman à clef but cannot accurately be described as such, for the fun of a roman à clef is in being given a key that opens doors on a world we usually may observe only through the keyhole, doors that politeness or official secrecy keeps closed. The works I will examine lack both keys and locks; they offer no real access to the private rooms of the famous people they portray, for their characterizations are so fantastic or so intimately detailed that no sensible reader can accept them as direct accounts of literal reality. Instead of conveying the pill of historical fact in a sugar coating of fiction, such writers openly ignore, revise, or contradict accepted facts; instead of simply filling in the gaps in the historical record—coloring in the rigid outline of a historical persona—they may transform the persona into a three-dimensional sculpture or, alternately, exaggerate and exploit its cartoon qualities. They offer not a rational recon-struction or re-creation of history but a new creation in which historical figures may, like any other fictional material, be altered to suit the purposes of the work.

Underlying this new sense of the plasticity of historical fig-ures is the view that identity and what we call "reality" are no less constructs of language than are the most fantastic fictions. These writers would argue that it is impossible to distinguish, on linguistic grounds, historical or biographical facts from fictional "factoids": those invented or selected details of envi-

ronment, chronology, and thought that give fictional characters fullness and plausibility. To the extent that we have seen
history as defined by factual research, the equal treatment of
verifiable facts and created factoids represents a challenge to
our concepts of history and truth. And to the extent that we
have seen character as fixed, documentable, and empirically
knowable, such empirical skepticism equally challenges our
concepts of identity and, ultimately, of the necessity of historical accuracy in the representation of historical figures. If there
is no "real person"—if the public persona is itself a fiction, not
an objective representation of a coherent individual—then
fiction writers can freely improvise upon or reinvent the
"facts" of a person's life.

These writers feel no obligation to the factual record about
a historical figure, for they see facts as dead until transformed
by imagination. Of his "research" for *Ragtime,* for instance,
Doctorow has said, "Certain details were so delicious that I
was scrupulous about getting them right. Others demanded
to be changed, people's lives demanded to be mythologized"
(Clemons 76). Insufficiently "delicious" facts "demand" to be
changed: what statement could indicate more astonishingly
the demotion of factual truth in this revised epistemological
hierarchy? Fiction is now seen as providing a special kind
of truth that may actually be obscured by facts. As Ursule
Molinaro's Cassandra says, "I've come as close to the truth as
facts would let me ... facts oppress the truth, which can
breathe freely only in poetry & art" (105, 120). In a similar
vein, Marx comments to Engels in Alan Siegler's *Comrades,*
"exact representations are always fakes" (121). Factual accuracy, it is argued, produces only a shallow realism like that of
the figures in a wax museum, which, though accurate to every
measurement and every mole, are too rigid and static either
to convince or to inform. Mimetic fiction's devotion to the
illusion of reality, which is so easily destroyed by recognizable

inaccuracies, is unnecessary slavery, for "Fiction can't be aware of its own limitation—indeed, it has no limitation—unless it puts itself forward as fact" (Brophy 191).

The reception of these books has sometimes been confused by attempts to judge them on historical grounds, and they have been attacked for the "lies" they perpetrate. But such critiques ignore the authors' foregrounding of the fictional nature of their "histories." Eve Babitz warns that *Slow Days, Fast Company* is "entirely a work of fiction. Names of actual people are used solely as a literary device. . . ." William Bayer insists that his *Visions of Isabelle* is "not a biography. It is a novel, a fantasy, based on the life of Isabel Eberhardt . . . it contains distortions and inventions devised to serve the telling of a story." In Keith Abbott's *Rhino Ritz,* Hemingway, Fitzgerald, Gertrude Stein, and Alice B. Toklas search for Sherwood Anderson, who has been spirited away by the owners of a Japanese amusement park; the preface announces, "All of the characters who are famous and might sue me are dead so they won't. All those not dead are friends, though sometimes their names have been used independently of their actual bodies." That familiar disclaimer "Any resemblance to real people, living or dead, is entirely coincidental" has been replaced by one quite different: "Any resemblance to real people is entirely intentional. Any resemblance to truth is intentionally misleading."

Together with this tendency to foreground and valorize the unique powers of fiction has come a changed characterization of the fictional process. Realist and formalist metaphors of the artist as scientist, as passive soil for the growth of a creative "germ," or as crucible or catalyst for inevitable processes, are being displaced by older, less orderly ones: the artist as medium who contacts the spirits of the dead, as sorcerer who conquers evil spirits by manipulating their images, as alchemist, as magus of a dream world revealing the strange essence of experience. The sense of power with which these writers approach the formerly intractable material of the historical figure is a measure of how much has changed in our views of self, of fiction, and of truth.

The present study is intended less to develop a single thesis about this multifarious phenomenon than to provide a survey of its varieties. I begin with a four-century overview of attitudes toward historical figures in fiction, showing that the seemingly experimental techniques of recent decades resemble common fictional practices of the Renaissance and seventeenth century and indicating the aesthetic and epistemological shifts leading to the exile of historical figures from serious fiction. According to the aesthetic of realism, historical fiction has been seen as presenting nearly insurmountable difficulties to the serious artist. But these difficulties and restrictions are tied to certain assumptions of the modern age: that fiction is (or can be) distinguishable from fact, that documentable subjects should be treated only in objective or factual ways, and that, indeed, rational objectivity is possible. The supposed difficulties are also bound in significant ways, it should be emphasized, to the presence of the historical *figure,* for many writers who object to historical fiction have written about past times without any sense of artistic restriction. It was primarily the conspicuous presence of recognizable historical characters and the events in which they were significant that has been seen as problematic. A look at earlier views of the relationship of character, truth, and art suggests that these objections are relatively new and far from unassailable.

My next three chapters examine the different ways in which historical figures are being used in today's fiction, beginning with relatively realistic treatments and proceeding to those more stylized and fantastic. Chapter 2 considers examples of the *fiction biography:* a focused, fully fictional treatment of a limited period in the life of a single historical figure. The employment of modernist and postmodernist literary techniques overcomes the traditional obligations to completeness and objectivity in biography. A sense of the mystery of identity and the contingency of fact allows the fiction biographers to trust their intuitive sympathy or communion with the subject. Facts here provide only a jumping-off place from which William Styron, Rhoda Lerman, Frederick Buechner, and Michael Ondaatje leap toward a pararational or postrational truth about personalities with whom they have become willingly or unwillingly entangled.

Historical figures are appropriated even more boldly by writers of the satirical, skeptical, really anticharacter fictions that have been called "mockhistorical" or "pseudohistorical," and that I will, for convenience, call *fiction histories* in Chapter 3. Bored with individual psychology and wishing to anatomize the ills of an entire nation, E. L. Doctorow and Ishmael Reed reduce historical figures to simplified types in a satirical exploration of aspects of American culture transcending specific historical contexts. To these writers, historical figures are interesting not as unique, historically significant individuals but as representatives of unchanging patterns of human behavior. Playing on readers' preconceived notions of historical figures, they use inaccuracies, indeterminacies, and anachronisms to collapse history and emphasize similarities between modern times and times past.

By far the most adventuresome uses of historical figures occur in antimimetic *recombinant fiction,* in which characters from myth, popular culture, literature, and history coexist in completely ahistorical fantasias. Reduced to pure personae, the historical figures are important counters in a metafictional game confusing the boundaries between all epistemological categories and forcing readers to recognize their own complicity in the reading process and in the preservation of the myths of power that accumulate around public people. When characters from different levels of "reality" coexist within a single fictional realm, our trust in comfortable epistemological divisions is shaken. Here I will demonstrate the pitfalls and potentials of the recombinant mode in two science fiction series, the Riverworld books of Philip José Farmer and Robert Nichols's *Daily Lives in Nghsi-Altai,* and in the works of the punk novelist Kathy Acker.

However confidently contemporary writers justify their indifference to literal truth, those who treat *living* people may find that the law does not yet share their postmodernist insouciance. My fifth chapter explains the legal principles under which fictional treatments of living people may be ruled libelous. Robert Coover's *The Public Burning,* with its outrageous representations of a fictional character named Richard M. Nixon, demonstrates the extent to which libel law regarding public figures may support writers who argue that celebrity personae are media-created fictions, saturated with ideology, and that a fiction writer's revision or distortion of such personae is a justifiable form of commentary upon public matters and public myths.

The reappearance of historical figures in contemporary fiction is a fascinating symptom of the epistemological and aesthetic upheavals of our time. The technique is far more than a response to the challenge of nonfiction in a time when the daily news is, as Philip Roth noted in one well-known essay, more fantastic than the products of the most fertile imagination. In a variety of literary contexts, the presence of the historical figure signals our questioning of the artificial boundaries between truth and lie, history and fiction, reality and imagination. This presence invites the readers of today's fictions to recognize and accept the daunting and exhilarating knowledge that we can reshape the malleable realities of our dreams, our selves, and our world.

# The Character
# of Truth

# 1

## Precedents

ALL FICTION IS scrap art compiled from old conversations, rumors, memories, and visions, which are cut into patterns and stitched together or simply relabeled like old bottles, retaining their original shapes but wearing new names and containing different potions. From its beginning, the novel has evidenced this acquisitive itch to capture and fix the things of the world, and it has directly claimed a referential truth with lies ranging from the familiar assertion "Only the names have been changed" to the subtler persuasions of recognizable small truths: real cities, streets, and parks; the minutiae of fashion, furniture, card games, slang, and music; and the details of real events. In the earliest English novels, all this baggage of realness included real people, recognizable historical figures, dead and alive, who were treated with full fictional freedom. But when stricter distinctions between fact and fiction developed, such figures were felt to endanger the mimetic illusion and so were exiled from serious fiction. From the Renaissance into our own time, fictional uses of historical figures have reflected changing assumptions about truth, history, character, and the fictional experience.

## The Historical Figure in Renaissance and Elizabethan Fiction

Many Renaissance writers and critics saw historical subjects as entirely suitable to imaginative literature, though they differed over whether treatments of such subjects must remain historically accurate; and here the influence of Aristotelian poetics can be felt. Though some of Aristotle's contemporaries thought a historical plot unimaginative, Aristotle himself cautioned only that events depicted should have the "tragic quality" and should "conform to the law of the probable and possible." He saw no reason why a historical plot centered on historical characters could not show these qualities. His Renaissance followers sometimes extended this view by actually requiring historical materials, at least in the higher genres. Castelvetro's 1590 translation of the *Poetics,* for example, argued that a historical subject is superior to a wholly invented subject, for if poetry is a "likeness of or resemblance to history," it follows that the "plot of tragedy and epic should accept things which have actually happened and which are common to it and to historical truth. For the plot of these two kinds of poetry should include action not simply human but also magnificent and regal." Such plots and characters *must* be tied to history, for "to introduce new names of kings and to attribute to them new actions is to contradict history and fame and to sin against open truth." Castelvetro's argument implied that any changes or additions to history would reduce the reader's belief in the events portrayed.

Perhaps more typical was Boccaccio, who justified even the *inaccurate* use of historical figures, considering it no failing that poetic fiction is most often "quite out of harmony and agreement with the literal truth." Of the anachronistic presence of Dido in Virgil's *Aeneid,* Boccaccio argued that it was necessary "to attain the proper effect." Virgil needed a character worthy to receive Aeneas on the shores of Africa; he chose

Dido because she represented the type of character he sought and because her "execrations at her death" (69) prefigure the Roman conquest of Carthage and glorify Rome. That Dido actually lived several generations after Aeneas, said Boccaccio, was irrelevant to the poetic effect.

Such disregard for factual accuracy reflected the notion that truth is moral and general rather than factual and specific; history is a "cyclical process of rise and fall, with the same human strengths and weaknesses being endlessly rehearsed in different surroundings" (Bannister 91). Historical actors in this cyclical drama are important only as instances of general human types that remain constant throughout time, and thus the verifiable particulars or "facts" of their lives are far less significant than the general patterns they represent. In addition, since the governing criterion of historical truth at this time was the absence of controverting evidence, authors of historical dramas or cautionary biographies such as *A Mirror for Magistrates* (1559) felt free to alter historical fact "with current political situations in mind. It is on the assumption that history repeats itself that political mirrors of history can be used to explain the present" (Campbell 125). Both history and biography were regarded as branches of rhetoric, intended more to persuade than to inform.

When this view that truth transcends the specific facts of any particular historical event came into conflict with a nascent historicism, the result was the mix of fiction and fact in many of our tradition's earliest novel-like narratives, some of which bear a startling resemblance to the anti- or pseudohistorical novels of the 1970s and 1980s. In the preface to *Ciceronis Amor* (1589), Robert Greene stated his intention to "pen downe the loves of *Cicero,* which *Plutarch,* and *Cornelius Nepos,* forgot in their writings." Claiming the power to create memories of what was "forgotten" by Cicero's contemporaries, Greene implies that those histories themselves were imaginative creations that any imaginative writer might attempt to complete. Thomas Lodge combined elements of legend, romance, allegory, and novella in his treatment of another historical figure, *Robert Second Duke of Normandy* (1591). Ballad makers who invented stories about historical subjects were common enough that William Kemp complained of them in his *Nine Days' Wonder* (1600); his targets included Thomas Deloney, a populist and propagandist for the working classes and for the new middle-class pride. Deloney wrote not only ballads but books that we would call novels, using historical figures to establish the plausibility of his stories in *Jack of Newbury* (1597) and *Thomas of Reading* (1599). Indeed, as Lennard Davis has discussed, ballads and novels were so closely related at this time that the term *novel* was at first used interchangeably with *newes, nouvelle,* and *coranto* to describe the news ballads that were the primary form of journalism in the sixteenth century. These ballads, often recounting the story of some famous criminal, consistently claimed to be both "newe" and "trewe," though they generally were clearly neither.

One of the most intriguing of these pseudofactual narratives was Thomas Nashe's *The Unfortunate Traveller* (1594). Nashe's fictional protagonist Jack Wilton is compatriate to and commentator upon a number of recognizable individuals from recent history. As page to Henry Howard, earl of Surrey, Jack follows Henry VIII's war to the continent in 1513; exchanging identities, he and his master chase women and adventure across the continent, encounter the "Pope's whore Juliana" in Italy, are framed and imprisoned for counterfeiting, and are rescued from execution only through the good offices of Henry VIII's representative John Russell. Russell is only one of many historical personages encountered: Jack meets Erasmus and "merry Sir Thomas More" in Rotterdam, for example, and sees Luther debate Carlstadt ("Luther had the loudest voice, Carolostadius went beyond him in beating and bouncing with his fists"). This protonovel is anything but a factually scrupulous "docudrama": Erasmus and More probably never met in Rotterdam, the historical Surrey seems never to have traveled to Italy, and Russell was never in Venice. And Nashe included historical events from as late as 1534 in a memoir supposedly ending in 1520. Promising in his preface that his "phantasticall Treatise" would give only "some reasonable conveyance of historie," Nashe foregoes both the respectability of a true chronicler or historian and the fantastic freedom of the romancer. As Robert Weimann has written, "by tentatively subsuming such historical material under the 'fained Image' of fiction, Nashe could not but make this fiction historical and the history fictional: to interrelate, on highly uneven levels of discourse, the 'phantasticall' and the historiographical, *fabula* and *historia*" (17).

Nashe's intertwining of the two modes produces a peculiar tension that feeds the disturbing power of his narrative, a tension that must have been even more remarkable when the book was published, given the power of the Howard family and their likely objections to such a scurrilous depiction of one of their most admired scions. Even less audacious treatments of important public figures could be dangerous to the writer. In 1596, Deloney's printer was arrested in connection with a ballad portraying Queen Elizabeth as talking with a group of starving workers, taking pity on them, and ordering an end to the famine. The arrest warrant charged that Deloney's ballad "aroused discontent among the poor and showed disrespect for Queen Elizabeth by presenting her as 'speaking with her people dialogue-wise in very fond and indecent sort'" (Ashley and Moseley 313). Though Deloney had intended to praise a monarch who cared for her people, the authorities felt that the queen's power was endangered by any manipulation of her image. Deloney was on safer ground when he depicted Elizabeth's father, Henry VIII, as joking and dining with Jack Winchcombe and his family in *Jack of Newbury;* dead monarchs, it seems, are less vulnerable—or more tolerant—than living ones. Thus few early writers chanced an open portrayal of a living royal figure. But other public figures from history and from contemporary life became even more common in fiction of the next century.

## The Historical Figure in the Seventeenth Century

Like our own time, the seventeenth century was a period in which received truth was severely challenged by cultural, technological, and ideological change; its narrative practice was influenced by "doubts and skepticism about a universe that is no longer certain" (Stephanson 36). On the one hand, Puritan attacks on the value of fiction encouraged the story-teller to seek "a way of making his tale in some sense historical and so acquiring for it the unquestioned praises of history"; on the other hand, non-Puritan aesthetic theory valued the "distinctive poetic function of 'making'" (Nelson 93). Throughout the century, distinctions between fact and fiction seem to have been of minor interest to fiction readers, fiction writers, and the government. Although concepts of factual truth certainly existed and were increasingly of concern to historians, only moralizing critics seemed truly concerned about whether narrative depictions of historical figures were accurate. The result was a heady mix of fiction and history in both serious and popular narrative.

Sir Philip Sidney had written his poetic *Arcadia* (1590) with little reference to contemporary people or events; his niece Lady Mary Wroth would produce *The Countesse of Montgomeries Urania* (1621), a roman à clef of scandals in her own family that were no secret to any member of court society. Historical figures also appeared under an allegorical guise: although names were changed in Sir Percy Herbert's *The Princess Cloria* (1661), which examined the events of 1640 to 1660, the book's frontispiece clearly identified the historical subject as Charles II. Herbert, like other Royalist chroniclers of the Protectorate period, found the allegorical romance an appropriate mode in which to address events that seemed as unbelievable as those in any purely fictional romance. To these writers, neither straight chronicle nor pure allegory was adequate to express their responses to historical events and characters whose philosophical and political reverberations were still being felt. As Herbert wrote in his preface, "the common Occurances of the World, do not arrive always at a pitch high enough for example, or to stir up the appetite of the Reader, which things feigned may do under the notion of a *Romance*" (quoted in Salzman, 157–58). History, even that of regicide and fratricide, must be heightened or stirred up to be effective; romantically named but still-recognizable historical figures, taking part in fictionalized events, allowed the writer to focus and dramatize general issues raised by specific historical events.

English fictional fashions at this time were strongly influenced from abroad; over half the novels published were translations of foreign works, many of which centered more directly on historical figures. Most popular from about 1640 to 1665 were heroic novels such as Madeleine de Scudéry's *Artamène, ou Le Grand Cyrus* (1649–53) and La Calprenède's *Cléopatre* (1652), epic accounts of the grand passions and heroic conflicts of known historical figures. These writers considered a mix of fact and fiction morally superior to either straight chronicle or straight fiction; by serving the goal of *vraisemblance,* the historical figures would contribute to the moral effect of stirring fictional images of noble behavior and notable villainy. Renaissance views of history and character were still current with many readers of the heroic romances, and so it is not surprising that roman à clef elements surfaced, as with de Scudéry's recognizable portraits of contemporaries in *Le Grand Cyrus* and *Clélie* (1654–60). If human qualities and characters repeat themselves endlessly through time, any portrait of a great hero of the ancient world will necessarily suggest a great hero of the contemporary world. In fact, though showing some respect for historical accuracy, these stories reflected the concerns and conversations of the salons of the précieuses more than those of the courts of ancient Persia or Greece; their use of history was essentially decorative and dramatic. Later in the century would appear more accurate works, such as the Abbé de Saint-Real's *Dom Carlos* (1672). Historical love stories would come so much to emphasize history over love that writers "were often writing biography rather than fiction" (Mish 290).

But faked memoirs, histories, and letters, purporting to present the "secret histories" of famous individuals of the past or the present remained vastly popular on both sides of the Channel. In England, the 1660s saw the appearance of "criminal biographies," longer prose versions of the ballad biographies of contemporary highwaymen, con artists, or thieves that had long made up an important component of popular lower-class reading. Though presented as the historical individual's memoirs, they often resembled earlier jest books and rogue pamphlets and frequently reused materials from such works. From this ground would grow Defoe's *Captain Jack* and *Moll Flanders* and Fielding's *Jonathan Wild* in the following century. Offering a more elegant thrill was the *chronique scandaleuse*, an intimate but libelously fictional account of the love affairs of living persons; Bussy-Rabatin's *Histoire amoureuse des Gaules* (1665) provided the model for this subgenre. The French-English cross-fertilization would reach its ultimate expression when a Frenchwoman who had never visited England, Madame d'Aulnoy, detailed the duke of Buckingham's amorous exploits in *Memoirs of the Court of England*.

The extent to which readers of these pseudobiographical novels believed that they were actually reading a famous aristocrat's letters or a first-person account of events at the highest level of society is difficult to determine. Certainly, those able to buy books were well-to-do and relatively well educated, hardly a gullible group. And the claim to historicity—the "editorial" description of how a manuscript or letters had been found or the narrative assurance that a story was entirely true—was a device dating back into the Middle Ages, shopworn enough to be a frequent target of parody (Nelson). It seems likely that most readers maintained a certain skepticism even as they lost themselves in these "historical" or "biographical" tales of passion and scandal. We might call this willingness to enjoy the artificiality of the false history a willingness to suspend *belief;* it created a readership prepared to understand more sophisticated uses of historical figures in the service of epistemological and cultural critiques.

## The Historical Figure and Social Critique

Scandal chronicles, with their casual disregard for literal truth, often capitalized on the worst kind of libelous titillation. In some cases they were intended simply to discredit the writer's political opponents by portraying them in immoral or embarrassing activities. But in the hands of more skilled and ambitious writers, pseudobiographical treatments of recognizable public figures were used to critique official truths or values and even to foreground the arbitrariness of all narrative constructs. These writers played on the literal truth of certain actions and characters in order to compel recognition of the truth of their critiques of the society those characters inhabit.

It would not be extravagant to describe as metafictional the techniques of the French "libertine" novelists, most notably Cyrano and Tristan, whose autobiographical fantasias call into question the very nature of verbal truth. Representing themselves and their friends in wholly invented and sometimes fabulous adventures, they "maintain a distance from the events of their lives that allows them to mingle what actually took place and what they imagine as having taken place . . . so that in the long run all notions of true and false become inoperative. For them, the reality of an event is less important than the presentation of that event as real" (DeJean 41). These freethinkers were extremely alienated from orthodox society; their self-contradictory personal histories as well as their use of intertextual allusion challenged the concept of a "true history" and demonstrated the fictionality of all narrative. Their motivations and tactics anticipated by three hundred years the similarly provocative pseudoautobiographies of Celine, Henry Miller, and recent postmodernists such as Sukenick and Acker.

The aristocratic Madame de La Fayette also challenged official history, if in more subtle ways. A notice on the title page of her first work, *La Princesse de Montpensier* (1662), includes this deceptively modest statement: "The Author having wished, for his own diversion, to write adventures invented for the sheer pleasure of it, felt it would be more fitting [*à propos*] to take names that are known to us from history than to use the names we find in novels, being certain that the reputation of Mme de Montpensier could not be harmed by a story so clearly incredible" (quoted in Guetti 211). Only a few decades after the death of Madame de Montpensier and other historical figures whose families would have been among her prospective readers, La Fayette casually appropriates their names and certain of their circumstances—their public personae, if you will—and plays with them in an openly fictional story of adulterous love. Her reluctance to admit authorship or discuss her techniques has left us with little information as to why precisely she felt it would be "more fitting" to use historical names. But La Fayette's technique is considerably less decorous than the prefatory notice suggests; her use of historical figures is "the very type of forgery which seeks to usurp historical truth, replacing it with a rival, alternative truth" (Guetti 213).

One of few seventeenth-century novels still widely known today, La Fayette's *La Princesse de Clèves* (1678) is another such forgery. Here, the princess's intimate conversations with the queen-dauphine Mary Stuart, her uncle's intrigues with Queen Catherine, and the baroque rivalries between the factions of the queen and of the king's mistress, Diane de Poitiers, provide ironic counterpoint to the exquisitely pure love affair between Madame de Clèves and the Duc de Nemour. The novel was considered "unbelievable," implausible, by its first readers and was also criticized on formal grounds; critics such as Valincour and Bussy-Rabatin reproached La Fayette for having written "a text that was neither entirely a novella nor entirely a romance" and argued that her interpolation of stories about "such figures as Marie Stuart and Anne Boleyn did not seem to fit in" (Lyons 384). But perhaps the real reason for these objections was that La Fayette's subjugation of history to fiction—as when she reschedules the death of Henry II, a major turning point in French history, to coincide with and reinforce her fictional crisis—initiates a radical reassessment of the importance of public and private histories and proclaims that both are linguistic constructs with no necessary relation to truth.

Most successful of the English writers who learned from these French models was Aphra Behn, who wrote two of only six "best-sellers" between 1660 and 1740 (Day 78). One of these, the posthumous *Histories and Novels of Mrs. Behn* (1696), contained her translation of J. B. de Brilhac's *Agnes de Castro*, which recounted King Pedro I of Portugal's love for his wife's lady-in-waiting. The other, her three-part *Love-Letters Between a Nobleman and His Sister* (1683–87), offered a pointed social critique in the guise of a scandal chronicle. It was the first original epistolary novel in English and perhaps also the first full-scale nonfiction novel. Though Behn herself received few profits, the work was remarkably successful in its own time and in the eighty years that followed: it went through at least twelve editions before 1740, was published as a weekly serial in 1735, was versified, and was reprinted in full as late as 1765. Its stylistic model was the famous "Portuguese Letters" or "Five Love-Letters from a Nun to a Cavalier" of 1669, the factual status of which is still a matter of debate.

In the extravagantly emotional *style portugaise*, Behn wrote a series of letters between two prominent lovers whose scandalous affair had become public only a year before her book appeared: the elopement of a notable Whig, the earl Forde Grey, with his wife's younger sister, Lady Henrietta Berkeley, at the same time as he was taking part (it was believed) in the Rye House plot to assassinate Charles II. Part I of the book is a remarkable psychological re-creation of the process by which "Philander" lures his young "Sylvia" away from her parents' home and her "Cruel Honor." The letters between Philander and Sylvia trace in subtle detail the fears, desires, and conflicts of a young woman facing her first lover and the prospect of exile from the security of her family. No literate person in Behn's time could have read these love letters as other than a representation of an actual series of events. Some contemporary readers seem to have accepted the letters themselves as real; in fact, in one early copy of the book, the names of the real-life models are penciled in alongside the romantic aliases (Goreau 276). Part I was received with such enthusiasm that Behn continued with *Love-Letters from a Nobleman to His Sister* (1685) and *The Amours of Philander and Sylvia* (1687); these trace the lovers' flight to the Continent, their growing estrangement, and "Sylvia's" final transformation into an unscrupulous and most politic lover, as well as "Philander's" part in the Duke of Monmouth's rebellion against his uncle, James II.

Far more than just a scandalous potboiler, Behn's accomplished epistolary novel also demonstrates a fascinating use of near-pornographic "history" as a means of commenting on political events, reaching levels of sophistication and intensity in a historical fiction that would hardly be matched until our own century. In the single historical figure of Forde Grey, Behn saw embodied all that she, a passionate Royalist but a radical thinker on many social and sexual issues, detested in her society. And in her account of Grey's intrigues, she fuses predatory Restoration sexuality with political opportunism and cowardice. Through explicit and implicit parallels between the seduction plot and the political plots, she radically revises the equation of politics and sex so common in Restoration poetry. To the Wits' equations of sexual conquest with military glory and sexual failure with treason and shame, Behn opposed an equation of the sexual "triumph" of libertine exploitation with treason, opportunism, and cowardice. For in the long-postponed climax to part I, the night on which Philander finally gains access to Sylvia's bed, he is impotent. The eventual consummation of their passion, by comparison, is anticlimactic. In her mischievous application of the "Incomplete Enjoyment" theme, Behn satirizes the emotional impotence underlying both sexual and political betrayal. The concurrent treacheries of one of the most intriguing rascals of her day offered material for fiction that could not have been surpassed by pure imagination. Understanding the broader significances of Grey's amorous escapades, Behn offered a critique of all of contemporary society through her fictionalization of events and emotions in the lives of public figures. Her exploitation of the mythic dimensions of private lives would be as completely at home in the literary climate of the 1980s as it had been in the 1680s.

## The Historical Figure Under Realism

Despite the ongoing fame of pseudohistorical fictions such as Behn's *Love-Letters* and the later scandal chronicles of Tory opposition during Walpole's time, the eighteenth century saw the gradual disappearance of historical figures in fiction, due to a combination of historiographical, legal, and aesthetic changes. First, the increasing power of rationalist and scientific approaches to knowledge led to more rigorous standards for historical study, established by scholars such as Jean Mabillon, whose *De Re Diplomatica* (1681) set forth principles for the dating and authentication of documents. The extremes of this new "scientific" approach to information can be seen in John Craig's *Rules of Historical Evidence* (1699), which described a historical geometry capable of mathematically calculating the probability of truth by factoring in such figures as the number of witnesses to an event or the distance of the historian in space and time from the initial occurrence. Craig's Proposition XIV, Theorem VI, for instance, postulated, "Historical probability transmitted by one historian, and through only one series of witnesses, although it continually decreases, nevertheless in no given time utterly vanishes." However idiosyncratic, Craig's ambitions reflect a major change in general attitudes toward historical truth. Truth had become time- and place-specific, documentable and quantifiable, rather than cosmic and cyclic: truth had been historicized.

These attitudes were reinforced by government decree in 1704 and after, when all criticism of the government was ruled libelous and the definition of libelous linguistic practices was enlarged to include "encoded" treatments of historical figures such as satire, allegory, and use of nicknames and initials. These rules tended to discourage, if not completely suppress, political pseudohistories of the sort Behn had written. Delariviere Manley was arrested for her attacks on the Whigs in *The New Atalantis* (1714), and Eliza Haywood was threatened with prosecution for her satire on Walpole in *Eovaai, Princess of Ljaveo* (1736). In addition, after a 1724 revision of the Stamp Act, current factual narratives ("news") became taxable, although history and pure fiction remained exempt. Thus, particularly in narratives with contemporary settings, clear dis-

tinctions between fact and fiction became more necessary. To
prevent angering the censors or incurring the tax, novelists
restricted their stories to those with no specific contemporary
reference or political significance; to maintain the appeal of
"newes" that made the new novelistic narratives so popular,
they made unverifiable truth claims about unrecognizable
characters and events. The foreign or classical names that
had sometimes marked historical characters were replaced by
names that could very well be those of some real persons, but
that were too common to be traceable to any particular real
person. Faked memoirs or letters of historical figures were
abandoned for the obviously spurious historicality of "edited"
memoirs or letters. And what had been at first a practical
expedient came to be seen as aesthetic necessity. As Barbara
Foley has said, "realistic verisimilitude, previously a by-prod-
uct of the claim to veracity, became the central determinant
of mimetic conventions" (*Telling the Truth* 119).

Defoe's career well illustrates the gradual clarification of the
boundaries between fiction and history in the prose of the
eighteenth century, and the resultant allocation to each form
of a particular realm of truth. Defoe's first works of popular
narrative were criminal biographies of contemporary figures.
Moving to "purer" fictions late in his life, he claimed that the
first *Adventures of Robinson Crusoe* (1719) were literally true,
but "Crusoe's" preface to his *Further Adventures* claims that the
story is both allegorical and historical. The "editor" of *Moll
Flanders* admits to tampering with the text and asserts only
indirectly that the story is true. By the time of *Roxana,* the
truth claim is clearly false; the author has purportedly based
Roxana's story on the testimony of her first husband, who
leaves her early in the novel and so could not know the intimate
details that follow.

In the early "nonfiction novels," the presence of historical
figures had operated as an implicit truth claim, similar to the
editorial and narrative truth claims that served several uses.

First, the truth claim appeased censors who considered fiction as nothing more than corrupting lies and felt that writers should depict only events supporting religious doctrine. A true story, obviously, was not a lie and presumably would reflect the moral order of God's world. The truth claim could also answer critics who denigrated novels for belonging to no established—that is, classical—genre or for lacking verisimilitude; a true story would belong to the established genre of history; and truth, "being stranger than fiction, need not obey mere laws of *vraisemblance*" (Mylne 58). But more so than other kinds of truth claims, the historical figure is open to evaluation and challenge from any skeptical reader and thus is at odds with the techniques of formal realism that establish in the reader a type of belief not based on factual truth but yet capable of being weakened by falsifiable claims (McKeon). Because the verisimilar effect of the historical figure depends upon its congruence with preexisting and possibly conflicting images in readers' minds, it is particularly open to falsification.

In fact, though it has been commonplace to consider the truth claims of eighteenth-century writers such as Defoe and Richardson as defenses against Puritan attacks on frivolous fictions, many writers seem to have been less concerned with moral or legal safety than with their narratives' power to convince. By contrast with stories openly based upon real people, the quasidocumentary forms of the fictional memoir and letter were both unverifiable and unfalsifiable, relatively immune both to legal charges and to objections on the grounds of inaccuracy. These objections, it should be stressed, become important only when a culture seeks factual accuracy, as opposed to general truth, in portrayals of real people.

Thus, with the tandem development of a more rigorous historiography and a fiction characterized by formal realism came the eclipse of the historical figure that was to last until our own time. Henry Fielding, the last of the British novelists to uphold the classical tradition, was advocating an already outmoded view of truth in 1743 when he introduced *The Life of Mr. Jonathan Wild the Great* as a "narrative . . . rather of such actions which he might have performed, or would, or should have performed, than what he really did; and may, in reality, as well suit any other such great man, as the person himself whose name it bears" (29). Despite the vogue for the historical novel from about 1830 to 1850, accompanying the nationalistic and revolutionary spirit then on the rise, such "great men" as Jonathan Wild rarely would serve as protagonists for major writers after Fielding's time. Scott is, of course, the major English writer in the historical form, and many important novelists of his century made at least one attempt at historical fiction: Melville with *Israel Potter,* Thackeray with *Henry Esmond,* Dickens with *Barnaby Rudge,* and Eliot with *Romola.* But these writers tended to downplay the historical or biographical component of their characters, even when offering historical evidence for the plausibility of their events. And all tended to restrict historical figures—what Lukács calls the "world-historical individual"—to the sidelines; on the fictional characters are focused the real narrative energies.

Though historical fiction has never lost its large popular readership, the form has suffered from "neglect, even contempt" (Shaw 9) under the reign of realism, particularly in works where historical figures are prominent. Many writers and critics have argued that the form is inherently inferior, offering the childish delight of recognition rather than the more sophisticated pleasures of formal perfection, which have been seen as difficult or impossible to achieve with historical subjects. Historical figures have been thought to restrict the writer's imaginative freedom, to blunt artistic precision. Even the great Manzoni, whose *I promessi sposi* is one of the triumphs of the form, eventually rejected the historical novel on the grounds that factual truth is incompatible with the unified belief created by great fiction. The form of the historical novel, he wrote, "inevitably calls for a combination that is contrary to its subject matter and a division contrary to its form . . . its premises are inherently contradictory. . . . A great poet and a great historian may be found in the same man without creating confusion, but not in the same work" (72, 126). The historical novelist thus must either deceive readers or incur their doubts in order to create a unified artistic work. Although many realist writers have described the novel as a form of history— Balzac a "history of the human heart," James a history "as the picture is reality"—by this they have meant a sort of history generalized enough to allow full artistic freedom. The true artist, they have said, should be liberated from the slavery to chronology, the known conclusion to the story, and the "dry and repellent nomenclatures of facts" (de Balzac vii) that were seen as characteristic of historical writing.

According to the commonplaces of realism, the direct or extensive use of historical figures inhibits the writer's ability to imagine the subject in a beautiful way. James insisted that reality is always transformed in the "crucible" of the artist's imagination into something quite different from its original state and that the more minute and suggestive the original germ for a work, the better the completed work was likely to be. Even in *The Aspern Papers,* which more than any other of his works is tied to a historical character's situation, James was far more interested in the atmosphere of an imagined past, the suggestiveness of the situation, than in the actual experiences of Claire Clairmont. In his feeling that a meeting with the woman would have restricted his artistic freedom, in his willing subjection to that "odd law which somehow always makes the minimum of valid suggestion serve the man of imagination better than the maximum" (*Art of the Novel* 161), James expressed the belief, still current in many circles, that characters based too closely on real people are doomed to fail, in part because the author is not sufficiently ambivalent toward them: "they exemplify and give expression to nothing but their author's desire for self-justification" (Bayley 230).

Of course, writers have never stopped using real people, in disguise, as fictional characters. But under realism they have preferred to deny their models, prizing the transformations they have accomplished and seeing the obligatory name change as a badge of their transformative artistic powers. Kingsley Amis, while acknowledging that no writer can "truly invent anyone or anything," claims, "the closer the likeness of the real interesting person, the less interesting he will be in the novel . . . the novelist may well start from a real person, as George Eliot may have started Mr Casaubon from Mark Pattison. But then he became Mr Casaubon, because he had to do things Mark Pattison did not do" (847). The realist aesthetic assumes that a recognizable historical figure in fiction must not "do things" its model did not do in real life; it follows that historical figures can be used only in very limited ways.

Recognizable historical figures have thus been relegated to the secondary positions of contributing to period ambiance or creating a reality effect around the fictional characters. Just as that Baker Street address has led many readers to conclude that Sherlock Holmes really existed—and to send him birthday cards there—Henry Esmond's encounter with jovial "Dick the Scholar," who turns out to be Richard Steele, makes that supposed memoir more convincing. For any reader not an expert historian, the presence of recognizable historical characters raises the possibility that all other characters may be similarly historical or "real," and our imaginative engagement with the story makes us want to accept that possibility. The a priori reality of recognizable names and historical people— "real names" and "real people"—can reinforce the created reality of the fictional people.

But if the realist illusion is seen as contingent upon a historicist obligation to accuracy, historical figures become problematic. In order to establish verisimilitude, the historical figure must be immediately recognizable, preferably by appearance as well as by reputation. Such a character—a monarch, a head of state, or a national hero—may even go unnamed and simply be described in such a way that the average reader will know who is passing by. No obscure figure, however historical, can aid verisimilitude, for he or she does not evoke the note of recognition that causes the fictional world to intersect the historical world in the reader's mind. An identifying description is a poor substitute for the reader's independent knowledge; if we must depend upon the author for knowledge of a historical character, we respond to that character almost exactly as we would to a fictional one, accepting what we are told as true within the confines of the book but reserving a certain skepticism about its validity outside the book.

Since the verisimilar effects of the recognizable figure depend upon shared stereotypes in the minds of numerous readers, the portrayal of a historical figure must not conflict with what is commonly known or might reasonably be expected of the original. If the fictional portrayal clashes with this preexistent mental portrait, the effect of increased reality is lost. Particularly where national legends are concerned, the reader's conception is strong and resists significant alteration. This is not to say that a convincing portrait must remain within the bounds of documentable facts. Historical novelists have always described historical characters in places where they could not have been, talking to people they could never have met. As Lukács notes, Vigny and Hugo characterized great men "by means of historical, or *even invented,* anecdotes" (72; my emphasis). Nor must a portrait accord in every particular with communal expectations. However, any variation must be reconcilable with those expectations, reconcilable with the historical persona, as distinguishable from the historical person. The latter is the human being we can approach, though never fully know, through the public and private records that are the resources of a biographer; the former is that same person as idealized or vilified in the public imagination, an image projected officially through public acts and unofficially through rumor, caricature, and satire. A skillful historical portrait in the realist mode must attempt to approach the person without significantly modifying the persona. In *Israel Potter*, for instance, Melville presents a John Paul Jones who is near-ridiculous in his coxcombery and bravado and a Benjamin Franklin whose endless advice giving nearly exhausts the patience of the reader as well as of Israel. Yet both characters finally contribute to the glorification of American virtues (Jones's bravery and Franklin's resourceful intelligence) that seems the chief purpose of these fictionalized memoirs, and as a result they merge successfully into the personae, the nationalistic communal characterizations, on which they were based. Had Melville challenged the readers' idealized versions of Jones and Franklin, his historical characters would not have increased belief in his equally but not recognizably historical protagonist.

Paradoxically, although historical characters can strengthen the overall sense of reality, they will be less convincingly alive than the more psychologically complex fictional characters, to the extent that the portrait accords with public myth and expectation. In some cases, novelists expect the name alone to serve as the primary characterization, standing before us like the first descriptive paragraph introducing a new fictional character. More successful historical characters will be built and presented in the same way as fictional ones, through dialogue, physical appearance, contrast, and so on, and serve the usual functions of fictional characters as well as provide plausibility props. But in the context of a realistic narrative, there is often, mixed with the delight of recognizing a familiar figure, a more or less equal dismay at the encounter, for the historical character is felt to be of a different order of existence than the fictional character. Thus its verisimilar effects can be cancelled out by the challenge it poses to the mimetic illusion.

One sometimes feels that the author has been subjugated by a preexistent character; the effect is something like that of a ventriloquist: one hears the communal voice speaking through an inanimate dummy. Under realism, writers have been fooled or forced into thinking that the historical character is more real than other real things, somehow immune to re-creation. An author who assumes that any character is a completed, solid entity rather than material to be shaped often loses interest, having been self-excluded from the process of creation, and the historical character has often suffered as a result.

With the modernist challenge to realism early in this century, writers found formal methods of subjugating communally created characterizations (bearing, like all characters, the stylistic marks of their age and creators) to an individually created style and work, and the suppression of the historical figure began to decline. The first movements were cautious. In the *USA* trilogy, for instance, Dos Passos avoided extended direct interaction between fictional and historical characters; although a fictional character may mention having heard Bill Haywood speak or having seen Pancho Villa, the real people rarely come directly on-stage to talk with, dine with, or sleep with the fictional ones. Similarly, Dos Passos's minibiographies are structurally separated from the fictional passages, and in these biographies the techniques of compression, irony, and rhythmic repetition ("he had confidence in railroads, he had confidence in communications, he had confidence in transportation, he believed in iron") subjugate the communal characterizations, such as that of Andrew Carnegie as the kindly tycoon who endowed libraries, to Dos Passos's artistic purposes. Once such techniques had begun to dismantle the mimetic illusion, historical figures could not but appear in any highly personal and political view of history.

A number of influences may help to explain the increasing use of real people, dead and alive, as fictional characters in the 1970s and 1980s. Legal changes making it more difficult for public figures to win libel cases certainly encouraged the audacity with which a number of writers lampooned media figures and politicians, most notably Richard Nixon. It is also tempting to speculate that television, with its conflation of news and entertainment and its constant interruption of mimetic narrative for hucksterism, has produced an audience far more tolerant of fragmentation and surrealistic juxtaposition in aesthetic experience; the modal confusion of mainstream TV is not unlike that "news/novels matrix" Lennard Davis described in seventeenth-century England. But when we look at fictional practice and listen to writers, the explanations that most often recur are the views that identity, like reality itself, is a fiction and that no fiction can provide an exact rendering of experience, unfiltered by consciousness, perception, or language itself. If this is so, the traditional change of names to protect the innocent or the guilty may be, in Robert Coover's phrase, only a "cowardly lie" to protect the novelist. The result is a new willingness to display failed attempts at knowledge and confess to character assassinations. The presence of real people in fiction today occurs in so many different contexts and serves so many different intentions that no single explanation can adequately account for the phenomenon. But what is clear is that a familiar taboo has lost its force, and a very old tool has again found its place in the novelist's bag of tricks. The chapters that follow will consider the variety of ways in which contemporary writers are calling up the spirits of the dead and manipulating the images of the living to explore the limits of history, politics, culture, art, and truth.

# 2

## Raising the Dead: Fiction Biographies

THE TRADITIONAL BIOGRAPHICAL novel has often been a dreary item, relying upon the panache of a famous subject to maintain interest, packed full of tedious expository and analytic passages, indulging in exhibitionistic display of its background research, and attempting simultaneously to get cozy with the subject—to bring him or her down to earth—and to trumpet the subject's greatness ("Little did Anna Magdalena know that her sweetheart would one day be world-famous as JOHANN SEBASTIAN BACH"). The disjunctions between the historical materials and an embarrassingly contemporary narrative idiom often leave one with the impression of having attended a costume party, and a low-budget one at that. Until recently, most of our finest writers have avoided biographical fiction, because the form has been thought to entail the same obligations that apply to nonfiction biography: factual accuracy based on exhaustive research, objectivity based on emotional distance and expressed through restraint of style, and scope covering the whole life, from birth to death. When these obligations are applied to fiction, the goal of the fictionalized biography becomes simply "to represent faithfully the actual facts and only to fill in what will add to the appreciation of historical figures or to the reader's enjoyment in learning history. An author fails if he does not report the facts" (Crittenden 336).

That fiction and biography are not inherently inimical forms was dramatically demonstrated by their ubiquitous cross-fertilization in prose narratives before the development of modern objective biography in the eighteenth century. Earlier biography, with a few exceptions such as Suetonius' *Twelve Caesars* and certain passages in Roper's *Life of More,* had been intended to inspire readers to ethical behavior through the presentation of ideal character types; its chief goal had been to instruct rather than to inform in any factual sense. Such exemplary biography could comfortably contain both documented truth and rumored, intuited, or invented truths, for selected inventions, exaggerations, and omissions would serve and even enhance the moral effect of the life. Though the fictional memoirs and criminal biographies of the seventeenth century lacked this moral goal (despite a certain cautionary value in the gallows confessions of the rogue-heroes), their authors evidenced a similar disregard for any strict boundaries between imagined and documentable truth. It was with the *Life of Johnson* that the combined fictional and historical impulses underlying biography split decisively; for though Boswell wanted to create a rounded, convincing portrait of his revered friend—to keep him alive, if you will—he aimed at an objective portrait, essentially expository and analytic rather than fictional despite its frequent dramatic scenes. The emblem of the modern biographer is Boswell taking notes, observing rather than dreaming, recording rather than speculating, and this model operated to subordinate biographical elements in fiction of the following centuries. In the enormous and enormously popular Victorian expansions of both forms, the distinction held: fiction as an imaginative art must remain subordinate to the historical art of biography, and a fiction writer treating an openly historical subject was obligated to the same accuracy, objectivity, and completeness that were the biographer's goal and that make the effects of a good biography quite different from those of a good novel.

Chief among these obligations, of course, is absolute faithfulness to the factual record; conscientious biographers have aimed, in their writing if not always in the creative process that precedes it, to be dispassionate, to produce a narrative "calm and measured and judicial" (Edel 81) and, it goes without saying, *accurate*. The biographer is obliged to spend years in research, to remain within the bounds of the factual record, to inform us when something is missing from that record or cannot be explained, and to propose or suggest rather than to recreate directly in most matters of private life. According to Leon Edel, the biographer must be "neat and orderly and logical . . . [he] may be as imaginative as he pleases . . . in the way in which he brings together his materials, *but he must not imagine the materials*" (1). Of course, a good biographer does much more than simply collect and record facts and may create a more or less intimate "viewing distance" between reader and subject, but that distance will be measured out purely by the materials available: "the more intimate the evidence—letters, diary, reminiscences—the nearer the reader can be brought to the subject" (Kendall 10). Justice to a subject is thought best served by careful objectivity, and so biographers repress or at least restrain the frank partisanship, even passion, that they often develop after years of living with a subject. According to this view, the biographer must "outgrow the wish either to *be* or to transform the subject, either to usurp the subject's place or to rebel" (Young-Bruehl 422); however complex and intense might be the relationship between writer and subject, that relationship should not be evident in the writing and should never significantly reshape the facts.

From this follows the abstracted and tentative language of many biographies and of biographical novels written upon the same premises. According to Park Honan, "style in the novel easily becomes inventive, exuberant, diverse, comparatively 'free,' whereas style in biography is more rigidly determined— so that one false, imaginative flight, one novelistic description of the Edinburgh housetops, for example, or of what Scott supposedly felt when in love, undermines the authority of a Life of Scott" (114 n.). Biographical authority, that is, resides in the author's refusal to let the imagination "fly"; only the earthbound language of reason convincingly conveys the effect of truth in our fact-bound epistemology. The effect of such stylistic restraint is to reduce the reader's emotional involvement, just as the writer's involvement has been restrained by reason, logic, and rules of evidence. True, there are novels that proceed in the same tentative way—indeed, in which the narrator's uncertainty about the protagonist contributes to the impact of the novel. A novelistic narrator may certainly display the same objective, coolly evaluative stance that one finds in a mainstream biography, and the relationship between a biographer and an enigmatic subject is not unlike the ambiguous relationships of Nick Carraway and Gatsby or Quentin Compson and Sutpen. But the omniscient narrator of biography is obliged to maintain a *tone* of objectivity as well as an appearance of it; ambiguities must be either resolved or frankly confessed as failures of the biographical enterprise.

The antifictional force of the biographer's historical conscience and scientific detachment is compounded by the implicit formal obligation to trace a subject's progress from birth to death; if "one volume concerns The Middle Years, you can be sure there will be others about The Early Years and The Later" (Rose 115). Even biographers who tamper with chronology and use novelistic techniques of flashback and juxtaposition tend to accept the necessity to present the whole life and thus to summarize, select, and generalize in order to render that life intelligible as a single process. The standard biography compresses sixty years into six hundred pages and thus is more generalized and less shapely than we expect novels to be. Not even a relatively uneventful year can be adequately treated, in a novelistic or psychological way, in ten pages, and so any novelist who accepts the biographer's obligation to completeness is forced to dilute the emotional and sensual intensity of the material. This problem was largely responsible for the artistic failure of Melville's *Israel Potter,* one of the rare attempts at fiction biography by a classic American author and a book almost universally evaluated as less than classic Melville. Though many early critics, preferring the book to the "morbid" or "perverse" *Pierre,* praised its comedy and its lively characterizations of Benjamin Franklin and John Paul Jones, they found it tedious after the first half, the point at which the novelistic sense of time began to compress into biographical time.

But recent excursions in the genre demonstrate a general rejection of these long-accepted obligations. Far more than books "based upon the life of " or "about" some famous individual, they are novels convincing and memorable on their own terms, in which the biographical element can come to seem almost incidental. The familiar label "fictionalized biography" seems to imply that the fictional component is superficial, a thin overlay; I prefer to call these works *fiction biographies* as a way of emphasizing the primacy of fiction in their makeup. The fiction biographers have cast off the hampering obligations that biographers and biographical novelists have long accepted but that have lost their force, at least in fiction, as a result of contemporary views that truly objective historical truth does not exist and that the intuitive methods of fiction may provide truths more valuable than those built on and restricted to exhaustive factual research. Accepting and valuing the fact that fiction is always a distortion of reality—that reality is always itself a fiction—a variety of serious writers have chosen historical figures as protagonists.

Their subjects vary widely. Some choose the invisible people of history: the man who manipulated the famous chess automaton in Thomas Gavin's *Kingkill,* a German negotiator at Compiègne in Thomas Keneally's *Gossip from the Forest.* Others expand or explode the myths surrounding legendary figures: Francine Prose demythologized and then remythologized *Marie Laveau,* the nineteenth-century queen of New Orleans voodoo, Speer Morgan revived *Belle Starr* as a woman more complex and interesting than the gun-toting outlaw mama of legend; and Jay Cantor has meditated upon the life and *The Death of Che Guevara.* Their motives are equally varied. Some have become intellectually intrigued, some more personally and emotionally involved, with a subject. Some, after attempting traditional biographies and becoming frustrated with the inadequacies of the technique, turned to fiction as a more legitimate truth, as Sartre's Roquentin turned to fiction from history. Some wish to flaunt their skills by applying them to knottier materials than those of the straight novel: they aspire not to fill the gaps in the biographical record with plausible speculations but to overwhelm the biographical facts with the flow of imagined facts to which the former give rise. Skeptical about historical or biographical objectivity and generally distrustful of facts, all make large claims for fiction, both as a way of approaching truth and as an endeavor worthy in itself. The best of these writers overstep the boundaries of research and of reason and move right inside the heads of their subjects and the people around the subject. The resulting works retain both the fascinations of fiction and the fascinations of biography: the simulation of a particular real life, not just of "life." They approach their subjects with a combination of fascination for the actual historical figure and confidence in their own abilities to resurrect that person, to share the person's experiences and even to exchange identities.

This current upsurge in fiction biography is a natural outgrowth of developments in straight biography that have legitimized more audacious moves into the historical subject's head. The two forms have always had a great deal in common. Like a novel, a biography is made up of many small details of ordinary life that the writer hopes to shape into a coherent whole; both aim not merely to inform the reader of the events of a life but to simulate a life in such a way that the reader may share it. Both forms offer the pleasures of gossip and of eavesdropping and thus satisfy the seemingly universal human curiosity about the lives of others. Gamaliel Bradford sees this curiosity as based on the twin components of human identity and human difference: the pleasures of recognizing that one's own deepest experiences are shared, the novelty of experiencing passions and obsessions not one's own. And, in fact, writers in both forms have used dramatically similar terms to describe the ways in which a subject may declare itself and take possession of the writer in an intimate, almost occult union. Flaubert felt that he had become Madame Bovary; similarly, Leon Edel describes the biographer as undergoing a sort of "alchemy of the spirit . . . becoming for awhile that other person, even while remaining himself" (7). Many a biographer claims to achieve an intuitive sympathy with the subject that can nearly "annihilate the centuries, the spaces, the deceptions of change, the opacity of death" (Kendall 151), and all insist on the necessity of imagination in the creation of a good biography, on the essential deadness of facts without that inspiring force.

The biographer and the fiction writer have become even more close in our century, when the principles of depth psychology revealed by Freud significantly expanded the biographer's task to include the rendering of "not only the public and private events of a life but its intimate existential and perceptive textures, all adding up to the whole sense of a person," a project that Justin Kaplan has termed "extravagant" (2). Since we now tend to locate the true meaning of a life in the private springs of public actions, any biographer who undertakes to present a life must attempt to provide knowledge that cannot be established irrefutably upon facts; work-ing more or less from speculation, the biographer finally resur-rects a spirit that could be the biographer's own shadow. More and more, biographies have come to read like psychological novels, and once biographers had entered the domain of the novelist, it was inevitable that serious novelists would reenter the domain of the biographer, for the novels written between the lines of modern biographies are rarely satisfying works of fiction.

And, in fact, biographical materials offer strong attractions to the contemporary fiction writer. For one, factual truth has a specific urgency that pure fiction cannot provide. Discussing "The New Biography," Virginia Woolf wrote that truth "stimu-lates the mind, which is endowed with a curious susceptibility in this direction, as no fiction, however artful or highly colored, can stimulate it" (229). To Woolf, the most difficult artistic problem of the biographical novel is that invented facts and verifiable facts may destroy each other when combined, the verifiable facts discrediting the imagined ones and the imag-ined ones making the verifiable seem dull or incoherent ("The Art of Biography" 225). The new fiction biographer solves this problem by creating a context in which the two sorts of facts, now indistinguishable from one another, serve equally the stimulative function of truth and the symbolic and evoca-tive functions of fiction.

A historical figure also offers an escape from the prison of selfhood, from the endless exploration of one's own conscious-ness. Speer Morgan has commented, "psychological realism became dull twenty years ago. . . . I'm more interested in larger tales . . . that reflect history and the world. . . . I'm looking outward as a writer" (interview). More so than a tradi-tional fictional character, the historical figure represents a true "Other" to the writer. The past is a far country; the historical subject can offer a simplicity and an oddness difficult to find in a contemporary subject, and this can open new possibilities for a writer fettered by the repetition, even the growth, of a personal style. For in re-creating the historical subject, even one with whom the writer identifies, the writer cannot simply re-create herself or himself. The fictional character, so intimately a child of the writer's mind, will often insist upon the family connection, will repeat the inherited gestures and expressions, will squint with the family myopia and sneeze with the family allergies. The historical subject, an adopted child, will be more recalcitrant, and this resistance can be blessing or bane.

## William Styron and the Politics of Fiction Biography

The first technically inventive approaches to fiction biography in this century tended to retain a certain cautious distinction between fact and fiction. Thornton Wilder's 1948 *The Ides of March*, for instance, which deals with the last few months of Julius Caesar's life, begins with a prefatory disclaimer not unlike those accompanying more recent fiction biographies: "Historical reconstruction is not among the primary aims of this work. It may be called a fantasia on certain events and persons of the last days of the Roman republic" (vii). But Wilder is careful to identify his departures from known fact: his preface tells us that he dated certain events seventeen years later than they actually happened, that he invented an association between Caesar and Catullus, and that the "conspiratorial chain letters" circulated by Caesar's enemies are modeled after the antifascist letters circulated in Italy in Wilder's time. He admits that, except for Catullus' poems and an excerpt from Suetonius, "All the documents in this work are from the author's imagination. . . . This is a suppositional reconstruction provoked by the inequalities" in the historical record.

Ten years later, Marguerite Yourcenar's magisterial *Mém-*

*oires d'Hadrien* would take a step further toward the free use
of history. Like a traditional biographer, she spent years exam-
ining contemporary accounts of Hadrian's life and reign, his
few surviving written works, the ubiquitous statues of his lover
Antinous, the villa where he died. She attempts to remain true
to those facts, and, like Wilder, she accompanies her fiction
with notes identifying those points in the story where she
has departed from history. But unlike her predecessor, she
emphasizes that her "reporting" of Hadrian's dreams, skepti-
cisms, private emotions, and fantasies—her assumption of
knowledge of a man dead thousands of years ago—is no more
ambitious than any novelist's assumption of knowledge about
a living person or even about herself: "My father's life is more
unknown to me than that of Hadrian. My own existence, if I
had to write it down, would be recreated from without" (323,
my translation). Her comments reflect the growing sense that
all character is a fiction, constructed by imagination as well as
observation, and that the process of reconstructing a historical
subject differs very little from the process of constructing a
wholly fictional character.

Yourcenar and others like her had not yet pushed these
conclusions to their ultimate implications; their sense of responsibility to historical accuracy, their reluctance to relinquish all claim to the "prestige of fact" (Rose 124), left them
vulnerable to attack by critics dissatisfied with the accuracy of
the "biography" implied by the form of the fiction.

And so the freeing of biographical fiction from biography's
obligations has not been a painless process. One of the first
fiction biographies to achieve commercial and critical success
in this country was also one of the most controversial: William
Styron's *The Confessions of Nat Turner* (1967), published in a
volatile time that brought the book fierce attention from political as well as literary commentators. Indeed, fiction biography
always meets its most difficult challenge when the work comes
before a public with a political or ideological stake in the

presentation of iconic historical figures. Styron's interest in the rebel slave Nat Turner had dated back to his youth in the Virginia county where Turner's rebellion took place; he has described Nat's story as "the book I wanted to write when I started out writing" (Plimpton). Initially "overly smitten" with the violence of the massacre and drawn more to the melodramatic scenario than to the character of Turner himself, he was advised against the project by his Random House editor after the publication of his first novel in 1960 but continued to read about slavery and picked up the Turner project again in 1962. The next five years were devoted to a fictional rendering of the experience of slavery, an ambitious project and a dangerous one in several ways. Not least of these dangers was the low reputation of the genre in which he was working; Styron has said that he called the novel a "meditation on history" in order to "take the curse of the phrase 'historical novel' off the book" (Lewis and Van Woodward 52). Even more damaging to the book's prospects, he was attempting to enter the consciousness of a black slave—and not just any slave, but a figure holding real emotional and ideological significance for increasingly militant black Americans. Never one to shrink from a challenge, Styron blithely and almost naively tackled a subject that had come to be regarded by some as the exclusive property of blacks.

Though admitting that treating a black slave in the first person, which Sokolov has called "Styron's big gamble" (66), would be a challenge no other white writer had successfully met, Styron seems to have been remarkably confident of his ability to understand Nat Turner in this intimate way. "If you can sympathize with the dispossessed, you can certainly take on the lineaments of the Negro," he later remarked. He seems to have felt that transcending historical distance was the least of his technical problems, and in fact he made no effort to adjust his style to the historical subject: "I tried to write as spontaneously as I could in the form and language I would have written a contemporary novel . . . [though] trying to avoid obvious anachronism" (Plimpton 37). The resulting version of Turner is little different from "what a white man might be in similar circumstances. . . . Social conditions, not heredity and biology, set him apart" (Rubin 6), and the portrait is in many ways as ahistorical as it is color-blind. Though Styron vividly recreates nineteenth-century Virginia through accurate historical details of architecture, food, dress, and landscape, his protagonist's consciousness seems essentially of the twentieth century.

The insouciance with which Styron undertook the project is startling, particularly given his own account of the vast gulf between white and black in the modern South. In the essay "This Quiet Dust," which details his search for evidence of Nat's rebellion in the dusty roads and memories of Southampton County, Styron describes his early feelings toward blacks as "wobbling always between a patronizing affection, fostered by my elders, and downright hostility"; modern southerners, by his own account, have little real contact with blacks and no real knowledge of them. Any intimacy between the races is "rare and sporadic." He concludes that "to *know* the Negro, has become the moral imperative of every white Southerner" (136–38); the novel, then, was the record of an experiment in knowing that he believes to have succeeded. He has stated that it describes "the way Nat, as I lived his life, felt," a claim that would seem extreme if not for that qualifying "as," which admits that Styron's living of Nat's life is probably different from what someone else's would be. Yet he trusts his own intuitive understanding of Turner more than the historical accounts of Nat's life, which Styron sometimes sees as irrelevant to the truths he sought. Of his portrayal of Nat as unable to kill, he admits, "I do not know if this was true. This was naturally part of my insight as a novelist rather than anything having to do with the facts of the matter" (Lewis and Woodward 56, 54). The lack of solid facts, Styron argues, is "not disadvantageous to a novelist, since it allows him to speculate—with a freedom not allowed the historian" ("Quiet Dust" 139).

Styron's mainstream (that is, white) critics tended to accept the book on its own terms, praising what they saw as its full and realistic portrayal of slaveholding Virginia, its convincing representation of Nat Turner's mind and experience, and its novelistic power and inventiveness. By most accounts, Styron had confronted a monumental challenge and triumphed. The book's "big" subject made it into a literary event. Except for a few dissenters such as Wilfrid Sheed, who found the book faulty as a work of art, negative opinions centered on the book's genre, seen by some as inherently suspect. But the historian Herbert Aptheker's brief article in the *Nation* in October 1968 unleashed a series of vehement denunciations, generally from black critics, of the inaccuracy of Styron's picture of Turner and of slavery in the 1830s. As Aptheker wrote, the *Nation*'s request for his response seemed based on the assumption that a historical novel should "bear some resemblance to history" (375), and in fact, Styron's preface to the *Confessions* shares this assumption in its claim to have "rarely departed from the *known* facts" about Turner and his rebellion and to have remained "within the bounds of what meager enlightenment history has left us about the institution of slavery." Black readers argued not only that Styron's Nat Turner was not the Nat Turner of American blacks but that his portrayal of the black folk hero was an attack on black history and black people.

The reaction against the novel, "one of the most violent attacks in the recent history of American writing" (Anderson 158), culminated in the 1968 publication of *William Styron's Nat Turner: Ten Black Writers Respond,* a collection of articles arguing that Styron deliberately distorts the historical Turner in the service of racist ideology and politics. These writers object to specific factual inaccuracies in Styron's description of Turner, of slavery, and of blacks under slavery; moreover, they object to racist patterns in these inaccuracies and especially to the potentially harmful effects of these patterns on the contemporary civil rights movement. The vehemence of their responses, which sometimes degenerated into personal attacks on Styron's motivation and personality, shows the extent to which these reviewers found Styron's version of Nat Turner to be a real violation of their own manhood. I use the term *manhood* advisedly; it appears frequently in these essays.

In fact, Styron had consulted the most detailed nineteenth-century sources on Turner: the relatively brief *Confessions*, supposedly taken down verbatim in Turner's jail cell by the lawyer Thomas Gray; Frederick Law Olmstead's 1856 *Journey in the Seaboard Slave States;* and William Drewry's 1900 *Southampton Insurrection,* largely based on newspaper accounts contemporary to the rebellion and on interviews with people who remembered it. But Styron departs from the record at several significant points, most of which serve certain theories about revolutionary psychology and about slavery in America: notably the "Moynihan thesis" of the absence of the father in the American black family; Stanley Elkin's "Sambo thesis" of slavery, which holds that blacks were so demoralized and dehumanized by the conditions of slavery that they were unable to resist and did in fact resemble the compliant and childlike slaves of southern myth; and Erikson's psychoanalytic theory that the "traditional revolutionary" is "puritanical, repressive, and sublimated" (Plimpton 38). Though the Turner of the original *Confessions* describes himself as having been educated by a mother, father, and grandmother to whom he was very close, Styron's Nat has little contact with his father and is educated by the white family that owns him. Drewry says that Nat's mother was a wild African woman who had to be restrained from killing her child to save him from slavery; Styron attributes this action to Nat's maternal grandmother, who in his account dies shortly after the birth of her only child. Gray's Turner frequently helps other slaves plan thieving expeditions; Styron's Turner, contemptuous of his fellow slaves, rarely associates with them. Olmstead says that Turner had a wife; Styron's Turner is a celibate whose only sexual experience has been a homosexual one and who fantasizes about raping white women. Gray's Turner says he escaped from his master for a month and returned of his own free will; Styron omits this episode. Gray describes, with reluctant admiration, an unrepentant and still defiant Turner who, when asked whether he felt his imminent execution showed he had been wrong, responded with a question of his own: "Was not Christ crucified?" Styron's Turner, by contrast, is defeated, self-doubting, and cut off from God by his participation in the bloody rebellion.

Styron's account of the rebellion itself and of Nat's followers similarly diverges from early historical records. Styron fabricates the characters of two of the fellow conspirators, Hark and Will, out of whole cloth; Hark, described as a "black Apollo" by one contemporary source, is in Styron's version completely cowed by white power, a Sambo in the presence of any white. Will, depicted as an efficient but not unusually bloodthirsty killer in the historical sources, becomes a raging maniac who challenges Turner's leadership and whose thirst for blood is exceeded only by his hunger for "some of that white stuff"; he rapes several women before axing them. But contemporary newspaper accounts of the rebellion make no mention of rape, and Gray's Turner says "we would not do to their women as they had done to ours" (Higginson 176). Styron sees the rebellion as basically a failure, on the grounds that plantation slaves did not join in with Nat in numbers as great as might have been expected and some actually fired upon the rebels. But according to Aptheker, Turner actively recruited only six men and the other several dozens joined spontaneously; at only one plantation were slaves reported as defending their masters (Higginson 181). Drewry says that blacks knew of, but did not denounce, Turner's planned insurrection. Styron also describes many repressive slave-control measures as resulting from the rebellion; historians show that these measures predated the rebellion.

Finally, Styron's critics objected to his portrayal of the slave system itself and of the effects of slavery on its victims. Styron does portray slaves, on the average, as ignorant, filthy, and acquiescent creatures, slack-jawed and childish, with little real longing for freedom and less ability to resist their enslavement. He depicts freed blacks as worse off than most slaves, though Drewry says that the freed blacks of Southampton County were prosperous, and Frederick Douglass and many other slave autobiographers describe their hatred for their condition and their continual scheming to escape it. Styron shows the blacks as having no culture of their own and makes little attempt to draw upon the powerful traditions of black religious rhetoric and of music, to say nothing of the stories of slaves who had successfully resisted or escaped, an oral tradition from which one might expect Turner to have drawn strength and comfort. Styron's Turner, in other words, represents a white man's imagination of what slavery might have been like: he lives in complete isolation, cut off both from those people (all white) with whom an intelligent man could find intellectual companionship and from those (all black, and ignorant) with whom his race aligned and associated him and to whom his race doomed him. He despises his own people, in terms reflecting—it must be said—every possible racist stereotype of rolling eyes, lollygagging gait, mindless grins, and obsequious loyalty to the "massah." Occasionally Styron will present such behavior as role playing for the benefit of the master and the self-preservation of the slave, but more often he seems to see this degradation as the real state of blacks under slavery.

Styron appeals to his favored theorists and to his own intuitive skills when defending his account. He considers the available historical facts unreliable or at least questionable but feels that his own version of the reality of slavery was reliable and even "true," whether based on historical research or simply on fictional imagination. He claimed to have felt and honored an obligation to accuracy: "there is a basic responsibility involved. . . . You want to use the art of fiction to its ultimate degree . . . and at the same time you want to be faithful to the time and place." To twist historical events to serve contemporary parallels, for example, would have been a "betrayal" of his "own vision of Nat and his story" (Lewis and Woodward 52, 57). But the responsibility to history is a very generalized one. Calling himself a "student of history" rather than an historian, he writes,

I at no time pretended that my narrative was an exact transcription of historical events; had perfect accuracy been my aim I would have written a work of history rather than a novel, one of the advantages of which is its ability to allow a certain free play to the imagination . . . the book is neither racist nor a tract but a *novel,* an essay of the imagination, where the necessities of always questionable "fact" often become subsumed into a larger truth. (*Nation* 544, 545)

Styron seems to have had little sense of possible conflicts between historical faithfulness and fictional truth, feeling that his fiction could legitimately use "Anything that was possible," whether or not the possibility had a historical basis; "If that places fiction above history, I am willing to do so if it does no disservice to the spirit of the time. An out and out lie is not acceptable" (Watkins 60).

Just what Styron would consider an out and out lie is not at all clear, for at every point at which he diverges from the historical records, that is, at which he makes a statement that can be evaluated as truth or lie, he denies the accuracy of the records. He does quite freely embroider upon or tinker with those suspect "facts" in the service of the "larger truth" of his theories or of fictional effect, saying, for example, that he placed Nat under a benevolent master in the service of irony

("Truth" 546) and that he perpetuated the stereotype of the black man obsessed with white women because he thought it was "quite likely true," though there is little evidence to suggest that Nat Turner was plagued with such an obsession. Styron trusts his own goodwill, his own imagination—he describes one scene as having come to him "with no research and no correction . . . as if he had been a witness" (Watkins 63)— and his own gut reactions, yet he resists the validity of other intuition-guided "larger truths" built on the same set of unreliable facts. His fictional portrayal, he would claim, presents the complexity of the slave experience in a way that his ideology-ridden detractors cannot match.

Had this subject been treated in later decades by another writer, it very likely would have caused much less uproar. The political climate is so dramatically changed that the portrayal of a failed revolution and a neurotic revolutionary would now seem less a direct attack on blacks, whose revolution of consciousness and revolution of action in the ghetto uprisings were coterminous with Styron's book. But more important, Styron's book had presented itself as essentially true and was largely read and praised as such by the critical establishment; it thus took on potential political power in a highly politicized time, particularly when the awarding of the Pulitzer Prize placed an official stamp of approval on the work. As Mike Thelwell wrote, "the real issue is not whether or how Styron changed facts, but that an inaccurate view is being presented and accepted as responsible to the 'essential truths of history' " (403).

## Form, Style, and the Fiction Biography

Since Styron's book, dozens of excellent fiction biographies have appeared in this country and abroad. None has been met with an attack of the sort that greeted the *Confessions*. To some extent this is simply because no book tackling a subject as controversial as Nat Turner has become a best-seller. But the fiction biographers of the seventies and eighties have also initiated bolder adaptations of fictional technique to the biographical enterprise; their clear departures from the formal conventions of biography free the writers from those fettering obligations to factual accuracy that have so long inhibited treatments of historical figures. The new fiction biographers are much more likely to incorporate their own self-doubts, the tenuousness of their truths, as an essential part of the narrative itself, thus directing attention to the fictional qualities of the books. Fact and fiction must be seamless, or at least simultaneous. The means to this end are myriad. Biographical time is truncated; we receive a juicy slice of the life rather than a dessicated summary. The objective point of view is discarded for an intimate first person or multiple narrators. The style may become dense, poetic, or dialectal, calling attention to itself and thus calling into question its pseudofactuality. Numerous metafictional techniques serve the same function; once it has been made clear that the story cannot be entirely trusted as a historical account, it may operate effectively as an artistic account. Today's fiction biographer is careful to establish both the factual existence of the subject and the fictionality of the account. Writers who have chosen an obscure subject tend to establish factuality by including pictures, documents, or explanatory prefaces; such procedures are, of course, unnecessary with a well-known subject. Whatever the subjects, writers may also establish the tentativeness of their interpretations through passages of fantasy or direct authorial intrusion, through conflicting perspectives on the subject, and in some cases through deliberate and easily detectable lies, not the least of which are the detailed accounts of the subject's dreams, fantasies, and physical surroundings.

The most common first step is the step away from biographical time, away from the telling of a whole life. Typically, the fiction biography is limited to a crucial year or few years and thus may expand into realms where few facts will be available: the daily life, the inner life, the unrecorded experiences of the self. The fiction biographer also abandons the conventional biographical point of view, that of the omniscient narrator, in favor of multiple narrators or an intimate first person, both of which increase psychological intensity and discourage literal belief. Frederick Busch's *The Mutual Friend,* for instance, uses "voices" of Charles Dickens's tour manager, his wife, his housemaid, his mistress, and Dickens himself to present a complex, contradictory portrait of Dickens' world and of the man.

Metafictional devices are frequently used to create a context in which imagined fact and verifiable fact carry equal, and equally partial, authority, in which hunch and intuition mix indistinguishably with verifiable truth. Each fact or factoid must be treated as possibly true and becomes as stimulating as truth, but the explicit possibility of falsehood protects the writer from charges of deception and—theoretically—renders inapplicable the categories of truth and falsity. Thomas Gavin's *Kingkill* begins with a chapter called "False Facts." His first-person narrator frequently refers to and quotes from the "distorting prism" of the journal of his protagonist Schlumberger. The narrator, we finally learn, *is* Schlumberger. Similarly, Jay Cantor's *The Death of Che Guevara* combines passages from Che's Bolivian diaries with the comments and meditations of the friend who "edits" the manuscript.

Another common technique for subduing fact to the service of fiction is the use of a highly wrought, poetic language quite different from the language of fact. In some cases this shift from contemporary idiom can represent a real liberation for the writer, opening up a new pace, new tone, new mood. The much-lamented "exhaustion" of mainstream fiction—the sense of certainty and of redundancy and the sometimes empty experimentation that can result when writers are trying to find ways to surprise themselves—can be cured by the challenge of a noncontemporary subject matter. Just as some people find a whole new personality in speaking another language, a writer may find a new voice in the spiritual body of another, a real other, person. For novelists entirely at home with or at war with their own experience, the contemporary idiom and setting can provide all the resistance needed against which to hammer out art. But others, who may feel their own lives too private for revelation or too monotonous for free invention, can find more room to move with the historical subject: unknown, unknowable, and yet tantalizingly real; other, odd, and yet disturbingly familiar; dead, gone, yet still here, and lively.

One particularly successful case of this sort is Frederick Buechner's *Godric,* a fiction biography/autobiography of an eleventh-century saint. Buechner, an ordained Presbyterian minister who has written religious meditations and books on theology and the Bible as literature as well as nine novels, must have been attracted to Godric as a historical figure exemplifying the problem he had examined in several of his novels: how can a fallible human being attain holiness? The focal character of several of his books, published in one volume as *The Book of Bebb,* is Leo Bebb, a southern evangelist with all the marks of a charlatan (a business in mail-order divinity degrees, an interest in pious millionaires, and a penchant for exposing himself to small children) but also the marks of a true holy man: solemn conviction and, perhaps, ability to work miracles. Like Bebb, Godric is holy in spite of himself. His life is known today only through an official biography commissioned by his abbot friend Ailred and written by the monk Reginald; this real book contains words of self-condemnation that Buechner's Godric repeats: "Know Godric's no true hermit but a gadabout within his mind, a lecher in his dreams. Self-seeking he is and peacock proud. A hypocrite. A ravener of alms and dainty too. A slothful, greedy bear. Not worthy to be called a servant of the Lord when he treats such servants as he has himself like dung, like Reginald! All this and worse than this go say of Godric in your book" (21). Somewhere in the contrast between these rough words and the smoothness of the official life of the saint lay the truth of a real person whose life paralleled the fictional life Buechner had created in Bebb.

Reginald's biography is impossibly false, for he has snipped out "all the grief and ugliness" (132), has taken out all human meaning. No human being, saint or sinner, was ever so surely, so undividedly holy as the saint whom Reginald imagines. Says Godric, "I scoop out the jakes of my remembrance, and he censes it all with his clerkish screed till it reeks of mass" (6). Yet neither was any saint so sinful as Godric describes himself, and his self-loathing is itself, as Reginald sees, a sign of grace. Here as with Leo Bebb, the holiness is both undeniable and inexplicable: the saint sins, rages, despises, and hopelessly loves, like any human sinner, yet is visited by the Virgin, the Baptist, and the Savior himself. His transgressions include theft, fraud, rape, incest, blasphemy, and a kind of fratricide, as well as the spiritual sins of pride, impatience, intolerance, cruelty, and unbelief. And yet there is something else, which he himself never understands: his unwilling, unsought saint-hood. The leper he kisses and cures, he kisses as much in disgust as in pity; the pilgrims he receives, he sometimes drives away; yet they return, and bring others.

Thematically, the book is classic Buechner; stylistically, it is classically lovely but uncharacteristically lyrical. The language is alliterative, heavily accented, poetic in its strong verbs and archaic nouns. There is a melody here, light yet centered, that the books of Bebb, despite their word-play and acute images, lack. Against all theory and all expectation, the historical subject seems to have freed Buechner from matter-of-factness, instead of entangling him in a web of history. The marvelous, which might seem naive or sentimental in a contemporary setting, can here be affirmed without irony; released from the materiality of the contemporary world, Buechner finds a materiality of the word that is pungent and exhilarating. The language of the subject, the historical language, brings the same pleasure we find in the dialect of southern writers, black writers, and Jewish writers: sensuous sounds, not imposed on the subject but integral to it. Of course, Godric would speak like that; how else could he speak? Not in our idiom, certainly, nor in the formal cadences of Latin. And yet, of course, he did not speak like that, like an Anglo-Saxon poet, even though he was one, any more than our American poets speak in the tonalities of their poems. He is an imaginary creation, a fantasy, if you will, from a writer for whom fantasy does not seem his first or most congenial mode. His success suggests the ways in which a historical character may open up new possibilities for a writer.

## The Novel as Alembic: Rhoda Lerman's *Eleanor*

Close sympathy or similarity is the most common reason for an author's choosing a historical subject. But on occasion the obsession, far from being symbiotic, becomes a demonic possession, and an unwilling novelist becomes involved with a subject who will not be denied. Such a situation produced Rhoda Lerman's *Eleanor: A Novel,* which treats the life of Eleanor Roosevelt between 1918 and 1921. The book was, Lerman said in a 1981 letter, written "at great personal expense," because the attempt to "find someone about whom I had gotten in deep water" forced her into impersonating someone entirely uncongenial to her own personality. This alchemical transmutation was "a form of madness," accomplished only with great violence to herself, and thus offers a particularly intense example of the occult union between novelist and subject.

The book had begun as a conventional biography, a joint project with Roosevelt's eldest grandson. They began writing chapters like "Eleanor and Men. Eleanor and Women"; Lerman found this mode "a vaguely decent way to organize material but . . . cold as ice," but she persisted for a year. It was only after writing a dramatic monologue in Eleanor's own voice and watching the actress Jean Stapleton perform it that Lerman realized that she would never really understand Eleanor without actually *becoming* Eleanor, claiming identity with someone who, far from being her mirror image, had a very different personal style. "Squeezing" herself "into this depressed and depressing lady was a great effort," for her own characteristic style is comic, playful, explosive; Lerman felt "fettered" by Eleanor's style and "couldn't wait to get onto my own stuff, my own self."

How then did she achieve an exploration so full, so deep, so convincing that readers would describe her character as having a " 'reality' truer and more haunting than the most scrupulous notes of the biographer" (Taliaferro 98) and sense something "bordering on love and unabashed partisanship" (Maloff 14) in her treatment of Roosevelt? Lerman describes the process as both a form of madness and a form of magic and sees her own transformation into so opposite a soul as an alchemical process, dissolving her own personality "to 'marry' and bring another to life." In an unpublished paper on the works of Marguerite Yourcenar, entitled "The Novel as Alembic," Lerman describes the creation of a historical character as a far more radical process than a simple transformation of the facts of history or the materials of experience; the novelist must actually transform herself, become that other person, if biographical or autobiographical fiction is to transcend "the clumsy facts of history" (1): the further "an author dissolves himself, transports himself, kills himself to become the other, the more pure will be the artistic creation" (2). The novel itself is the alembic in which the author *becomes* the subject, a process the reader can repeat, becoming "deeply and permanently changed at the molecular level" by the divine marriage of souls (6). If the novelist writes as "the scholar not the witness," the "background becomes foreground" and the details overwhelm the subject (8). But if the author has truly witnessed, indeed, has *been,* the subject, the details the author includes will be integral to the character and the character will live, a spirit nourished on the lifeblood of the writer.

The alchemical language is more than simply an apt metaphor, for the principles of alchemy underlie Lerman's understanding both of her own experience as writer and of Eleanor's transformation from a "depressed, miserable, dysfunctional woman" (letter) to the great heroine she became. Alchemy was both a scientific system and a mystical philosophy, based on an analogy between the spiritual principles of the universe and the properties of physical substances, particularly the metals. According to H. Stanley Redgrove, the alchemist believed that all forms of matter "are one in origin, and are produced by an evolutionary process. The Soul of them all is one and the same; it is only the Soul that is permanent; the body or outward form, i.e., the mode of manifestation of the Soul, is transitory, and one form may be transmuted into another" (xii). Metals, like people, are constituted of body, soul, and spirit, the soul being "the inward individual spirit" and the spirit "the universal Soul in all men"(15). In order to transmute one element into another, the "body" of that element must be destroyed; this allows the development of "the essence within" (32). Just so, the novelist must dissolve her own identity, indeed her own "soul," in order to develop the spirit of the subject and then to distill the purified gold of the fictional character.

Lerman's means to this dissolution of self and this communion with the spirit of her subject were, like those of the alchemists, partly scientific and partly mystical. Much more so than Styron or Buechner, she could base her understanding on detailed research, including interviews of people who knew Eleanor Roosevelt and examination of her voluminous personal papers. But more important than these for the success of the novel were impressionistic and sensory routes to sympathy. "I was able to sleep in her bed, use her china, try on her clothes. I had great intimacies with her" (letter). Intimacies of scene and ambiance inform the novel: the smells of winter medicines cooking on the kitchen stoves, "creosote and camphor, chloride of iron, corn syrup, honey, stability, the tinctures and oils of childhood, babble and bubble away in mahogany brews in copper boilers" (49); Franklin playing with model ships, testy that the children's clutter invades his space; the ghastly visits to the World War I battlefields; the heat, discomfort, and indifferent crowds of the 1920 vice-presidential campaign; the brutal work involved in caring for Franklin during his illness. And these intimacies become the alembic in which the reader, too, is transmuted into Eleanor and shares her own perceptions of her transformation, a slow, confused soul-making that she herself cannot entirely explain. It is easy to say, with the biographer, that after Eleanor's discovery of Franklin's romance with Lucy Mercer, "Ended was the subordination to her mother-in-law and to the values and the world Sara represented; emergent was the realization that to build a life and interests of her own was not only what she wanted to do but what she had to do" (Lash 220). It is more difficult to show the erratic progress toward that new life, the half-comic attempts to reconcile conscience with aristocratic rearing, in scenes such as that depicting Eleanor leaving a reception at the Waldorf to stand outside in the cold, in her jewels and her evening gown, holding a picket sign with a group of striking Waldorf charwomen.

Though Lerman shares the understanding of Eleanor's development found in the major biographies, her fictional method allows one to experience that development as a more ambiguous and complex change. Joseph Lash, for instance, mentions that in 1919 Eleanor attended a tea for the delegates to the International Congress of Working Women, quotes a letter saying she found it "interesting and amusing," and tells that she invited some of those working-class delegates, women who would later become her friends, to lunch at her home. There is no suggestion that these experiences might have been awkward or troubling. Lerman, in contrast, describes the congress in detail, imagining Eleanor's embarrassment at the off-color jokes, the unshakable aristocratic bossiness that pushes her to correct the grammar of the women she talks to, her attraction to the sense of community she feels, and the caricatured version of the event she presents to Franklin at the dinner table so as to preempt *his* caricature of "the ladies who sucked on cigars and lived with each other" (192). Similarly, Lerman vividly imagines that lunch at the Roosevelt home:

With each tinkle of my bell, with each gleam on the silver sherbets and each creme on the three-tiered Meissen candy dish and each ring of crystal on the Marie-Therese chandelier over our heads and each trace of carving on the wainscoting of the dining room and the silver brackets of the gas lamps, with each of the things of my life—my curiosities—the bonds I had felt at the congress unravelled. . . . What I was embarrassed me. (195–96)

Lerman gives, in other words, the mixed emotions, the ambiguities, the body of the events she portrays; gives them in a way not accessible through the rational mind, made possible by the narrowed focus, the expansion of scene, that a novelist has time for and a biographer does not. But this intimacy was achieved only at enormous cost in time, energy, sanity, to the writer herself.

That expense, however, paid great fictional dividends, for

the voice she created is fully satisfying as a fictional character and equally satisfying, according to some of Eleanor's friends, as a resurrection of the personality they knew. The forced transmutation of author into subject and reader into subject is paralleled by the transmutation of Eleanor into a determined and self-determined force. The book's most persistent metaphor is that of the lead Eleanor feels is her essence: base, heavy, and poisonous. She longs to transmute this lead into silver, not aspiring to gold, Franklin's element. The references to lead are mixed with references to pregnancy and birth; Eleanor feels that her soul stirs within her like a child she must bring to fruition and bear in pain. Again the alchemical references inform the image in a more than superficial way, for "the great alchemical theorem . . . is one of universal development, which acknowledges that every substance contains undeveloped resources and potentialities, and can be brought outward and forward into perfection" (Redgrove 9). Lead, the basest of the metals, was a symbol of "sinful and unregenerate man" but yet, like all other metals, was "gold in the making." All metals were thought to "spring from some seed in the womb of nature" (Redgrove 11, 28). Eleanor's soul is her own child, a spirit seeded by the events that chance and luck force upon her and brought to birth almost unconsciously, when finally she sees, in FDR's polio, "the lead moving slowly, deepening in Franklin's limbs" (282) and she knows that she is freed to be herself at last.

The book is not a saint's life, and so it horrified readers who had idolized Eleanor and did not want to see their idol's image graven with human lines of fear, petulance, awkwardness, self-righteousness. But it is a human being's life, the life of a fictional character named Eleanor Roosevelt, who came to life, if we are to believe its reluctant creator, by living in that creator's body for three years, a long gestation. Whatever the fire that heated up this distillation, the product of the transmutation is pure gold.

## The Photograph Becomes a Mirror: *Coming Through Slaughter*

Rhoda Lerman found writing *Eleanor* difficult because of the contrasts between her own self and that of her subject. Fiction biography based on more natural identities and sympathies between novelist and subject can also be difficult, because "very private" (Witten 10). Such identities and sympathies underlie one of the most accomplished and technically interesting fiction biographies yet produced, a book that provides an instructive case study of the technical and personal issues confronting the fiction biographer. Though less known in this country, Michael Ondaatje is one of the best-respected contemporary writers in Canada. A productive poet, Ondaatje made his first foray into biographical writing with the poetic biography *The Collected Works of Billy the Kid: Left-Handed Poems,* a "collage of poetry, prose, photographs, and found material" (Scobie 5), which he later adapted as a stage play for the Shakespeare Festival at Stratford, Ontario. In 1976, Ondaatje won *Books in Canada*'s award for the best first novel by a Canadian for *Coming Through Slaughter,* a fiction biography of Buddy Bolden, one of the legendary figures of early jazz. Other jazz musicians mention Bolden as a great innovator and one of the most popular musicians in New Orleans during his brief career, but little is actually known about his life. The biography of Bolden by Donald Marquis is only 130 pages long, excluding appendices and bibliography. Despite exhaustive research, the book's two greatest contributions to knowledge of Bolden's life are negative: Marquis disproves the persistent legends that Bolden was a barber and edited a scandal sheet named *The Cricket.* Bolden's second wife, Nora, who was traced down in Waterloo, Iowa, in 1942 by the indefatigable jazz researcher William Russell, denied both stories, and her denials were corroborated by other reliable sources and by the fact that no copy of a newspaper called *The Cricket,* edited by anyone, has ever been found. Other than these two facts, Marquis's research in old New Orleans phone books, police records, jazz archives, and newspaper morgues produced pitifully few rewards: a few family addresses, a few death certificates, the knowledge that Bolden worked for a time as a plasterer, the marriage certificate of a wedding he witnessed (and thus the only known copy of his signature), his commitment papers, and the only newspaper coverage of his legendary career: one-paragraph items in two different newspapers describing his first attack of insanity, during which he hit his mother over the head with a water pitcher. Even more than most, this biography is full of qualifiers, of possibly's and perhaps's, and despite its brevity is padded with contextual materials, as chapter and appendix titles reveal: "Family History and City Neighborhoods," "Places Bolden Played," "Bolden's Sidemen and Contemporaries," "The Music and Musicians after Bolden Left," "The Family Up-to-Date." Many of the chapters about Bolden himself are formed largely of quotations from the many contradictory accounts of the man and his music, some of which Marquis then disproves and others of which he questions.

How much less conclusive was the "thin sheaf of information" (*Slaughter* 134) available to Michael Ondaatje a few years before this biography appeared! A single photograph, of Bolden's band in 1905, and even that mysterious, since whichever way it is printed some of the band members appear to be holding their instruments backward; a single page of facts, and even that full of questions marks ("Born 1876?"), of blanks ("Hattie _____ had a son by him"), of uncertainties ("Other teachers were possibly . . ."), and, as it turns out, inaccuracies. In fact, certain details very important to Ondaatje's interpretation of Bolden are either mistaken or simply and admittedly invented. Yet these inaccuracies do not discredit this book as they would a traditional biographical novel, for the book clearly establishes that biographical accuracy is not its goal, and, indeed, given the scarcity of information, is not even possible. The enormous gaps in the biographical record grant so much freedom for invention that one might expect Ondaatje to have retained at least the few facts available. But Ondaatje found even these to be restrictive or irrelevant: "While I have used real names and characters and historical situations I have also used more personal pieces of friends and fathers," he says in the acknowledgments that conclude the book. "There have been some date changes, some characters brought together, and some facts have been expanded or polished to suit the truth of fiction." By announcing but not specifying the changes, Ondaatje establishes that the purpose of the book is not to convey information about Buddy Bolden. Here he differs from earlier fiction biographers such as Yourcenar, who were careful to identify the false leads in their accounts and thus also to identify the more reliable information. He also differs from mainstream biographical novelists, who tend to insist that their novels are consistent with the historical record; in such books, the reader learns about the subject and about history—indeed, the purpose of many such books seems to be to make history fun for those people who would not find it interesting if taken straight. By contrast, in *Coming Through Slaughter,* we learn very little about Bolden except that he existed. What we do learn about is Ondaatje's version of Buddy Bolden, which does not merely extrapolate from the historical record but openly contradicts it. Ondaatje describes the book as having "a totally mental landscape . . . a landscape of names and rumours. Somebody tells you a rumour and that becomes a truth" (Witten 9). The indefinite article is significant: a rumour becomes *a* truth, not *the* truth. It is one of several possible truths, each of which must be at least partially false.

The historical Buddy Bolden was born in 1877 in New Orleans and spent his youth there. He learned to play the trumpet around 1894 and became the first of the "kings" of the trumpet in jazz, leading a highly successful career between 1900 and 1905. At about this same time, the odd little photographer E. J. Bellocq was taking his portraits of the Storyville prostitutes, though there is no reason to believe the two men ever met. Bolden had two common-law wives, Hattie Oliver and Nora Bass; when not involved with these women, he lived with his mother and sister. In early 1906, he began to have psychotic episodes, brought on at least in part by heavy drinking; he was arrested for insanity in March and released shortly thereafter. His last job as a musician was a Labor Day parade that year; at some point, he dropped out of the parade, "either from exhaustion, or perhaps more likely, from some conduct that caused concerned musicians or friends to take him home" (Marquis 117). About a week later, he was arrested for the second time; after his release, he spent several months just sitting around the neighborhood drinking. In March 1907 he was again arrested, spent two months in the House of Detention, and was then committed to the state asylum at Jackson. He died there in 1931 and was buried in an unmarked grave in Holt Cemetery, New Orleans.

Ondaatje's novel begins in the spring of 1906, with occasional flashbacks to Bolden's life as barber and as editor of a scandal sheet *The Cricket*. Police Detective Webb (a fictional character), a friend of Bolden's, learns from Nora that he has been missing for six months and sets out to find him. In his two-year-long private investigation, he talks to former Bolden band members such as Willie Cornish and to the photographer Bellocq, whom Nora blames for Bolden's disappearance. Eventually he finds Bolden at Shell Beach, where he has been living with Robin and Jaelin Brewitt (also fictional). Webb urges Bolden to return to New Orleans and to his career. Bolden spends a few weeks alone at Webb's cottage on Lake Pontchartrain, trying to escape the trap of fame that Webb has set for him; finally he returns to New Orleans and five days later goes mad while playing in a parade in April 1907.

In June he goes to the asylum, and here the novel essentially ends, except for one scene years later between Webb and Bella Cornish.

For all its inventions, the novel clearly and immediately establishes that it deals with a real person. The first page of the novel is the picture of the Bolden band, with Bolden identified, accompanied by a quotation from Bolden's friend Louis Jones describing his popularity. The first section of the book describes "his geography" as it appears today: "The various homes of Bolden, still here today, away from the recorded history. . . . This is N. Joseph's Shaving Parlor, the barber shop where Buddy Bolden worked" (10). Throughout the book, clearly set off from the fictional sections, are pieces of history: quotations from interviews with old jazzmen; popular song titles of the time; descriptions of Bellocq's photographs; a list of a dozen band names, too exotic to be invented: the Diamond Stone Brass Band, the Old Excelsior Brass Band, Kid Allen's Father's Brass Band; many specific dates and addresses; a one-page résumé of the facts of Bolden's life; an interview with Lionel Gremillion, chief administrator of East Louisiana State Hospital, and selections from his history of that institution; and transcripts of taped interviews with the musician Frank Amacker.

Yet most of these factual items are undercut in one way or another. The real interviews are set up on the page in exactly the same way as imagined interviews, recognizably imagined because the language is poetical and the speakers are not , listed under the interview credits on the copyright page. The photograph, we are told, "is not good or precise" but is the "only photograph that exists today of Bolden and the band" (66). The interview with Gremillion is frustratingly unspecific: "Wasn't much communication between whites and blacks here and so much information is difficult to find out. No black employees here" (137). Gremillion speculates that Bolden may have had an "endocrine problem" but can shed no real light on his madness. The selections from Gremillion's history of the hospital describe general conditions there but include only two references to Bolden: the negative results on a Wassermann test and the date of his death. And Frank Amacker, an old man with a failing memory, has little to say for Bolden's playing except that he was the loudest of the good trumpet players. Thus, the facts feel considerably less certain than the fiction, which proceeds by the flat assertions of most fiction: she did, he thought, he felt, she said.

But even this certainty is undercut by shifts in point of view that continually catch the reader off-guard. The narrators include an omniscient researcher-author offering historical background and externalized descriptions of characters such as Bellocq; Buddy Bolden, sometimes in third person and sometimes in first person; detective Webb, in third person; the various first-person voices of the interviewed musicians; and finally, and most startling, the author speaking in his own voice, describing himself confronting the "desert of facts" that is Bolden's life, the elusiveness of the man, the "complete absence of him" from those places he frequented, and then the author's own identification with him: "When he went mad he was the same age as I am now."

"The photograph moves and becomes a mirror. When I read that he stood in front of mirrors and attacked himself, there was the shock of memory. For I had done that. Stood, and with a razor-blade cut into the cheeks and forehead, shaved hair. Defiling people we did not wish to be" (133).

The shock of remembering Bolden's activities as his own, and the immediately felt sense of "we-ness," seem to have given Ondaatje the freedom to create a Bolden out of "personal pieces of friends and fathers" and of himself. For to learn that one's own most private or extreme moments have been shared by another is to be encouraged to believe that the boundaries between people, the limits of selfhood, are not as impermeable as we assume. Ondaatje speaks directly to

Bolden:, "[I] Did not want to pose in your accent but think in your brain and body" (134). Thus the project of understanding another becomes equally the project of understanding oneself: one's present options, one's potential futures. This same sort of identification appears more briefly in *Billy the Kid,* in the poem that identifies the gunman's hands with the writer's hands: "and my fingers touch / the soft blue paper notebook / . . . I am here with the range for everything / corpuscle muscle hair / hands that need the rub of metal" (72), and also in the uncaptioned childhood photograph of Ondaatje, Michael the Kid, that ends the book.

Such identification, at first the motivation for the biographical quest, becomes its technique as well, a route to knowledge, and it is when treating the most intimate and crucial experiences of Bolden that Ondaatje uses the first person: the vital setting of the barbershop, the love-making with Robin Brewitt, the violent fight with Tom Pickett, the long retrospective soliloquy at Webb's cabin, the final parade, and the trip to the asylum, after which the narrative fades into the distance of third-person accounts by peripheral characters and of historical records, which say so little. It is as if Ondaatje were unable or unwilling to violate the privacy that he sees as the motivation of Bolden's "madness," whether real or feigned. But he seems to have felt that the first person, the assumption of identity with his subject, was necessary if the most impossible parts of the account were to be convincing, and so the most purely invented sections are told in the most strongly assertive form: I did, I thought, I felt. When first reading the novel, one feels these shifts into first person only because of the increased intensity they bring, but at the end of the book, one is forced to rethink all of those passages, for the last paragraph of the novel is one in which the "I" could be either Bolden or Ondaatje: "I sit with this room. With the gray walls that darken into corner. And one window with teeth in it. Sit so still you can hear your hair rustle in your shirt. Look away from the window when clouds and other things go by. Thirty-one years old. There are no prizes" (156). Twenty pages earlier, Ondaatje had emphasized connections of age and emotions between Bolden and himself. Here, the setting suggests Bolden in the asylum, as do certain images associated with Bolden throughout the novel. But the tone is more lucid than the Bolden of the last previous first-person section: "Laughing in my room. As you try to explain me, I will spit you, yellow, out of my mouth" (140). This confusion of author and subject, coming at the end of the book, casts much of it into doubt even as a fictional account of Buddy Bolden's life, for many of the first-person experiences attributed to Bolden are anonymous enough, unconnected enough to the specifics of his career, his friends, or his family, that they could as easily be read as "personal pieces" of Ondaatje himself.

Many gratuitous factoids, public and private, connect Ondaatje and Bolden. Certain connections are obvious only to readers who can recognize Ondaatje's favorite poetic motifs and images when they occur in Bolden's mind. But even the few details about Ondaatje available to anyone who sees the dustjacket of the book tie him to his version of Bolden. According to the jacket blurb, he "lives with his wife . . . and children and dogs in Toronto"; the photo shows a man in a collarless shirt. Now, though the only pictures of Bolden show him in a stiff dress collar, Ondaatje says, "Nora's habit of biting the collars of his shirts made him eventually buy them collarless" (49). And though Bolden's son from his first marriage was living with his first wife, and though he had only one child by his second wife, in Ondaatje's account both children live with Nora and Bolden's role as father is emphasized: he walks his children to school every day, giving "himself completely to them during the walk, no barriers as they walked down the washed empty streets one on either side, their thin cool hands each holding onto a finger of his" (13); he automatically goes in to comfort a crying child at night; and he has recurrent nightmares of his children's dying. According to Marquis, the historical Bolden was an "idol to the children in the area" and "was not star-struck and always had time to talk" (95), but there is little evidence that his own children received much attention—indeed, after a few years he no longer provided any support for his son—or that he would be so obsessed with their safety. And the fictional Bolden shares Ondaatje's "well-known love of dogs" (Scobie 10), picking up a stray when he is staying at Webb's cabin; the historical accounts mention no dogs in any context.

However, these private jokes are only minor versions of the manipulation of facts that happens on a much larger scale throughout the novel, in the service of Ondaatje's central understanding of Bolden as an extreme case of the problems facing any artist in this century (Witten 10), the understanding that drew him to Bolden initially: "Why did my senses stop at you? There was the sentence, 'Buddy Bolden, who became a legend when he went berserk in a parade.' . . . you like a weatherbird arcing round in the middle of your life to exact opposites and burning your brains out . . . There was the climax of the parade and then you removed yourself from the 20th century game of fame" (134). Already at this point, at least as he describes it, Ondaatje had begun to conceptualize the life, to perceive Bolden as the victim of a game Ondaatje himself was resisting. His desire to illustrate an artist's conflicts between improvisation and order, in life as in music, and between the purity of private art and the intoxication of public art determined which facts he selected, which he "expanded and polished," which he distorted, and which he invented.

Ondaatje's use of those persistent legends, Bolden as barber and as scandal sheet editor, is intricate and fascinating; from them he draws several central images and an idea of Bolden's music not really suggested by the historical descriptions of his style. Since these legends, which Bolden's biographer goes to such pains to disprove, are stated as fact in most earlier sources on Bolden, Ondaatje presumably took them at face value as facts with good fictional resonances. Ironically, these suggestive "facts" were already fictions, the first based on Bolden's habit of hanging around barbershops and his close friendship with a barber, Louis Jones, and the second based possibly on the existence of another Bolden who was something of a gossip. The N. Joseph Shaving Parlor on the corner of First and Liberty in Bolden's old neighborhood, which Ondaatje identifies as the place where Bolden "probably worked," *is* Bolden's place of employment in the novel. Actually, the shop was owned by Bolden's friend Jones at the time; Nelson Joseph and his brother did not take over the place until about the time that Bolden went to the asylum. But in *Coming Through Slaughter*, this very ordinary shop becomes a magical environment that both enthralls and enslaves Bolden, providing him with material for *The Cricket* and for his music but also restricting him into its routine. Ondaatje sees Bolden as caught in the impossible trap of trying to maintain a music that was always new, formless except for the form of the mood behind it. Before his disappearance, he keeps a life that is finely balanced, finding the "certainties he loathed and needed" (78) in Nora's "delicate rules and ceremonies" (15), while exercising his anarchic improvisational impulses in the barbershop and through the trumpet. To his clients in the shaving parlor, who come with a need for the solace of confession, Bolden "freely gave bizarre advice just to see what would happen. . . . Days later furious men would rush in demanding to speak to Bolden," who "instead of accepting guilt" would "quickly suggest variations. . . . He loved it. His mind became the street" (42). As he works on his clients, Bolden savors their powerlessness and their trust of him, knowing that he could at any time, with a slight movement of the hand, drop burning soap in a man's eye or cut his throat. Surrounded by mirrors, green plants, Audubon wallpaper, and the ice fogging the windows of the "only cool place in the First and Liberty region" (47), he balances chaos and control and gathers the stories he will print in *The Cricket* and play on his trumpet, "his whole plot of song covered with scandal and incident and change. . . . Up there on stage he was showing all the possibilities in the middle of the story" (43).

The barbershop also furnishes several of the book's recurrent images, most importantly the "tin-bladed fan, turning like a giant knife all day above my head. So you can never relax and stretch up" (47). Though providing comfort, it also provides a limit; it cramps Bolden's style. Stephen Scobie has pointed out a possible pun here on the "fan" who adores the musician but also forces him to maintain a single rigid posture (13). But the fan is also related to Bolden's own self-destructive impulses, and it finally provides the symbol to describe the "suiciding" of Bolden's mind: "Bolden's hand going up into the air in agony. His brain driving it up into the path of the circling fan" (136). The other image furnished by the barbershop is the blocks of ice that melt all day long in the windows of N. Joseph's to cool this room; this coolness is repeated in the Brewitts' house and in references to Robin's hair, breath, and touch—a private version of the anarchy he courted at N. Joseph's since he and the Brewitts have "no order" among them—and represents the evanescence of human relationship and human endeavor. In their last time together, Bolden thinks that he and Robin "give each other a performance, the wound of ice. We imagine audiences and the audiences are each other again and again in the future. . . . We follow each other into the future, as if now, at the last moment we try to memorize the face a movement we will never want to forget. As if everything in the world is the history of ice" (87). Ice, of course, has no history that can be traced, only the history of melting and evaporation, leaving no sign that it existed, just as in "Holtz cemetery the high water table conveniently takes the flesh away in six months" (134) so that the "history" even of Bolden's body has become the history of ice.

*The Cricket,* as Ondaatje imagines it, is wholly unedited, equally respecting "stray facts, manic theories, and well-told lies" (24). It contains excessive references to death—freak accidents, murders of passion—reflecting Bolden's obsession with all the ways that death can surprise a person. But its method is to fix the chaotic flow around him. It was, he thinks in retrospect, "my diary too, and everybody else's" (113), briefly making sense of situations that would have changed again by the next issue of the paper. After his disappearance, his plunge into silence and privacy and a life without theories, Bolden sees the newspaper as only "the crazyness I left. Cricket noises and Cricket music for that is what we are when watched by people bigger than us" (113–14). Bolden has become bigger than he was, by escaping the cramped room of fame, escaping the false sense of his own significance, and returning to the eternally unpredictable, eternally improvised, edge of music and of experience.

It is not difficult to see how these two legends came together in Ondaatje's mind as clues to the man's personality: a barbershop, one of the most sociable places imaginable, where men would sit and gossip as they waited their turns; a broadsheet made up of gossip and scandal, of public improvisations upon improvised daily lives, the lives as formless and fluid as most lives, except those in novels and biographies. Together these two legends provided one-half of a life; the other half is silence, isolation, anonymity in the asylum, where no one knows, or knows anything about, anyone else. To represent the opposing forces that finally snap Bolden in the parade, Ondaatje arranges a constellation of characters, some real, some partly real, some completely imagined, whose gravitational power draws and repels Bolden. On the side of order and ceremony:

his wife Nora Bass, who provides for a time the secure base for his improvisations, and Webb, the detective who likes to play with magnets, who never loses anything, who tempts Buddy back into the world after his self-imposed exile. On the side of silence and chaos: Bellocq, the artist who scorns fame, who tempts Buddy into a "mystic privacy" (64) and "out of the world of audiences" (91); and the Brewitts, "The silent ones. Post music. After ambition" (39), who help Buddy to recover the "fear of certainty" that had been the essence of his jazz.

In creating the Brewitts and Webb, Ondaatje does nothing very different from what most fiction writers do when they create representative characters to act as foils or doubles for the protagonist. Even his version of Nora Bass is almost entirely imagined, and suited to the fictional purposes as much as any figure tailor-made to the author's desires by the author's mind. But his use of E. J. Bellocq is more intriguing, because it is in so many ways *not* an imaginary construct, but reconcilable with the historical evidence (again rather sketchy) about Bellocq himself. Other than Bolden himself, Bellocq is the only well-developed historical figure in the novel. Like Bolden, he is an enigmatic figure, though their career progressions were reversed: Bolden, popular in his own time, is now generally unknown; Bellocq, an obscure commercial photographer during his lifetime, has now become respected through the exhibition of his work at the Museum of Modern Art and through Louis Malle's film *Pretty Baby*, which was loosely based on the mood and subject of Bellocq's private pictures—the women in the Storyville brothels. Ondaatje's "Acknowledgements" list Bellocq's pictures as "an inspiration of mood and character," but he gives no other direct clues to the "Private and fictional magnets" that "drew him and Bolden together" (158) in the fictional world, except perhaps his description of Bellocq's photos. Ondaatje sees in these a kind of intimacy or privacy: the photographer alone in a room with the woman, so silently attentive that he forces her into a passing grace or beauty, waiting until "she would become self-conscious towards him and the camera and her status, embarrassed at just her naked arms and neck and remembers for the first time in a long while the roads she imagined she could take as a child" (54). In contrast to the almost compulsively sociable Bolden, Bellocq seems to have preferred to be left alone and to create his art alone; he showed his pictures only to the few people he liked and trusted.

He and Bolden, then, are opposites that must have come together in Ondaatje's mind and so come together in the novel. The author was faced with a puzzle: an outgoing, idolized, creative young man goes insane at the peak of his career, and withdraws into the silence, anonymity, and stasis of an asylum, "dropped into amber" (134) for the remaining twenty-five years of his life. The process of unpuzzling the puzzle is analogous to working a mathematical formula in which certain quantities and relationships are given and others must be deduced. To Ondaatje, Bellocq was a key, an alternate artistic and personal style, a functional version of the silence that Bolden preserved in madness. Bellocq's privacy and self-sufficiency free Bolden from the false sense of his own significance that is encouraged by public admiration. So short that "he was the only one who could stretch up in the barber shop and not get hit by the fan," Bellocq offers "mole comfort, mole deceit" (91). And Bolden follows Bellocq's lead, finding that mole comfort with the Brewitts. Others (Scobie, Solecki) have traced the intricate imagistic motifs by which Ondaatje establishes conceptual relationships between Bellocq and others in the constellation of characters, so I will not repeat them here. But it is worth emphasizing that in Bellocq, as in Bolden himself, Ondaatje found a historical character so suggestive and complex that a name change would have seemed a sham, even an insult to that person. And this despite the changes Ondaatje does make in the historical record, in particular, a fiery suicide for a man who died naturally some thirty-five years later than this fictional death in which he sought something "to clasp him into a certainty" (67).

As an inspiration of "mood and character," Bellocq's photographs probably inspired Ondaatje's version of Nora Bass, who in real life was a good Baptist, "lively and attractive" according to Marquis, but in the novel is a former prostitute, one of Bellocq's subjects, who yet had "managed to save delicate rules and ceremonies for herself" (15). The most striking of Bellocq's portraits are of women who could fit this description, women who had salvaged a certain dignity and reserve. As a group, the pictures are startlingly contemporary, despite the outmoded costumes. Like Ondaatje's novel, these pictures do not force awareness of the time elapsed since these people were alive. Neither the novel nor the pictures suggest that dead people are easier to understand than live ones, and so they preserve what Yourcenar called the mystery that "before being that of history must have been that of life itself" (344) and they avoid oversimplifying their subjects into types, whether the type of the whore or the type of the mad artist. Bellocq did this by allowing each woman simply to be herself; Ondaatje does it by allowing his character to be in some ways his (Ondaatje's) own self, attributing to him entirely contemporary, recognizable sensations and ambiguities rather than recognizably historical ones. The book, in other words, has no period flavor, at least not in its fictional sections: items of furniture, of clothing, of architecture are simply chairs, shirts, cottages, and this reinforces the sense of identity between author and protagonist. Only the barbershop is archaic. The "mood" suggested to Ondaatje by Bellocq's photographs must have been that of the generally shabby and simple settings of the pictures and of the novel; many of Bellocq's models are posed against a white or black background, a wall or a cloth hung over a line, and this monochromaticism is repeated in the "white room" and the "black room" that describe states of mind for Bolden.

Bellocq's pictures are "windows" (59) for Bolden, offering escape from the room of self and of sameness that reputation made "narrower and narrower, till you were crawling on your own back, full of your own echoes" (86). To a modern viewer, these pictures are windows out of the present time, offering a seemingly unbiased view of the anonymous women living in 1912, and thus of that world of 1912, which seems so distant (and feels distant in a novel like Doctorow's *Ragtime,* which exaggerates and exploits period details) from today. Oddly enough, that particular description of Bellocq's pictures probably comes from another historical detail to which Ondaatje several time refers: according to Louis Jones, Bolden used to urge his band members to play louder, in order to lure the audience away from the neighboring park where another band was playing, by saying, "Come on, put your hands through the window. Put your trombone out there. I'm going to call my children home" (Marquis 62). In this poetic phrase, Ondaatje found one of his major poetic motifs, or at least the legitimization for his use of personally significant images to describe the experience of another person: the complicated imagistic structure of rooms, corners, windows, and mirrors.

According to a ward attendant at the state hospital, Bolden used to go and stand by the window when he played his horn with the hospital band (Marquis 128).

It seems that even the smallest details of a true life, when allowed to roll around in a writer's head, begin to form wholes, aesthetically satisfying, intellectually provocative, yet still tied to the historical reality from which the details came. Even in a case like this where the details were so few, it was necessary to select, to focus upon bits of the legend. A different writer might have concentrated on Bolden's legendary popularity with women; another might have given more space to the musical career; another might have described the conflict between Bolden and his less unconventional wife, who eventually left him as a result of his erratic behavior; another might have examined the madness itself. Ondaatje chose details, seemingly less dramatic, that appealed to him and from which he was able to construct a complete aesthetic structure. Or perhaps it would be more accurate to say that those details chose Ondaatje. Whatever the "private and fictional magnets" that drew him to his subject and to these particular facets of his subject, Ondaatje did not allow his artistic impulses either to be intimidated by the authority of the truth or to simulate historical truth. It is the mixture of factoid and fact, of absolutely convincing psychological development and yet absolute refusal to claim real knowledge, that resolves the dilemma of the writer, drawn to a historical subject, who wishes neither to mislead readers about the accuracy of the account nor to undervalue the truth of fiction.

According to Phyllis Rose, biography "aspires" to the condition of the novel, and novel and biography today are converging as writers of both forms lose their superstitious respect for objectivity and facts. Certainly, fascinating experiments in both forms have blurred a boundary line that once seemed self-evident (and that still exists in the hallucinations of certain conservative critics). How do we classify, for instance, a work like Julian Barnes's *Flaubert's Parrot?* Is it novel, biography, meta-biography? Barnes's Charles Bovary-like protagonist searches for the real parrot that Flaubert describes in "A Simple Heart"; he searches too for some reliable way of seeing and writing about Flaubert but finally concludes that there are only ways, and all of them tenuous: "Sometimes the past may be a greased pig; sometimes a bear in its den; and sometimes merely the flash of a parrot, two mocking eyes that spark at you from the forest" (112). The least durable components of the past, human beings leave behind few solid artifacts by which to know them, but that "flash" of their having *been* does speak to us, spark at us, from the pages of these new fiction biographies that pursue the truths of their vanished lives.

# 3

# Fiction Histories and
# the Death of Progress

THE FICTION BIOGRAPHERS' faith that a historical individual can be known, intuitively or poetically if not rationally, shows a continued trust in the existence of personal identity and the intrinsic interest of psychology. Whatever their doubts about the historical method, these writers still focus upon identity in process and hope to understand and resurrect the spirit of the historical individual. Most fiction biographies present believable portraits, using fictional techniques to probe the meanings of a particular historical life.

But to another group of contemporary novelists, historical figures are interesting less for who they were than for what they represent. These books, which have been called *mockhistorical, antihistorical,* and *pseudohistorical,* and that I will here call *fiction histories,* are immensely varied, and any generalization over such broad ground is of necessity overextended. But they share an ironic distance from the historical characters and the use of inaccuracies and anachronisms to create what might be called a suspension of *belief.* Unlike a mainstream historical novelist, who seeks to bring history to life for contemporary readers—to establish immediacy, intensity, and believability—these writers discourage either immersion in the historical scene or identification with the historical characters. Real people in the fiction history function as cultural types; their presence contributes to the writer's satirical analysis of the culture that produced them and, by implication, of contemporary culture as well.

In the historical novels of the nineteenth century, historical figures also carried a significance more than individual and more than simply antiquarian. Lukács discusses, for instance, the presence in Scott's novels of the "world-historical individual" embodying the interaction of historical forces at a particular world moment. The popularity of historical novels in that century accompanied the rise of nationalism throughout Europe; writers sought to understand their nations by understanding the national past, and the historical novel often has served as an "ideological screen onto which the preoccupations of the present can be projected for clarification and solution, or for disguised expression" (Shaw 52). The Renaissance Florence of Eliot's *Romola* or Browning's dramatic monologues reflects thoroughly Victorian concerns. But such works had as premise the notion of history as process, the "pastness" of the past; the present was seen as an outgrowth of the depicted past, not a repetition of it. This historicist assumption shaped two motivations of traditional historical fiction: the desire to make the past "visible, intelligible, coherent" (a goal served also by historiography) and the desire to "take refuge from the present" (Aiken 37) in a world that is comforting simply because it is distant from our own.

Both desires are defeated by the new fiction histories, which violate the tacit "reading contract" of historical novels implied by Manzoni's statement, "one can do nothing with historical truth but represent it plainly as such" (76). The traditional historical novel has generally shared with history the assumption that historical materials should be treated only by statements of documentable accuracy. In history, this contract is honored by the inclusion of what Philippe Carrard has called the "testimonials" that "certify, or warrantee, the truth of the information that the historian is presenting" (1): citations from archival sources, footnotes referring to such sources, and "iconographic documents" such as photographs and maps. The combination of such testimonials with statements made by the historian make history "a kind of collage, or patchwork, where statements are taken from here and there and then rearranged" (Carrard 7). Historical novels have always incorporated a great deal of verifiable or "testifiable" information, based on research very similar to that of the historian; though rarely marking the boundaries between documented and invented materials, they have under realism felt bound to some degree of accuracy when representing historical events and figures.

But fiction histories are not intended to be good history or even to look like good history. Like the fiction biographers, their writers feel no obligation to a sound historical method: to research the subject exhaustively, to evaluate the reliability of information, or to present facts in the context in which they occurred. They refuse even to confine themselves to plausibility in their depictions of a historical figure's words or actions, for they see all history as essentially fictional. Like most modern historians—with the exception of the *Annales* school, who believe that historical inquiries and results can and should be replicable (Fischer 113)—they recognize that history is less a science than an art, in which certain facts are selected from a much larger body of data to serve the historian's biases, hunches, and theories. A fact becomes a "historical fact," says E. H. Carr, only when some historian decides it has importance (68). If history itself is a construct, the fiction historians see no reason not to play with and even invent facts and to draw upon facts a historian would consider trivial. The historian tends to focus upon documentable events and phenomena such as laws, reforms, wars, inventions—all those things our theories tell us have tangible, traceable influence—and to set aside other facts that the novelist considers equally important constituents of experience. The historian may be interested in the fact that Henry VIII was a bad husband "only insofar as it affected historical events" (Carr 69). But the fiction historian will see Henry's penchant for connubial executions as itself a historical phenomenon, perhaps even an amusing one, that may have affected historical events in ways more subtle than whether or not the king made a poor decision after a sleepless night over a decapitated wife.

The fiction historian is also aware, perhaps more so than some historians, that "all the facts" can never be known, that despite the cartons of notes a scholar can accumulate on almost any subject, the public record of even the most publicized event or the most scrutinized life will include only a small part of "what really happened." The historian prefers primary evidence, documents and original texts, a strong base of evidence from which conclusions may be drawn, and believes that a rigorous logical evaluation of fact is the most reliable method for discovering truth. The fiction historian, on the other hand, is interested not only in what can be more or less proved to have happened but also in what might have happened, in this world or some amusing invented version of it. The fiction historian employs the free imagination to describe possible thoughts, meetings, and actions for which no evidence could exist. Instead of a plausible account of recorded events or even a plausible extrapolation filling gaps in the record, the fiction historian creates an openly unverifiable, blatantly implausible and even indefensible version of what might be called an epoch's internal experience, the hidden structures it shares with our own time.

The fiction historians differ from their predecessors in the historical novel, who also examined the past for the purposes of the present, in their lack of faith in the concept of historical process and factual truth. According to Avrom Fleishman, the "ultimate subject of the historical novel is . . . man in history, or human life conceived as historical life. . . . What makes a historical novel historical is the active presence of a concept of history as a shaping force" (11, 15). In the historical novel, history is treated seriously as an ongoing process, the working out of the fate of humankind. The historical novel emphasizes our differences from the past, so that we may know history and not be "condemned to repeat it." But in the fiction histories, history is essentially static, a realm of endless and absurd recurrence that is more appropriately a subject of black humor than of sober consideration. Rather than showing us our origins, tracing a coherent development of which we are the result, the fiction histories show a past that has never departed, a "present which contains all time" (Bryant 246), and depict "all history as mindlessly destructive, all destructiveness as impelled by the same underlying forces or motives. . . . The course of history itself is seen not as a weighty, momentous development in experienced time, but as an abstract scheme of contentless data" (Alter, "New American Novel," 46–47).

Setting out to debunk both specific historical accounts and the myth of historical progress, the fiction historians reverse the traditional practice of using the historical figure as a plausibility-building link between "real life" and that of a fictional protagonist. Violating our expectations of such characters, they ignore, trivialize, or transform their political and cultural significance, reducing them to comic cutouts or simply to common citizens. At work here is what Cushing Strout has called the "*voracious* imagination that ignores, defies, parodies, or reorganizes history because it no longer finds it coherent or explicable" (424). Vonnegut's Hitler is deeply moved by the Gettysburg Address, and his Eichmann beams a saintly smile. Marc Behm's Goering is a "jolly dancing bear" (21), a drug addict who visits his Jewish dentist incognito. Richard Grayson's Hitler, wearing denim and carrying a backpack, visits his lover Ellen in New York; she calls him a "sadist" when he throws her into the swimming pool. Jerome Charyn shows FDR's White House through the eyes of a halfwit sailor, Oliver Beebe; we learn about Roosevelt's "triskaidekaphobia" (fear of the number thirteen) and Stalin's stand-ins, but little or nothing about the world events they shaped. Russell Banks's Che Guevara can be found at the Plaza, in New Hampshire, and at Kitty Hawk. Public life and politics are "domesticated" (Tobin); the implication is that such matters, finally, have no meaning, since the story of the species is nothing more than an endlessly repeated farce.

The inaccurate and anachronistic use of historical facts and figures in these works serves a pedagogical purpose based on this nonlinear concept of history. The writers invite comparison between their fictional versions of the past and their personal visions of the present, luring readers to see in the fictions their own present histories. An impossible-to-untangle mixture of seemingly accurate detail and possibly fantastic invention prevents the reader from trusting any detail as true; the close interaction of historical characters with fictional ones, the frequent impossibility of distinguishing little-known historical characters from wholly fictional ones, and the tight way in which historical events are interwoven with imaginary ones finally produce in the reader an "anxiety of critical reception" (Knorr 226) quite different from the effect of historical novels that differentiate between fact and fiction and "always give facts where facts are known" (Sale 21). Since the tactics of the fiction history make it impossible to recognize factual truth, readers can neither read purely for information nor evade the contemporary significance of the story, dismissing the book as about a time that is over, dead, and therefore safe. By defeating these automatic responses, the fiction history can force readers to internalize the implications of the historical material.

Recognizable historical figures provide one very effective way to maintain this simultaneous awareness of past and present. Historical characters cannot be imagined in any other time than their own; especially if they are famous, we will have a dated visual image of them and a sense of their "pastness" that cannot be easily ignored. Yet they are still a part of our world, in the sense that they continue to exist as clear images in our minds. The manipulation of such images, in conjunction with fictional details that oppose them, establishes the sense of anachronism by which these writers evoke the "haunting continuity of the past in the present" (Foley 96). In the Greek, *anachronism* means "against time," a definition that might be expanded to read "against history." For one must know history to be able to recognize anachronism; indeed, history must exist before anachronism exists, because a judgment that something is anachronistic assumes that certain objects or ways of thinking belong to a particular time and to no other. The writer who purposely uses anachronism is subverting that assumption, arguing "against time" by rejecting the historicist assumption that every time is unique. Conscious anachronism is a kind of metaphor in which the presence of the anachronistic object or idea establishes an equivalence between the original, "correct" context and the new, "incorrect" one; thus, like inaccuracy, it leads readers to recognize similarities between their own time and the past. In these fiction histories, the ephemera of a time are seen as manifestations of cultural or universal impulses that vary superficially but remain essentially unchanged through time.

If inaccuracy and anachronism prevent the reader from taking a purely consumeristic interest in the factual aspects of the book, ironic distance from the characters prevents a purely psychological, apolitical reading. This distance is achieved through the caricature or stereotyping of fictional characters and the direct commentary of a narrator, most often third-person omniscient, on the action and the characters. In Thomas Keneally's *Gossip from the Forest,* for example, a novel dealing with the negotiations at Compiègne after the First

World War, the omniscient narrator "enters" the sleeping quarters of Foch in a section entitled "Our Last Viewing of the Marshal": "Now that the monolith is asleep, we can take our final view of him. From this time onward we shall more accept than examine him: acceptance will be our only recourse, for he will not change or sprout unexpected limbs at the conference table. . . . Tonight as any night and even in the dark there is a faint nimbus (having to do with innate success) about the head" (108–10). Such comments discourage identification with the characters, even with Erzberger, president of the German delegation and protagonist if any character can be so designated. The subject of the book is not Erzberger's experience of futility, but the peacemaking process itself, set in the forest that comes to symbolize the uselessness of the war and the immorality of the treaty. Keneally's forest is as much a character as are his human beings, who are either bewildered victims or smug victors fueling revenge with their sense of moral superiority.

Modern history may be no more insane than ancient history, but we can know about it in much greater and more distressing detail, a fact that has helped to produce these urgent absurdist fictions suggesting that the human race has learned no lessons, made no progress, and hoping that if we cannot see the idiocy of the present day, perhaps we can recognize that same idiocy in its earlier appearances. From this perspective, the individual is important or interesting only as he or she reveals these recurrent communal urges. Perhaps this explains the frequent appearances of figures from Nazi Germany; the enormity of the Nazi crimes has already distanced us from these people, already turned them into symbols and types of a massive evil that remains a problem in modern consciousness: the ability of ordinary people armed with an efficient technology to carry out extraordinary cruelties. But whether stressing the demonism or the banality of evil, the fiction historians examine large problems by manipulating the images of small people (some of them famous) whose careers embody those problems. The historical figures, dehumanized or generalized in order to establish their conceptual significance, find their importance as ideas rather than as individuals.

## A Novelist's Revenge: *Ragtime*

One of the few fiction histories to have found significant commercial success is E. L. Doctorow's *Ragtime;* the lives of its fictional characters are intimately bound up with those of famous historical characters who interact freely in ways completely unsupported by historical testimonials or even by probability. Tom Wolfe's judgment that the book "would hardly have been noticed" if Doctorow had not used real names (Flippo 34) ignores the delights of its aesthetic surface and its wry, rhythmic style, but it is true that the use of historical figures was perceived as unusual and was exploited in the publicity for the book. The original jacket blurb touted "Its characters: three remarkable families whose lives become entwined with people whose names are Henry Ford, Emma Goldman, Harry Houdini, J. P. Morgan, Theodore Dreiser, Sigmund Freud, Emiliano Zapata. . . . Nothing quite like it has ever been written before." Of course, books "quite like" *Ragtime* have been written before, if not often quite so stylishly. In fact, the central incident of the book is based on Kleist's nineteenth-century novella *Michael Kohlhaas*, whose imprisoned protagonist is visited by Martin Luther just as Doctorow's Coalhouse Walker is visited by Booker T. Washington (Knorr).

Doctorow's works have all been concerned with history in one way or another: *Welcome to Hard Times* with the end of the frontier, *The Book of Daniel* with McCarthyism and its aftermath, *Ragtime* with the first fifteen years of this century, and more recently *Billy Bathgate*. They demonstrate a growing impatience with the conventions of the novel, especially with the assumed necessity to conceal fiction's ties to reality. *Hard Times* is recognizably historical only in its setting. *The Book of Daniel,* by contrast, is clearly based on the Rosenberg trials, though Doctorow named his family Isaacson and made one of the children a girl instead of a boy. Extrapolating from a real situation, the author "begins with their family situation but imagines in his own way the consequences of such trauma" (Emblidge 401). In *Ragtime* he makes a clear break with the convention of disguising historical figures. Like *Ragtime,* his later novels have resisted both the psychological concerns of the modern novel and the historicist assumptions of the traditional historical novel.

Doctorow has not been silent about why he used history in *Ragtime.* First, he wished to enlarge the scope of his fiction beyond personal experience and by extension beyond private experience. "Storytelling has been appropriated by sociologists and psychologists. . . . Even when they report the weather on television, they dramatize it." As a result, the novelist "is pushed into the realm of personal experience—a very small preserve" (Gussow 12). To escape this restrictive preserve, Doctorow maintains distance from both the historical characters and the fictional characters in ways that preclude psychologizing. The recognizable names of the historical characters suggest concrete, verifiable individuality by referring to individuals the reader knows to have existed, but the fictional development of such characters counteracts this suggestion of individuality by generalizing their significance. The purely fictional characters are similarly distanced by generalized names (Father, Mother, the Little Boy) that establish them as types. None of the characters is fully individualized: the narrative line always takes precedence over the personal stories. And that narrative proceeds in such a way as to undercut the "pastness" of the setting. In writing about the past, Doctorow has said, "you are really writing about the present. . . . Croce said that all history is written for the needs of the present, the purpose of the present. I think that is true of fiction that deals with historical materials as well" (Lubarsky 15). This double angle of reference toward past and present is established largely through the prism of historical characters: obvious historical "artifacts" that can also be developed as types still existent in the present. Such figures thus function quite differently than the "world-historical individuals" of the classic historical novel, whose individuality responds to a unique configuration of forces converging at a particular moment in history.

Doctorow develops significant private lives for only two of his historical characters, Harry Houdini and Evelyn Nesbit, and this psychological development serves primarily to establish the two as American types. The escape artist Houdini attracts an audience of the disinherited and disaffected: soldiers, workers, immigrants, poor people. The people of the upper classes "did not respond to his art" (26), because unlike the poor the rich find escape easy. To them, Houdini is only a freak, like the circus freaks Mrs. Stuyvesant Fish invites to a dinner party at which he is to entertain. But to the poor, he is a hero acting out their desire to escape the impossible traps of their lives. His "self-imposed training, his dedication to the perfection of what he did, reflected an American ideal" (27), the Horatio Alger dream of success through hard work and persistence. Houdini himself is "almost totally unaware of the design of his career, the great map of revolution laid out by his life" (29). His life is revolutionary because it suggests that escape is possible. He walks through brick walls as solid as ghetto walls; he wriggles out of straitjackets as tight as the bind of poverty; and he does it all, seemingly, with nothing but the resources of his own body, the sole resource of most of the immigrants. And today, the narrator informs us, "fifty years later, the audience for escapes is larger than ever" (49). By such interpretive comments, he warns us that even so seemingly irrational and unimportant a phenomenon as the popularity of a magician may have meaning for our own time.

Doctorow also gives specific contemporary significance to Evelyn Nesbit, the poor actress and chorus girl who is drugged and raped by the famous architect Stanford White (designer of most of the buildings mentioned in the novel), and who later finagles a marriage with the unbalanced millionaire Harry K. Thaw by blackmailing him with evidence of his abuse of her. When Thaw killed White, the subsequent trial made Nesbit notorious. Doctorow's Emma Goldman calls Nesbit "one of the most brilliant women in America, a woman forced by this capitalist society to find her genius in the exercise of her sexual attraction" (46), "a daughter of the working class whose life was a lesson in the way all daughters and sisters of poor men were used for the pleasure of the wealthy" (71). Doctorow fictively illustrates this interpretation of a life seen by others as purely Machiavellian by portraying her as infatuated with a little immigrant girl she meets on the street. The cynical, wealthy woman sneaks away to Hester Street to spend time with this child and her prematurely aged father, an obsession expressive both of Nesbit's sense of shame and of her loneliness. She feels a "strong kinship with the departed mother" (41), who had been driven away by her husband because she had prostituted herself to her employer to get money for the family. Evelyn identifies with the woman in both of her roles, Mameh and whore; she dresses shabbily and covers her head with a shawl, like an immigrant woman, to make her visits to tend the child. She lives for a time in this fantasy family, "insane with the desire to become one of them" (43). The public image of Nesbit brings guffaws and catcalls when Goldman mentions her name in a speech; Doctorow humanizes this image, showing her crying after losing her urchin, showing also the remarkable innocence of the famous scarlet woman. As Goldman says to her, "It would shock you to know

. . . in what freedom I've lived my life. Because like all whores you value propriety" (49).

Doctorow also generalizes Nesbit as "the first sex goddess in American history," created by the media and inspiring motion-picture dabblers with the idea of the star system:

> They realized that there was a process of magnification by which news events established certain individuals in the public consciousness as larger than life. They were the individuals who represented one desirable human characteristic to the exclusion of all others. The businessmen wondered if they could create such individuals not from the accidents of news events but from the deliberate manufacture of their own medium. (71)

Such constructed personalities are even more dominant today, as Edgar of Doctorow's play "Drinks Before Dinner" complains: "human character, like a precious resource, is allocated to fewer and fewer individuals. These are political figures and wealthy beautiful people, film stars and TV talk personalities" (40). Doctorow describes Edgar as preoccupied with "the corruption of human identity . . . the weak Self that loses its corporality to the customs and conventions and institutions of modern life" (xv). The public personalities of *Ragtime* are as much victims of this corruption as are the ordinary people not allocated that precious resource, for their "personalities" are only fictional creations. Thus our fascination with "real" famous people, with which Doctorow plays in *Ragtime*, is in fact an unacknowledged hunger for fiction.

Doctorow often debunks these near-mythic characters simply by letting them speak the American idiom. Houdini's first appearance is imposing: his impeccable dress, the chauffeured automobile, the description of his skills and of his following. So his response to learning that Father is going with Peary to the Pole is startlingly banal: "Keeping the home fires burning ain't so easy either" (9). He is, after all, just Erich Weiss, another slum kid trying to make good. Similarly, the fabulous Evelyn, the most talked-about woman in America, tragically lovely, impenetrably mysterious, sees a beautiful little girl, falls in love with her, and says, "Hey pumpkin." To Morgan's long and pompous exposition about reincarnation and the similarity between individuals of a species, Ford replies, "the Jews . . . ain't like anyone else I know. There goes your theory up shits creek" (122). Morgan himself, another "classic American hero, a man born to extreme wealth who by dint of hard work and ruthlessness multiplies the family fortune until it is out of sight" (115), maintains his dignity until the climactic night inside a pyramid, when instead of his expected encounter with the spirit of Osiris, he encounters some very material bedbugs.

We know very little about these characters' pasts, about the environment and experiences that might explain their personalities: how Ford got his great idea, why Younger Brother is so melancholy, why Houdini is driven to ever more daring escapes. The answers are suggested only in the most general terms. Like the characters in *Drinks Before Dinner*, these characters "only have their being from their position in the dialogue" (xvi); they have only the minimal history that exists in the minds of the readers. We may recall a photograph or a phrase. We know that Morgan was a tycoon, Ford an automobile manufacturer, Goldman an anarchist. We may even know a good deal about one or more of these characters. But we are unlikely to know enough to evaluate the truth of the statements the novel makes about their actions, politics, personalities, and influence. Just as with purely fictional characters, we are largely at the mercy of the author, who is free to lie without penalty.

One reader described the book as offering a "voyeuristic expedition into the private, psychological lives of people we could never really encounter in this way" (Emblidge 404). Presumably, he refers to the historical characters; but is not this sentence an accurate description of what we find in any novel? For our access to the "private lives" of Morgan, Ford, et al, can hardly be considered access to a real private life; Doctorow's version of the private life of Houdini is every bit as imagined, as invented, as is his version of the private life of Mother or Father. We might more accurately say that Doctorow's use of historical figures offers the illusion of such voyeuristic access, an access even more illusory than our access to characters who are wholly the author's creations and pretend to be nothing else, and about whom, presumably, the author can know everything.

Doctorow generally confines even this illusion of access to the actions, not the psychology, of the historical characters: Peary's pedaling his playing piano with his toeless feet, Ford's fingering Morgan's gold plate, Goldman's delivering a speech. Like the fictional characters, the historical figures are distanced by terms that emphasize a sociological or cultural significance transcending the difference in time. Doctorow explains, "I wanted to write a very rigorous narrative . . . and I realized in doing so that I had to sacrifice a good deal of the wisdom of the modern novel, which is its ability to psychologically explore the interior lives of its characters" (Lubarsky 152). We might not agree that "rigorous narrative" precludes psychological exploration. But certainly the attempt to generalize in fiction, to reveal parallels between the past and the present, requires this sacrifice. For, of course, the past and the present are not the same, really: Archduke Ferdinand was assassinated for different reasons than was Kennedy. Though Garvey raised black armies in the twenties, black resistance to racism in 1910 was not of the sort instigated by Coalhouse Walker. The "reliable sentiment" of patriotism in 1906 was as different from the patriotic upsurge, half-cynical, half-sincere, in 1976, as flags flying before private houses are different from eagle wastebaskets. Like any analogy, the analogy between the past and the present must be oversimplified in order to be illuminating.

The past-present analogy would be discouraged by an interiorized presentation of character, which proceeds by piling up details that make the character seem more and more individual simply by this mass of particularities. The novelist who wishes to establish parallels between one time and another must use characters who can transcend their own time. Historical characters are admirably suited to this need, for they combine the fact of a real, verifiable individual, someone who really existed, with the generalized qualities, the simplifications, that we attribute to any public personage and to which we respond in those personages. Our perceptions of such people are already simplified; the novelist can play with those simplifications, emphasizing the qualities that best serve the analogy being established. The name itself produces powerful associations to which the writer may add invented or real facts that emphasize the figure's typical qualities. A general analysis ("you are a creature of capitalism"), not unlike those one might find in a history book, establishes the general significance; the historical character's involvement with fictional characters provides a private life, an individual significance, and so complicates the generalized version. Similarly, the generalized non-names of the fictional characters evoke general characteristics and roles that are complicated but not displaced by the experiences of the characters and by their contact with historical personages and events.

That we are always fully aware that the book is not a reliable history is reflected in some of the terms that have been used to describe it: a "romance" (Kramer), an "anti-history" (DeMott), and Doctorow's own term, "fictive nonfiction" (Gussow), the opposite of the nonfiction novel. Doctorow freely admits his lack of interest in conveying information about these people and their time and says that the book was "proposed" to him by a

set of images. . . . I looked at enormous numbers of photographs of the period. . . . I also read a little bit, but I won't dignify the process with the word "research"—which to me implied exhaustiveness, systematic attention to everything. There were some things that I happened to learn about and use and others that I looked over which didn't interest me. The process of selection was totally idiosyncratic and irrational. (Lubarsky 151)

He describes the book as a "novelist's revenge" on the fact-oriented disciplines that have usurped the novelist's storytelling role: "It defies facts. Give 'em all sorts of facts—made-up facts. . . . My book is a false document" (Gussow 12).

Such "made-up" facts have always figured in fiction: a fictional "detail" is simply a small bit of concrete information (a date, a place, a name) that appears verifiable and would be verifiable if the fictional characters were real. We can find the addresses of some of Dickens's characters on a London map of today; we could, presumably, check the tombstones of a cemetery where a character is said to be buried to verify the dates of birth and death. A historical name is another such fact, for the existence of such a person is verifiable, as are that person's actions and politics to some extent. So the name of a historical figure invites the impulse to verification in a way fictional names cannot. Yet the events of this book are so fantastic that they undercut this impulse almost immediately. When Houdini first appears, his overheated automobile stops in front of the house of the ideal middle-class family; they invite him in, they have tea, and everything is decorous and friendly, but then the little boy tells him, "warn the Duke," a comment later explained when Houdini meets Archduke Frederick of Austria, soon to be assassinated. He hadn't been warned. Such fanciful incidents, combined with an intricate plot that eventually entwines all the famous characters with the lives of the family members, leads the reader to abandon hope of gaining historical information and to dismiss as irrelevant the question of truth. Doctorow does not know whether Morgan and Ford, who in *Ragtime* form a club of two, ever met, but, "if you ask me whether some things in the book 'really' happened, I can only say, 'They have now!'" (Clemons 76). Truth thus becomes a question of memorability rather than verifiability; if these "meetings that never happened" (Gussow 12) seem fitting, believable, then they do happen: in our minds.

This book, billed as a historical novel and delighting readers with its abundant trivia about the time (which one critic called a "method for giving the feel of a historical moment—as distinct from information about it" [Stade 1]) is highly anachronistic. Emma Goldman's feminism, though true to the bold rhetoric of that great wave of suffragism, echoes to our backward-hearing ears the feminist rhetoric of the nineteen-seventies, and her urgings to Evelyn Nesbit to free herself of restrictive corsets and, in modern terms, "get in touch with her body" sound much like the urgings of prophets of the human potential movement today. Mother's feminist awakening, after she has taken charge of the family business while Father explores the North Pole, is a familiar plot to readers of "Mad Housewife" novels. The takeover of J. P. Morgan's library by Coalhouse Walker's gang of black militants "belongs more to the style of 1970 than to 1910" (Sale 21). Mother's Younger Brother, who joins Walker's group and later makes bombs for Pancho Villa, could be one of the disaffected middle-class youth of the sixties. Father's sense of displacement upon returning from his expedition, his sense of exclusion from his family and mystification at the new generation represented by Coalhouse, parallels the lives of many contemporary Fathers whose wives have discovered independence and whose children have rebelled. The external trappings of the time also parallel the time in which the book appeared. The patriotic paraphernalia of Father's flag and fireworks business replicates the red, white, and blue glut of the Bicentennial, preparations for which were cranking up when *Ragtime* was published in 1975. Houdini's interest in seances, the immigrant ghettos, and the nosy reporters who torment Evelyn Nesbit all resemble phenomena of the seventies. One parallel might even support the author's claim to "prophecy," for the *Ragtime* interest in Egyptology was matched by the Egyptian fads that followed the King Tut exhibition in 1976–77.

Doctorow's versions of many of these phenomena, however, are gently mocking. Goldman's "loosen up" speech to Nesbit, given while she is massaging her, is climaxed by the appearance of Mother's Younger Brother, who bursts out of a closet wildly masturbating, certainly in touch with *his* own body. Mother's feminism is exaggeratedly mild; where before she had accepted sex as a domestic duty, closing her eyes and holding her hands over her ears, she is "not as vigorously modest as she'd been. She took his gaze. She came to bed with her hair unbraided" (93). Yet she still finds it "distasteful to see the outlines of maleness" under his wet bathing costume. In sympathy with the "proto-Black Panther" movement (Foley 97) that avenges the desecration of Coalhouse Walker's Model T, Younger Brother soberly makes himself up in blackface to show his solidarity, and in his revolutionary activities in Mexico, he always keeps with him, in a gesture of reactionary romanticism, Evelyn Nesbit's shoe. Such actions and events that remind us of our own time are distanced by the period paraphernalia, so that one must eventually realize that a Volkswagen Rabbit will someday induce as much nostalgia as a Model T, that the "dress for success" suit is as much a period costume as the summer whites of the prewar era, and that the causes we take so seriously may someday seem quaint.

The book is full of suggestions about the fluidity of life, including human character, and of the "haunting continuity of the past in the present" (Foley 96). Ford makes his fortune on the principle of "interchangeability of parts," a principle Morgan recognizes as applying also to the workers. Tateh makes his fortune by exploiting the "value of the duplicable event" (111). The little boy, who seems at times to be the narrator and the organizing intelligence of the book, listens to his grandfather tell stories from Ovid and considers the possibility that the "forms of life were volatile and that everything else in the world could as easily be something else. . . . It was evident to him that the world composed and recomposed itself in an endless process of dissatisfaction" (97–99). Just so, Doctorow's fiction composes and recomposes the forms of life. Yet though the forms are volatile, the basic materials remain unchanged. In Doctorow's world, change and identity are illusions; these families could be any families, their stories duplicated by those of "hundreds of thousands of Coalhouse Walkers in this country" (Gussow 12). Though all things seem mutable, though on "this watery planet the sliding sea refused to be fixed" (68), there are certain consistencies, recognizable through repetition. Personal identity, too, is both consistent throughout time, since types repeat themselves, and mutable. As Warren says to Joe in *Loon Lake*, "perhaps we all reappear, perhaps all our lives are impositions one on another" (177). This concept of character justifies the free use of historical characters, for if identity is shared or repeated, characters are significant for typicality rather than individuality. Readers who understand this will find no cause for distress in the book's historical inaccuracies and irreverence, for its significance is ahistorical, even antihistorical, and universal rather than specific. The historical characters are Doctorow's chief means to that end.

## The Novelist as Necromancer: Ishmael Reed

Sharing some of Doctorow's aims though not his fictional methods is the black novelist and poet Ishmael Reed, who began mixing fact and fantasy as far back as 1970. His *Yellow Back Radio Broke Down,* a parody of the old yellow-back western novels and of radio dramas, is ostensibly set in the old West but reflects the psychedelic culture and youth rebellion of the sixties; historical characters making appearances include Nelson Rockefeller, George Gershwin, Mae West, Martha and the Vandellas, Lewis and Clark, Dick Gregory and John Wesley Hardin. Reed's later novels have continued to use political, cultural, and pop-cultural figures in a mix far more eclectic and wildly anachronistic than Doctorow's.

A proponent of what he calls the "Neo Hoo-Doo Aesthetic," Reed rejects the prescriptiveness of the old Black Aesthetic, particularly its progressive bias and insistence on social purpose in art (Mackey). The rejection of the latter quality may seem to contradict the strong social purpose of Reed's own art, but his only article of artistic faith is that art should have no creed. According to his "Neo Hoo-Doo Aesthetic," art is like gumbo: "The proportion of ingredients used depends upon the cook!" Reed shares with the old Black Aesthetic its renunciation of Western culture, Pan-Africanism (artistic if not political), and interest in black folklore and the oral tradition. He sees the writer as a conjure man who can affect the world by manipulating symbols of it, just as the voodoo witch doctor destroys an enemy by manipulating a doll image. The novelist is also a necromancer, gaining the ability to foretell the future by knowing the past. "Necromancers used to lie in the guts of the dead or in tombs to receive visions of the future. . . . The black writer lies in the guts of old America, making readings about the future" (O'Brien 133).

Although Reed's use of voodoo terminology is less insistent than it once was, certain concepts remain useful for understanding his books. Voodoo is a pluralistic religion, in which there is always room for one more *loa*, or spirit. Frequently a *loa* takes possession of one of the faithful, manifesting its presence by characteristic smells, colors, actions, or requests. The possessed worshipper actually becomes, for a time, the *loa*. The world is understandable in terms of the interplay of *loas*. Just as a *loa* will manifest itself at different times and places and through different people but still remain recognizably the same, specific people and events are manifestations of recognizable, recurrent impulses. Reed claims to have "synchronization ability," or "insight into the similar forces emanating from disparate entities or mediums" (*Shrovetide* 131). This faculty resembles the ability, long attributed to all successful artists, to see the universal in the specific, but Reed's worldview is hardly Platonic: for him, history is neither a progressive linear sequence nor a static state, but the periodic recurrence of essentially identical impulses through superficially dissimilar people and events.

Of *Mumbo Jumbo*, written in 1972 and still, I believe, his best novel, Reed explained that he began by writing about Richard Nixon but decided to write instead about the Harding era, in order to transcend the "particular political event and make a statement about American civilization as a whole" (O'Brien 132). He saw many similarities between the two eras: unpopular foreign involvements in Haiti and Vietnam, postwar economic crises, upsurges in black literary activity, threats to civil liberties, and the political scandals of Teapot Dome and Watergate—parallel even to the "burning of papers in the Harding affair" and the famous lapse in the White House tapes. The similarity that provided the central idea for the novel that resulted was the "epidemic of 'negromania' sweeping through America." *Mumbo Jumbo* is many things: a detective novel, a fund of information on the twenties (accompanied by a five-page mock-scholarly bibliography), and a "humbling" of Judeo-Christian culture (*Shrovetide* 131, 133). But its central purpose is to expound a wildly paranoid theory explaining all of history, from ancient Egypt to the present day, in terms of a struggle between two opposing camps. On one side are the followers of the fertility god Osiris; Reed calls this camp "Jes Grew" because James Weldon Johnson once wrote that the first "Ragtime songs, like Topsy, 'jes grew'" (*Mumbo Jumbo* 11). The enemies of Jes Grew follow the monistic religion of the sun god Aton. The "carriers" of the Jes Grew epidemic in the twenties are the forces of song, color, dance, sex, and freedom. Their opponents are the Atonists: repressive, gray, inhibited, whose creed is "Lord, if I can't dance, no one shall" (65). Although Reed makes much of Osiris' blackness and the Atonists' pale faces, the Jes Grew-Atonist opposition is not, strictly speaking, a black-white opposition; rather, it is the struggle between exuberance and control, joy and self-righteousness, pluralism and monism. According to Reed's wackily sober reading of history, the Crusades were Atonist wars against Jes Grew; the witches burned in Europe in the Middle Ages were Osirians; Milton was an Atonist, as was Cromwell. Freud was sent to America to diagnose the Jes Grew epidemic. Both world wars were Atonist Crusades. Woodrow Wilson sent the Marines into Haiti in an attempt to wipe out the source of the ragtime epidemic; Harding, an Atonist puppet elected on the "No More Wiggle and Wobble" ticket (17), was assassinated by the Atonists because, being part black, he "caught" Jes Grew and began locking himself in the Lincoln bedroom to listen to Fats Waller records on the Victrola. The crash of 1929 was engineered to stop Jes Grew by Walter Mellon, the American head of the Atonists' military branch, known as the Wallflower Order because they were those poor souls of whom no one had ever asked, "May I have this dance?" Hitler, the "young lad who killed 14 at a Protestant Bible Study camp" in a "Wotanian seizure" and writes articles for the Atonist magazine (74), had been chosen by the Atonists for "a go at the Grail" (155). The rebellion of white youth in the sixties against the Atonist values of sobriety, reason, hard work, and conformity was one more resurgence of the Jes Grew spirit.

The central historical event used—and abused—in *Mumbo Jumbo* is the 1915–34 occupation of Haiti by the U.S. Marines. Most readers, unfamiliar with this episode in American history, will wonder to what extent Reed's account is warped or exaggerated. The answer is difficult to find, because the records of what actually happened in Haiti are necessarily incomplete or biased: the sources are generally either the same Americans who oversaw Haitian education, customs, agriculture, and civil policy for the nearly twenty years of U.S. presence or upper-class Haitians eager to downplay the amount of public discontent (see Balch, Kelsey). But some answer may be found in the condescending tone of many American reports, which emphasized the "ignorance" and "immorality" of the Haitians, deplored their seeming contentment with poverty, and depicted their religion as "superstition." These reports depict the American presence as beneficial and benevolent, bringing progress to a backward country. Though not denying that American soldiers occasionally abused their power, the reports generally attribute the worst abuses to the Haitian gendarmes.

The purpose of Reed's book is to rewrite the history of the occupation, less by revising the facts than by displacing the official interpretation of them. To advance his revisionist interpretation, he provides a presumably knowledgeable spokesman: Benoit Battraville, the leader of the Haitian guerrilla fighters known as Cacos. As Battraville tells the story to the conjure man Papa La Bas, what the Atonist-controlled American press calls the "mob murder" of President Vilbrun Guillaume Sam (the incident that precipitated the uninvited Marine landing in 1915) was actually a community "punishment" of a man who "could not do malice with style," having "randomly massacred" whole families in prison (133). Far from missionaries of civilization, Benoit's Marines are ignorant crackers who go about breaking up voodoo ceremonies, raping women, shooting Cacos as a "sport," and "rampaging the country-side machine-gunning 1000s of people." The 1918 rebellion led by Charlemagne Peralte was defeated, says Benoit, because the Marines were "tipped off" by Peralte's mulatto secretary, a man who was "trained in France and possessed by the white man's loas" (136).

To Benoit, the "achievements" of the American government are mystifying or simply wasteful. Take, for example, the roads built with forced labor, a practice generally credited with sparking the guerrilla resistance. To the Atonists, the highways are the marks of progress and modernization. To Benoit, they lead "to nowhere" and have no other use than to provide a place that the Occupation forces can "speed upon in their automobiles, killing dogs pigs and cattle belonging to poor people." The highways are just one more imposition of Western culture on a people with its own culture, an imposition expressive of deep-rooted American neuroses. Benoit asks, "What *is* the American fetish about highways?"

"They want to get somewhere, La Bas offers. Because something is after them . . . They are after themselves. They call it destiny. Progress. We call it Haints, Haints of their victims rising from the soil of Africa, South America, Asia" (135).

Just as Papa La Bas redefines an American catchword, Reed redefines a whole world through his voodoo theory of history. While entertaining his readers with this theory, Reed also wants us to entertain the theory, if only long enough to question the "reasonable" Atonist version of history, past and present. His satire is so sharp that anyone who has suspected himself or herself of being a Wallflower (and who has not?) must want to disavow these dullards and their values. Reed wants to teach an attitude, not a body of knowledge. To do this, he first redefines the past, then conflates the past and the present, and then, by extension, redefines the present. If the past is crazy, and the present is like the past, the present must be crazy too.

The first premise of this syllogism is easily established by conventional fictional techniques. But the second premise requires more specialized tools. Reed most often establishes the identity of the past and the present through anachronism, in this novel usually introduced by uncaptioned contemporary photographs that the reader must connect with the events of the narrative. One, for example, shows John Mitchell, Richard Kleindienst, John Dean, and a woman who could be Jacqueline Kennedy's twin standing on a balcony looking so disapproving and humorless that clearly they are Atonists. (Reed explains in another book that they were watching a Yippie demonstration: a Jes Grew uprising, of course). Another page offers two pictures: above, the four members of a contemporary rock group; below, a U.S. Army photo from the twenties of four men in civilian dress. Though the costumes and hair lengths differ dramatically, the two pictures have the same effect, for all eight men wear identical poker faces, expressive only in their aggressive stares. The dark colors and military cuts of the youths' leather jackets resemble the twenties tweeds; faces are obscured in both photos, by long hair or by hats. The implication is that the same men, obsessed with power and control, have followed Aton under many different guises.

Except for Battraville, historical characters in *Mumbo Jumbo* are generally relegated to walk-on roles: Irene Castle, a Jes Grew enthusiast in her early books, who later falls back to Atonist disapproval of jumping and shimmying; Attorney General Harry M. Daugherty, who delivers the "Plague edict. Pelvis & Feets Kontrols" (93); Cab Calloway, who runs for president on the Jes Grew ticket; Harding himself, appearing at a Harlem Chitterling Switch as president-elect. As such, they are only one part of the whole envelope of historical "evidence" that gives this book its mock-scholarly air. Since any credible historical work must have a listing of arcane sources, Reed includes a bibliography of such books as *Color Vision: An Enduring Problem in Psychology* and *The Conquest of Epidemic Disease*. His evaluation of historical characters according to the Jes Grew-Atonist theory extends the reach of the theory in a way at once both clearly farcical and fully serious.

Historical names are, after all, necessary in what purports to be a work of historical information, as opposed to traditional fictions, which offer themselves only as additions to history, private and previously hidden pieces of history. The history of any private individual need offer no familiar names to be believable. But *Mumbo Jumbo* pretends to be not "a history" but a reading of history itself: the broader scope necessitates historical characters. Reed offers a new angle (admittedly a very crooked one) on known history; by including familiar or documentably historical materials, he forces readers to consider the claims of the book even if only to dismiss them.

Reed's type characters, historical or fictional, lack even the limited psychological depth of *Ragtime*'s type characters. Their personalities reside solely in what they do and say, never in an individual style of doing and saying. They all talk alike—discursively, rather flatly—and their conversations are always conceptual disputes. Dress, rather than movement or feature, physically distinguishes them. Embodying impulses not strictly personal, they have ideas but no personalities. Not even Benoit, the one historical character who actually shares the stage with fictional characters, is presented as an individual: "A tall black man . . . wearing a red robe & a long necklace made of beads & snake bones. On his finger is a ring upon which a Dark Tower is ensconced" (132). After this description establishes his association with the powers of voodoo, only an occasional smile or a pause to take a drink of rum interrupts Benoit's night-long monologue about events in Haiti and the history of Atonism. He appears not as a historical individual but as a spokesman for the Osirian view of the Haitian intervention. Indeed, Benoit later admits that he was sometimes serving as the medium for a *loa*: "Agwe, God of the Sea in his many manifestations, took over when I found it difficult to explain things" (138). In this he is like all of the characters—all people, Reed would say—who embody or act out the universal impulses personified by the *loas*.

The fictional characters represent types with varying resonances into our own time. Abdul Hamid is a black Muslim, wearing a "bright red fez & a black pinstriped suit and a black tie emblazoned with the crescent moon" (33). His sobriety, puritanism, and intolerance of other beliefs are Atonist qualities, which Papa La Bas says are equally common in Christians and Muslims. He opposes Jes Grew as impractical, a distraction from the real problems of the black people, and it is he, not the white members of the inner circle of Atonism, who finally destroys the sacred Book of Thoth that gives Jes Grew its power. Woodrow Wilson Jefferson is a black kid from the country, enamored of Marxist doctrine, who becomes an Atonist flunkie. Hinckle Von Vampton (Carl Van Vechten?) is the white publisher who capitalizes on black writers, though despising their work and suppressing work not fitting his profitable, sensationalistic version of blackness. Thor Wintergreen is the rich white liberal who joins the third-world guerrillas stealing art treasures from Western museums and returning them to their origins; he later betrays the group when a policeman hostage convinces him that they are a threat to Western culture. Nathan Brown is the educated black poet whose work uses both black and white culture; he longs to "catch" Jes Grew but, presumably because of his Western education, has a little trouble getting it. All of these type characters are at least as familiar today as they would have been in the twenties.

*Mumbo Jumbo* is usually anachronistic in context and language rather than in content. Reed stays with his chosen time setting but consistently draws attention toward the present, in such a way as to create dual awareness of past and present. For example, when Abdul Hamid first appears, certain similarities tempt one to identify him with Malcolm X, particularly the fact that he was self-educated in prison. But then he prophesies the coming of X, a "someone" with the "red hair of a conjure man" who will "get it across" (39). Obviously Hamid cannot both be X and prophesy him. In a roman à clef, the fictional characters would refer to and be explained by the historical individuals on which they were based. But here, the fictional Hamid refers to an archetypal Black Muslim, embodied in the historical X among others, black or white, who evidence a certain intransigence and intolerance.

To the same effect, Reed plants occasional jokes that are funny only as they refer to the present. The Arch-Atonist Hinckle Von Vampton dreams of buying a summer home "in the Berkeley hills of that rising community on the West Coast where everyone goes about saying things like Well can you prove this? I mean don't you think we need evidence to this? Who's your source?" (141). The academic reader will get a very specific kick out of this jab at evidence-oriented inquiry and the contemporary academic community, a jab not limited to the California university where Reed was based when he wrote this book. Similarly, Papa La Bas's account of the history of Atonism includes a writer, placed somewhere between Cromwell and Freud, but whom we recognize as being of our time: "Well the mudslingers kept up the attack on Osiris, a writer Bilious Styronicus even rewriting Osirian history in a book called the *Confessions of the Black Bull God Osiris* in which he justified Set's murder of Osiris. . . . He was awarded the Atonist's contemporary equivalent of the Pulitzer Prize for this whopper" (172). Here the present-past analogy has no specific past equivalent: the William Styron of the sixties is placed centuries earlier only because that's where there was room for him in the narrative, not to draw a comparison between Styron and some other earlier writer. From Reed's antihistorical viewpoint, the date of Styron's book is irrelevant to the fact that it repeats a recurrent slander of Osirian heroes. As Malcolm Cowley remarked in a discussion of Thornton Wilder, "When history is regarded as a recurrent pattern rather than a process, it becomes possible to move a character from almost any point in time or space to another" (127). Our contemporary knowledge also produces the sense of anachronism (multichronism? synchronism?) with reference to Hitler, just a "housepainter in the balcony" (155) in the twenties. Here a historical individual who has taken on mythic proportions in our public consciousness points up the real political consequences of Atonist thinking, an effect much more slowly achieved when a novelist uses a fictional character to make a similar point. The historical name provides a kind of shorthand for an idea; instead of introducing a maladjusted lower-class youth and showing him rise to power, abuse that power, and lead a nation with him in his insanity, Reed simply claims that Hitler was an Atonist and establishes immediate connections between such recognizable horrors as the work of Hitler and such "benevolent" interventions as the American presence in Haiti—or Vietnam.

In *Flight to Canada* (1976), Reed's use of anachronism and of historical type characters is even more clear-cut. Set during the Civil War, it tells the story of a slave poet, Raven Quickskill, who has run away and is trying to get to "Canada," the land of legal, artistic, and personal freedom. Arthur Swille, Quickskill's owner, is an English-educated madman who keeps a collection of whips (and once flogged Queen Victoria when he found a copy of *Uncle Tom's Cabin* in her room), sneaks off at night for Poe/etic orgies with his dead sister, and drinks two gallons of slave mammy's milk for breakfast every day. Edmund White described the book as a caricature not of "the South as it ever was but as it exists in the image of some Southern writers and most Northern intellectuals—a land infatuated with death, sadism, Tennyson and feudalism" (248). Reed's satirical targets include Swille's wife, Ms. Swille, who stops feeding herself because it's "anti-suffragette" (20); Moe, the "white house slave," a junior executive who assiduously "Yassuhs" the massuh; Mammy Barracuda, the sadistic ruler of the mansion who has traded freedom for power; the "graffado" Cato, a Ph.D. in English who has fully internalized the slavemaster's values; Uncle Robin, Swille's shuffling old retainer, seemingly content in slavery, who embezzles Swille's funds, poisons Swille by feeding him Coffeemate instead of Mammy's milk, and inherits the whole plantation by means of a forged will; Princess Quaw Quaw Tralaralara, the Indian princess "under a white spell" (147) who does ethnic dances on the college circuit but wears western boots and denims and criticizes Quickskill for being too political; her husband, Yankee Jack the pirate, an artistic entrepreneur who talks like a liberal but uses an Indian chief's skull as an ashtray; 40s, a paranoid militant who locks himself up with his guns; and Stray Leechfield, the runaway who capitalizes on racism by offering himself as black buck for porno pictures and as "Slave for a Day," saying, "If anybody's going to buy and sell me, it's going to be me" (73).

The chief historical character is Lincoln, whose "yokel-dokel act" outwits Swille into financing the North. The Lincoln characterization evokes several twentieth-century equivalents. Like LBJ, he is crude and countrified but canny. Like Ford, he is mocked for his clumsiness, and he has "A most unusual First Lady. She said what was on her mind, sometimes embarrassing her husband" (98). And his televised assassination recalls that most publicized of killings, Kennedy's: "They replay the actual act, the derringer pointing through the curtain, the President leaning on one side, the First lady standing, shocked. . . . Her gown is spattered with brain tissue. A reporter has a microphone in Mary Todd's face. . . . Back to the party. Some of the people who had often called Lincoln a 'gorilla' and a 'baboon' were now weeping into the arms of others" (103). One critic even saw a "hypocritical and befuddled Nixon" in Reed's Lincoln (White 247). But as with the Black Muslim character in *Mumbo Jumbo*, the author has intentionally avoided establishing a single equivalence between Lincoln and some contemporary president: his target is not time-specific.

This novel adds anachronistic characters to the anachronistic perspectives found in *Mumbo Jumbo:* the prime minister of Canada, with his flower-child wife, is clearly Trudeau; Jefferson Davis has a manservant named Sammy Davis. But the chief anachronism is the setting. Though the historical people and events generally remain within the Civil War period, the trappings of the fictional world are contemporary: TV, helicopters, telephones, golf, a waterbed, elevators, gasoline, scuba diving, vitamin C, pickup trucks, Texas Instrument calculators, *The New Yorker* and *The New Republic,* Crisco, Betty Crocker, Greyhound, computers, stereos, Ford cars, Sears Roebuck, and Holiday Inn. The media's persistent presence provides a running motif: "a panel of newsmen is discussing the Emancipation" (56), *Life* magazine runs a photo special on Gettysburg, Barbara Walters and Harry Reasoner discuss the Canadian election. As Jerome Charyn suggests, the book implies "that the cluttered paraphernalia of our past, present and future are interchangeable, abused extensions of ourselves, flat and unreal" (5).

All of this works to evoke the "eternal present of slavery in America" (White 248). The slave master Swille lives in an archaic dreamworld of Camelot, Tennyson, and absolute power; he is in love with decadence, with death, with money and the power it will buy. The other characters, especially the runaway slaves, live in a thoroughly modern world of high technology and raised consciousness. But the archaic mind of the slave master dominates both blacks and whites. Laments Quickskill, "Slaves judged each other like the auctioneer and his clients judged them. Was there no end to slavery?" (144). Even after the war is over, Quickskill is pursued by Swille, who is not convinced by a small change like Emancipation that his right to own slaves has ended.

The disjunction between Swille's antebellum plantation and the modern setting outside it mirrors the presence in our modern society of thoroughly anachronistic attitudes and character types. The slave master still reigns, as he has for centuries. The multiple associations called up by Lincoln acknowledge the multiple American presidents who have both exploited and collaborated with the slave master. These equivalences, of course, are reductive. LBJ, like Lincoln, presided over enormous and potentially progressive changes in the legal status of American blacks; and, like Reed's Lincoln, many presidents have had both opportunistic and altruistic motives for their positions on the race problem, have had varying degrees of real concern for the blacks and real prejudices against them. But it is simply wrong to say, by such encompassingly general characterizations and analogies, that they are all the same, just as it is simplistic to equate Walter Mellon and Hitler in *Mumbo Jumbo*.

What is the value of such reductivism? Obviously these books offer no reliable history and only the most generalized sociology or psychology. We may learn to recognize character types or typical ways of responding to an existing power structure, but we receive little insight into how that structure operates: how the types develop, how they interact, what happens when they conflict, what can change them. Simple recognition of a type must suffice, for only such simplified and indistinct types are so universally recognizable. The artist, the militant, the collaborator, the entrepreneur, slaves of all varieties, are found everywhere, not only within the black community. Every community will contain opportunists, sincere but self-deluded crusaders, cynical self-exploiters and other exploiters; a more specific satire would lose its "one size fits all" applicability. The historical characters declare the historical relevance of the book; the reader, any reader, can then extend this relevance to modern times through both the historical and the fictional characters.

Unfortunately, *Flight to Canada* is marred by much dull language and editorializing; for example, when Swille's graffado Cato, the educated Christian black, is outlawing practices such as polygamy, Swille responds, "So you've just about ended

this heathenism, eh Cato? Their ethnicity" (53). Such a condescending in-text gloss destroys the fun of the fiction, yanking
it down to the level of exposition without offering the complexity of thought that is the pleasure of good exposition. The
problem here is not the satiric aims of the novel, or even the
novel's threatening to become an essay, for one of the high
points of *Mumbo Jumbo* is a long historical essay, Papa La
Bas's lecture on the history of Atonism, that is so lively and
intricately digressive that the didacticism goes down easily.
But in *Flight to Canada,* the expository content is broken down
into conversational exchanges between characters, conversations that have no other purpose than to delineate the characters' stances and their allegorical implications. These stances
are sometimes so simplified as to leave no room for invention
and the conversations so abbreviated as to provide no real
understanding. There are memorable characters in the novel
and many good comic moments, but the mixture of fiction
and social comment does not work well in this book, which
lacks both fictional unity (of plot or character) and conceptual
unity. In *Mumbo Jumbo,* fictional unity was provided by its
detective story plot and conceptual unity by its madly paranoid
conspiracy theory, the massive magnet that patterned all the
factual "filings" within its field. *Flight to Canada's* structural
model, the slave narrative of the nineteenth century, is dif-
fused by the many subplots and subcharacters. The book's
only conceptual basis is an analogy. However useful analogy
may be for illustrating ideas, its inherent incompleteness, ap-
proximateness, makes it inadequate as a controlling concept.

Reed's satire works well when he lets the images speak for
themselves, but oddly, this writer who claims the magical powers of prophecy, necromancy, synchronization, cannot always
resist moving into the antimagical mode of commentary and
explication. He seems not really to trust the power of his
fictional images. Of course, Reed had no intention of writing
a straight novel; he models his work on such improvisatory

forms as certain Muslim essays and jazz. But even jazz has an underlying chord structure upon which the variations develop. *Mumbo Jumbo* was a fine and exuberant old brass band, in tune and on the beat; *Flight to Canada* is like a street in New Orleans, on one side the blues, on another ragtime, with boogie-woogie and progressive jazz floating out of other windows and cellars, obscured by honking cars and shouts from passing drunks.

Both Doctorow and Reed use people from the past as a way of talking about the present, but the methods of the two writers are nearly opposite: Doctorow puts modern consciousness into period costume, Reed puts archaic consciousness into blue jeans and T-shirts. Doctorow's tone is ironic, Reed's farcical; Doctorow is restrained, Reed hyperbolic; Doctorow mildly improbable, Reed highly implausible. Perhaps they differ most of all in the impulses behind their fictions: Reed is ruled by his ideas, Doctorow by his images. As a result, Doctorow preserves at the sensual level the pastness of the past as well as its conceptual coexistence with the present. "The central thing about fiction," he has said, "is that it deals in specific images, specific sensations and events" (Lubarsky 152), and his book emphasizes those specific images and sensations over the general ideas they embody. Reed's fiction, though strong in specific images, does not deal with specific sensations or personalities. His historical characters are, to use his own voodoo terminology, zombies: corpses animated by a supernatural spirit, who do the magician's bidding and then return to the grave. Though they have the demonic energy and power of the tribal fetishes upon which they are modeled (*Shrovetide* 129), they have only the most stylized connection with the real people whose names they bear. And this stylization reflects Reed's particular concepts of character and history.

The two novelists share the sense that progress is illusion, that the world does not really change throughout history except in external ways. Doctorow stresses mutability, the eternal shifting of forms, and so in *Ragtime* he stresses the particular forms of that past time; Reed stresses recurrences, the immutable patterns underlying those shifting configurations, and his characters are more patterned as a result. But despite their differences in impulse and style, both wish to make their readers recognize certain essential qualities in the American consciousness, hoping that if we can resee present experience as a continuation of a past that we see as quaint or barbarous, we will recognize in what we have been "what we threaten to become" (Doctorow, "False Documents" 217). Though the look of the world has changed, dullness remains, racism remains, even hope remains. The shape of history in these novels is less a cycle than a wide, flat spiral, in which progress may be indistinguishable from backward motion, in which certain problems and opportunities eternally appear, disappear, and reappear in different guises. The lesson is finally that changes in styles of clothing, travel, architecture, or political leadership are merely ephemeral manifestations of more enduring realities.

# 4

# The Speculative Self: Recombinant Fiction

THE AUTHORS OF fiction biographies and fiction histories have challenged many philosophical and epistemological assumptions of realism, but their treatments of historical figures as coherent individuals or intelligible types within a unified historical context preserve a certain respect for concepts of individual identity and historical time. More radically antirealist are those fictions I will call *recombinant,* in which historical figures are torn out of their original realms and recombined in new, fantastic contexts with characters from pop culture, literature, and myth. At once unrealized and unrealizable, historical figures float in and out of these stories as if dreamed or hallucinated, serving a collagelike vision that may be satiric, speculative, magical, or mythical. The effect is disjointed, disorienting: the factual and the fantastic battle for predominance and the fantastic triumphs, finally discrediting even those "true facts" that share the stage. The juxtaposition of recognizable figures from different periods of history and different realms of reality ultimately cancels history and establishes some pure realm of language. These works flow from an artistic imagination "licentious" in the original sense of that word: that is, characterized by the taking of excessive license, the disregarding of limits. Their authors have relinquished the power to control readers' responses and shrugged off any obligation to sustain a mimetic illusion. Although some such writers are classified as experimental, there is nothing new about the use of real people as allegorical or fantastic figures, finding their meaning in what Coleridge, describing Spenser's allegory, called the "land of Faery, that is, of mental space," a domain "neither of history or geography . . . ignorant of all artificial boundary, all material obstacles" and showing a "marvellous independence and true imaginative absence of all particular space and time" (250). The recombinant use of historical figures in today's fiction is a conscious technique intended to provide readers with this marvelous independence of the categories by which we structure experience and attempt to separate fact from fiction, reason from imagination, and reality from art.

Realistic fictions, while pretending to refer to reality, often proceed as if introducing us to people we do not know: "Upon the lawn of an old English country house," about which we know nothing, "sits *an* old gentleman at the tea-table," we know not which, except as the sentence ("who had come from America thirty years before") and book continue. Like the "once upon *a* time there was *a* princess" of the fairy tale, such avoidance of definite reference establishes aesthetic distance between the reader's experience and the world of the fictional characters. We need to be educated about such characters; we have no knowledge of them that the writer can assume, even when they have appeared in other books by the same author. By contrast, recombinant fiction demands knowledge, imposes referentiality, requires us to recognize "Ty Cobb" or "Bella Abzug" or "Jack Benny" and to provide the corresponding characterization ourselves. Where the realist has only to tell us convincing lies, the recombinant novelist manipulates and revises, through the volatile processes of memory and imagination, fictions we hold in our heads and so makes us admit that the process of reading is the process of telling ourselves lies—and believing them.

The use of historical figures in fantastic settings finds its roots in the tradition of the "dialogue of the dead," developed most famously by the Greek satirist Lucian in the second century A.D. His *Dialogues of the Gods,* irreverent retellings of famous stories, depicts the divinities on Olympus as bickering, plotting, raging and whining. In Lucian's version of the "Judgment of Paris," for instance, the abashed shepherd boy begins to see the potential of his situation and insists that he cannot adequately judge the beauties of the goddesses as long as they are clothed. Lucian also exaggerates the human characteristics commonly attributed to the gods, as when Hermes, protector and patron of gladiators, heralds, and orators, as well as messenger for the gods and escort of the dead into Hades, complains about being overworked. In another dialogue, Charon and Mercury haggle over money Charon owes for boat supplies; Charon promises to pay as soon as a war or pestilence brings him more business. Such satires proceed by extrapolating from an incoherent set of fictions: if the demigod Charon can demand payment for the trip across the Styx, he must want the money for something, thus implying that money has a value in the underworld, that the gods sometimes run short of it, and that they use this concrete commodity for concrete purchases. Imposing a strenuous logic and literalism upon myths that illogical people persist in believing literally, Lucian encourages awareness of the fictitious nature of theology.

Lucian applied a similar perspective to heroes of history and legend in the *Dialogues of the Dead,* where the philosopher Diogenes and the Cynic Menippus serve as spokesmen for Lucian's own skepticism. Except for a sideways joke about Diogenes' tub, Lucian makes few references to the writings or ideas of these two men. Ragged and irascible, they alone of the dead seem at home in the underworld through which they wander, debunking myths and mocking those who bewail the loss of earthly happiness. Menippus, for example, questions Tantalus on his famous thirst: How can it be, since the flesh that "formerly rendered eating and drinking necessary, is buried in Lydia," that a "naked soul" can hunger and thirst? (17: 245). If none of the dead can drink, why should Tantalus wail that he cannot? He can no longer die from thirst, so what has he to fear? Similarly, Diogenes questions Hercules on how his body could have been both consumed in fire on Mount Etna and taken up to heaven, where he supposedly lives as immortal. Hercules claims that only his "form" is in Hades, while his true self is on Olympus; Diogenes then reasons that there must be three Hercules: the immortal in heaven, the mortal body that was burned, and the form in Hades.

Menippus and Diogenes encounter many historical or semi-historical figures whom Lucian treats as types. Midas, Croesus, and Sardanapalus, found crying over their lost wealth, embody the obsession with earthly goods. Great soldiers and rulers, particularly those who claim divine parentage, provide object lessons in the foolishness of both hero worship and god worship. Alexander, for instance, was reputed to be the son of the god Ammon; in Lucian's underworld, his real father Philip berates him for his bad behavior: "Now, Alexander, that you are dead, you will not perhaps deny that you are my son, for Ammon's son would not have died" (14: 235). In another dialogue, the emperors Hadrian and Alexander argue about who should take precedence in Charon's boat; after the mutual mudslinging is over, neither seems worthy of worship. Even Aristotle is demystified, when Alexander describes him as a charlatan who shamelessly flattered his prize student in order to get money from him.

These dialogues are light and general, certainly not intended as serious evaluations of historical figures. Though Lucian plays with well-known stories, his characters are only loosely based on their historical models, for the same actions that made them famous have also simplified them into types: the conqueror, the miser, the philosopher. The brevity and determinedly argumentative quality of the dialogues preclude precise historical commentary; though the comedy depends upon specific historical and mythical references, the lesson is finally the irrelevance of history and the absurdity of myth. The rich, the powerful, the beautiful, the famous, all come to be equal at last, unrecognizable skulls and bones in a realm where strength, pride, and wisdom—all encumbrances save laughter—must be left behind before one boards Charon's boat.

Lucian's dialogues have inspired hosts of imitations from Landor's *Imaginary Conversations* to Steve Allen's "Meeting of Minds" and Brigid Brophy's "The Adventures of God in Search of the Black Girl." And the fantastic conjunction of historical figures has not been confined to the dialogue form. Dante, of course, invited Virgil to accompany him on his spiritual journey, and the inmates of the *Inferno* included people still living as Dante wrote, as well as familiar characters from the past. Blake's Milton provides another notable poetic instance. Boileau and Pope both attacked poetic dullness in fantastic satires "arraigning persons by name" (Boileau 39) and claimed classical precedents as justification. Though Swift said that no satire that applies to only one age or nation is worth reading, he planted very specific contemporary references in *Gulliver's Travels* and even, in his exasperation with fools, killed the literary life of that fool Partridge by killing his literary persona, his name, in print. Common to all such improvisations is the sense that literature provides a free space of the imagination in which questions of truth and falsity simply do not apply.

Certain figures from pop culture and national history can still provide this sort of ready-made allegorical character. Even more than the fiction historians, contemporary writers in the recombinant mode see and exploit the historical person as pure *persona*, a convenient and concentrated code reference to an elaborate set of associations in the reader's and/or writer's mind. Such personae inhabit our minds along with other people more or less real to us, cultural clichés, personal icons, the stock characters of our secular mythologies. But in the modern era, the breakdown of cultural homogeneity has made impossible the building of coherent intellectual systems from such ready-made types. In a pluralistic society, the meanings a persona may carry to various readers differ immensely; our public mythologies are too chaotic, our commitment to various ideologies too changeable, for them to serve as the classical mythologies have done.

Writers such as Lucian and Pope wrote to a homogeneous audience, sharing important cultural and literary experiences as well as crucial metaphysical assumptions. They could evoke reliable responses to the type characters they presented, could know that readers would recognize and understand those types, even if only with the satirical appreciation that a self-conscious audience grants, with exaggerated hisses and cheers, to the characters of old-fashioned melodrama. In a more significant way, Dante's allegories were based on shared faith in universal design and in correspondence between material and spiritual realities. His grand allegorical structures asserted an equivalence between the narrative and the cosmic truth it portrayed. Dante placed real people in his imagined hell, because he and his readers found it possible to believe that all those people *would* be someday placed in just, symbolic relationships to one another. The conscious enjoyment of such allegory is located primarily in the full apprehension of a systematically built structure of parallel meanings; writer and reader in a Christian culture shared the moral or philosophical assumptions that made allegory a serious speculation on essential reality rather than just a game of decoding. Such shared faith is now rarely found. Modern writers and readers, unlikely to equate a cryptic but decodable narrative with a similarly structured universe, approach type characters with irony and allegorical structures with suspicion. Today's writers will find it difficult or impossible to build coherent intellectual structures from our culture's type characters and often have no desire to do so. Though their stylized historical characters may superficially resemble the type characters and allegorical characters of the past, the writers of today's recombinant fictions avoid transcendent meanings; their narratives cannot be "read" as allegory and their historical figures may ultimately represent little more than the impossibility of representation.

The recombinant use of historical figures in recent fiction occurs in two distinct locations. Writers of speculative fiction—science fiction and science fantasy—have often found historical figures useful for intensifying the peculiar combination of the familiar and the strange on which many of their effects depend. To quite different ends, postmodern writers have extensively used historical figures as part of their critique of realism, incorporating poststructuralist views of language, character, and experience.

## The Historical Figure in Speculative Fiction

The recombinant use of historical, literary, and mythical figures is familiar in both science fiction and its more romantic sibling, science fantasy, two modes carefully differentiated by those science fiction writers whose goal is a rigorously logical "extrapolation" of real possibility rather than what they see as the adolescent or simpleminded "swords and sorcery" mode of science fantasy. But the frequency with which the two modes are conflated by fans indicates that the reading experiences they provide are substantially similar. Readers go to science fantasy and science fiction alike for an experience of the marvelous, whether based on futuristic technology or on magic. The presence of recognizable figures in new contexts is one means of creating that experience of the marvelous. In John

Myers Myers's *Silverlock* (1949), for example, the shipwrecked hero drifts into the Commonwealth of Literature and encounters characters as varied as Prometheus, Job, Beowulf, Robin Hood, Manon Lescaut, Hester Prynne, and Moby-Dick. Other characters, such as Silverlock's bard-guide Widsith/Taliesin/Golias, the picaro Lucius Gil Jones, and "Faustopheles," are character composites built from types found in several national literatures. The story can be read as an allegory of how a brash young boor matures through contact with the great literature of the world. Myers encourages reader participation through recognition, for many characters go nameless at first and must be identified by physical appearance or by their adventures. Here, the use of ready-made characters allows the author to indulge in stylistic pyrotechnics as well as to display his erudition, for the characters speak and sing in the language and rhythms of their times.

Historical figures are particularly well suited to science fantasy, for these powerful fantasy figures can call up associations of magic and mystery more immediately than most invented figures. Poul Anderson's *A Midsummer Tempest* (1984) uses the postulate of parallel universes to combine historical and literary worlds. Anderson's protagonist is the historical Prince Rupert of the Rhine, who fought for Charles I in the English Civil War; but in this Rupert's universe, the Shakespearean plays are literal histories. Oberon and Titania, Ariel and Caliban appear and provide aid to Rupert in his escape from the Puritans, often in speeches written in blank verse and concluding with rhymed couplets. Occasional scenes in the "Tavern Outside of Time," an "interuniversal nexus"(137) where parallel universes intersect, provide the rationale for oddities in Rupert's seventeenth century such as the presence of the steam engine, but this rationale is incidental to the pleasures of language and incident the book provides.

Historical figures are equally at home in science fiction, which according to Darko Suvin's influential formulation is a "literary genre whose necessary and sufficient conditions are the presence and interaction of estrangement and cognition, and whose main formal device is an imaginative framework alternative to the author's empirical environment" (8). Through some narrative *novum*, which is "validated by cognitive logic"—that is, internally consistent and not impossible in physical terms—readers are led to compare the fictional world with their own world and to evaluate their world in terms of the other (63). Except in the case of "alternative histories," which project how history might have developed if some crucial event had not occurred or had occurred at a different time, the appearance of historical figures in science fiction has generally been engineered by some kind of time travel, as when Michael Moorcock's Karl Glogauer goes back in a time machine; meets a pathetic, near-insane Christ; and then becomes the historical Christ in *Behold the Man* (1969). Though science fiction purists currently scorn time travel as physically impossible, writers have been reluctant to give up historical figures, who are so well suited to that characteristic combination of "estrangement and cognition." The presence of familiar figures in unfamiliar contexts and the forced conjunction of figures from different time periods quickly set up a "feedback oscillation" (Suvin 71) between accepted reality and fictional reality, science fiction's way of forcing an examination and revaluation of accepted reality.

However, historical figures also present problems not found with a narrative novum less dependent upon readers' preconceived notions. Our interest in historical figures is a mixed response to extraordinary individuals and to the broader types they seem to represent, whether or not we are conscious of such broader connotations. These opposing urges to type and to individualize will clash when a writer attempts to use historical figures as types within the essentially realistic framework of science fiction, as opposed to science fantasy, which has already forfeited any strong mimetic component and thus may take full advantage of the peculiar qualities of historical figures. Two speculative series demonstrate the problems and potentials of the technique. In the mode of science fiction, Philip José Farmer's Riverworld series exemplifies the problems that arise when a writer, attracted to historical figures both as complex individuals and as representative types, yet determined to present a logically consistent recombinant narrative, is unable to reconcile his conflicting generic demands. Robert Nichols's utopian series, *Daily Lives in Nghsi-Altai*, recombines historical figures in a more self-consciously fantastic way; because Nichols exploits rather than resists the stylized qualities of his historical figures, his use of the technique is finally more successful.

### Of Two Minds: Farmer's Riverworld

The best-known science fiction series to "recombine" historical figures is Philip Jose Farmer's Riverworld, which began in 1971 with *To Your Scattered Bodies Go* and continued through *The Fabulous Riverboat* (1971), *The Dark Design* (1977), and *The Magic Labyrinth* (1980). The series's thesis situation is that all human beings who ever lived, excluding the insane, the crippled, and those who died before age five, have been mysteriously resurrected on the banks of a river some ten million miles long, which winds over the surface of an entire planet through valleys bordered by unscalable cliffs. The "lazari," all age twenty-five, are provided with food and clothing through devices called grails and do not age; if they die, they find themselves resurrected again at another place along the river. As the Riverworld inhabitants begin to form nation states, many of them extremely warlike, several people—including Samuel Clemens, Cyrano de Bergerac, Jack London, Tom Mix, and the British explorer Sir Richard Francis Burton— are visited by a "Mysterious Stranger," one of the "Ethicals" who have organized the planet, who tells them to attempt to reach the Dark Tower in the polar sea in order to foil the evil plan of the Ethicals. Though not convinced of the stranger's veracity, the chosen are sufficiently intrigued to attempt to reach the source of the river, if only to learn the truth about their situation. Traveling at first by the "suicide express" and later, as the resurrections stop, by Mississippi riverboats, balloons, and dirigibles (all these technological wonders developed from primitive tools in a matter of a decade, once the necessary metals were found!), the voyagers meet duels, double-crosses, and disasters, all the trappings, in short, of the typical adventure novel. Most die before attaining their goal, but Burton and his group, including his consort Alice Liddell Hargreaves (the putative real-life model for Lewis Carroll's Alice), enter the Dark Tower, learn its secrets, and help the renegade Ethical to save the world. The books, according to Russell Letson, "collapse time" so that "all human history can meet and interact" (125).

In his prefatory "Comments" to the 1980 reprint of *Riverboat*, Farmer insists that he is writing "science fiction, not fantasy" (xvii) and claims that the books' thesis involves no magic, logical contradictions, or crimes against the laws of physics. He presents the series as a realistic account of what would happen if those real people were to meet in that situation: "Though some of the names on the Riverworld are fictional, the characters are or were real. You may not be mentioned, but you're here" (*Dark Design* [5]). Farmer's concept therefore *requires* the appearance of historical figures, for if everyone who ever lived is on Riverworld, every reader will recognize some faces, and the only generally recognizable faces the author can offer are those of famous historical figures. But by thus insisting on the literal reality of his characters, within the bounds of the "parareality" that is fiction, Farmer becomes obliged to provide realistic psychological development, and this conflicts with his impulse to treat them as conceptual types and the narrative itself as a philosophical allegory.

There is a strong element of fantasy fulfillment in Farmer's use of historical figures, some of whom seem to be his own personal heroes. Indeed, who has not wished to meet some beloved character, real or fictional, in the flesh? A writer can "meet" such heroes by writing them into a book, as Farmer has done in his "biographies" of Tarzan, Doc Savage, and Sherlock Holmes; the Riverworld is an "encyclopedia of all of Farmer's childhood favorites, his hobbies and historical interests" (Tweet 374). But when hero worship motivates the treatment of a fictional subject, the author may be too dazzled by the name and the image it evokes to be able to evaluate his own version of the character. And so the Riverworld series sometimes degenerates into endless cameo appearances of the sort that Max Beerbohm lampooned in "Savonarola Brown," his parody of historical drama:

> Re-enter Guelfs and Ghibellines fighting. SAVONAROLA and LUCRETIA BORGIA are arrested by Papal officers. Enter MICHAEL ANGELO. ANDREA DEL SARTO appears for a moment at the window. PIPPA passes. Brothers of the Misericordia go by, singing a requiem for Francesca da Rimini. Enter BOCCACCIO, BENVENUTO CELLINI, and many others, making remarks highly characteristic of themselves. (131)

The opposite problem arises when Farmer assumes that his readers need education; the multiplicity of capsule personal histories makes some scenes read like a *Dictionary of National Biography*. To provide either the tinge of the marvelous or the shock of recognition, characters must be true cultural icons like the characters of commedia del l'arte: when Arlecchino appeared, everyone immediately knew him by his costume and knew what opinions, emotions, and problems to expect. In much the same way, the fans of television sitcoms love to see their favorite characters be predictably themselves, and they take much more delight in each repetition of a trademark gesture or phrase than in any new joke. The delight is multiplied when scriptwriters cross contexts by having a character from one show appear on another and be predictably herself or himself in new combinations with equally predictable and familiar characters. Farmer could have done something similar in his Riverworld, had he only defined his audience more narrowly and thus freed himself to explore rather than to explain.

His interest in the psychologies of certain characters, particularly Burton and Clemens, leads him to spend considerable time recounting their histories, thoughts, and dreams. Clemens, in particular, he attempts to develop beyond the stereotype of Mark Twain. Farmer's "Sam" is guilt-ridden, rather cowardly and vainglorious, grimly deterministic. He has nightmares about his "alter ego" Mark Twain, "an old man with bushy white hair and a bushy white mustache"; this grinning demon rides an enormous machine combining printing press, mint, and medicine show wagon that cuts off Sam's escape from some unnamed danger (*Labyrinth* 77). Only in a brief vision of cosmic oneness does Sam merge with Mark Twain. This concept of Clemens is intriguing. But unfortunately, such individualistic character development conflicts with the alternating type characterization. When seeking to replicate the famous Mark Twain humor, Farmer turns Clemens into a cigar-puffing comedian delivering one-liners more reminiscent of George Burns, or of the "Mark Twain" that Clemens played on his lecture tours, than of the Clemens who wrote the leisurely and cumulative humor of *Huck Finn* or *The Innocents Abroad.*

The problems with the Riverworld series are not in the concept itself, which could have provided an excellent basis for a philosophical meditation, in either an allegorical or a realistic mode, on the meaning of historical change, of cultural diversity, and of human nature. But Farmer seems unwilling or unable to confront these issues, other than by his characters' occasional speculations ("What is identity, anyway?"), which are nearly always phrased as questions and never answered, even when the meaning of the Riverworld is revealed. Though characters are introduced by their epochs and nations ("a woman from eleventh-century Prague") as if these differences were significant, most fade into identical speech patterns and behavior. Burton, Twain, Cyrano, and Hermann Goering are distinguishable personalities, with different views of life and of the Riverworld, but Farmer never places them into conjunctions that could develop some central concept; except for Clemens's petty jealousy of Cyrano, the major characters never significantly interact and cultural confrontations generally take place off-stage. Cyrano, for example, is for some time the lover of Clemens's Terrestrial wife Olivia Langdon; the first encounters between this filthy seventeenth-century Frenchman and the fastidious Livy could have been immensely funny, as Burton's struggles with his racism or Goering's with his crimes could have been immensely complex and pathetic. But Farmer simply alludes to or summarizes these changes and saves his real narrative energies for innumerable and interminable fights, policy debates, and ratiocinations about the origins of Riverworld. Most of these characters, with the exception of Clemens, finally merge into the single type of the adventure hero, who, whether carrying a lasso or a rapier, maintains his resolve, his courage, and his good humor through any danger. It is a world where men are men and where women, even those who are engineers or airship captains, shriek and sob at appropriate moments. And the adventures of the different characters are not shaped by their supposedly different personalities. As types, they are insufficiently conceptualized; as individuals, they are too much restricted by the type.

The series may succeed very well as formula adventure, but as serious science fiction it is disappointing, and as philosophical allegory it is far from complete (Cook). Farmer's conflicting impulses to characterize and totalize—to engage in moral or philosophical speculation—prevent him from doing either very well. He presents too many characters involved in too many episodes to be able to build convincing or interesting psychological drama; yet his overall design is inadequately structured for coherent intellectual drama. One could easily imagine a more lucid, schematic arrangement of characters and events to body forth the issues raised by the book's concept, or, conversely, a more modest, realistic presentation of a few real people responding to the imagined situation. But the two approaches are probably mutually exclusive. The failures of the Riverworld series are largely failures to recognize and accept the limitations of historical figures; because Farmer attempts to combine the puppet personae of recognizable historical figures with realistic character development, he is unable to benefit from the peculiar fictional advantages of historical figures.

## Robert Nichols's Recombinant Utopia

A more successful recombination of historical figures occurs in a less-known recent tetralogy: Robert Nichols's *Daily Lives in Nghsi-Altai: Arrival* (1977), *Garh City* (1978), *The Harditts in Sawna* (1979), and *Exile* (1979). This New Directions series represents a major accomplishment in utopian fiction (Capouya), though Nichols claims that the series was not intended as "utopian or as poetical anthropology. . . . It was meant as current events. . . . As a first step on the highway to progress and as a tuning fork held to what is human" (in Stoehr, R17). Nichols uses a trio of Western observers—William Blake, the Cuban filmmaker Santiago Alvarez, and Jack Kerouac (later replaced by William Morris)—to represent a "common wave band, a range of vibrations, through which 'Western eyes' *see*" the imaginary Asian country of Nghsi-Altai (*Garh City* 1). This anarchosyndicalist utopia is technologically advanced but sociologically primitive, having a folk culture's costumes, clan organization, and ritualized approach to daily life. Though the people have computers and other advanced equipment, they have chosen labor-intensive rather than capital- or material-intensive methods of production and still do much work with animals and by hand. The juxtapositions of monorails and water buffalo, Darvan and betel nut, high-rise apartments and rice terraces are as jarring as the opening statement that "Blake, Alvarez, and Kerouac have just awakened" (*Arrival* 1). Nichols introduces his three observers without fanfare and simply assumes that his readers will recognize them. We learn only that they have been invited by local shamans and sponsored by organizations such as the Cuban-American Friendship Society; the time is indeterminate.

Nichols uses this trio of visitors to complicate the classic structure of utopian fiction, in which an ignorant outsider, a stand-in for equally ignorant readers, arrives at an imaginary community, is educated in its ways, comes to perceive its superiority, and finally becomes a happy member. Nichols's three observers offer distinct, though all distinctly "Western," evaluative stances that prevent any simplistic celebration of the community's practices. And his narrative presents no systematic process of education. His outsiders ask questions, visit public works, and take notes, but their writings—reports, poems, what have you—do not cohere into a single consistent evaluation of Nghsi-Altai, for each sees in the new world the same elements he saw in the old. Even after years in this world, they remain foreign and find the country increasingly mysterious; as Morris says, "We are *between* worlds, the old and the new. And the borders of the one are as closed to us as the others" (*Garh City* 4). The historical figures, always less important to the narrative than are the activities and people of the country itself, are eventually relegated to "individuality freak shows" brought by the shamans to the free zone outside village boundaries, where crimes may be acted out and illicit emotions expressed. In their vaudeville performances, the westerners wear "masks of their own faces," behind which can be seen "only a kind of smokey vagueness"; when they step from the stage, they dematerialize, as if they exist only as masks and costumes (*Exile* 69–70). Similarly, in the fiction, they exist only in the exaggerated masks and costumes of the stylized characterizations that Nichols attaches to their names.

Alvarez, the Marxist revolutionary, embodies the officious and dogmatic enthusiasm of the theorist. He is interested in systems, in historical background, "production and property relations" within the specific framework of Marxist ideology (*Arrival* 37). He worries about malaria, sees everything in practical terms; when Kerouac describes "pilgrims stopped at the village pond to bathe ritually," Alvarez asks how he knows "they weren't washing their shirts?" (*Arrival* 12). Though at first popular with the village production officials, he soon finds them insufficiently progressive, and they sour on his lack of sensitivity. Determined to join what he sees as a successful Marxist revolution, Alvarez becomes a member of a communal household in Garh City, marries a local woman, joins a production syndicate, and works on "eradicating individualism" in his personality. But his Western-rationalist tendencies reassert themselves; soon he is agitating for streamlined manufacturing to increase factory output. As a result, he is tried for the crimes of "Productionism," antisocial behavior, and "going against harmony" (*Garh City* 56) and is punished by having both ears cut off. Alvarez's bossiness and nosiness, his earnestness and gung-ho Marxism, set him up as a likable fool, incapable of discarding preprogrammed theories in the face of a reality that cannot be explained in his terms. His punishment is described in a detached, comic way; because he has never functioned as a full realistic character, the violence against him is no more distressing than the stylized violence of Saturday morning cartoons. In the final book of the series, Alvarez has been chastened enough to recognize the difficulty of getting "below the surface" in any representation of reality (*Exile* 48), the very problem of a novelist attempting to prevent a utopian novel from reading like a technical report.

Kerouac, like his replacement William Morris, is interested in the present moment, the personal and physical. He is "all energy, a hard vigor. He plays soccer with the young men . . . [and] has made the acquaintance of some of the women—not easy in a country where the purdah shawl is worn" (*Arrival* 15). Kerouac responds through his senses; he adopts the native costume and prefers to "just sit" and let life pass before him. His real report is a notebook of stories, songs, and poems in the pure Beat style; his official report, an account of a dinner in a local household, is plagiarized from an anthropological work funded by the Ford Foundation. Kerouac dies at the end of the first volume, probably murdered as a result of his irrepressible curiosity. Morris will be sentenced to the stocks for taping local songs.

Nichols's Blake is not a syndicalist and dislikes the communal "bedlam" (*Garh City* 42). Equally impatient with the materialist and rationalist attitudes of his two companions, he sees no purpose to the self-criticism sessions Alvarez insists on holding and has little interest in Kerouac's description of life in a Jat household. Both Alvarez's theoretical analysis of the local economy and Kerouac's collection of local folklore, he complains, omit the "element of the marvellous" (*Arrival* 41). His own poetry made no attempt to *describe*—"The spiritual world was all my aim" (*Garh City* 73)—and as such he is closest to the spirit of the local culture, which forbids replication of reality through print, tape, or film. Blake frequently wanders away from his fellow foreigners, visits the shamans, learns to play a musical instrument, and comments mostly through extemporized poems. In the traveling show, he will act a "madman's part," declaiming the poetry of Walt Whitman and Allen Ginsberg, in an entertainment that leaves the local populace "warmed by fires that were in their own country illicit, of egotism, romantic challenge and scrappiness, and apocalyptic prophecy" (*Exile* 76).

Nichols' tone is more modest and whimsical than Farmer's,

his concept less grandiose, and this accounts in part for the greater charm of his imaginary world and his characters. But he is also willing simply to play with the personae, without attempting to develop real inner lives for these impersonations of historical figures. His references to the historical models are graceful asides, accessible to the knowledgeable reader but probably not even noticed by others; his depiction of Blake, for instance, as interested in blacksmithing and furnaces provides amusement for readers familiar with Blake's cosmic smith Los or his fondness for metaphors of manufacture in poems such as "The Tyger." One can miss such in-jokes and still enjoy the books, but some knowledge of the historical characters *is* necessary to understanding Nichols's satire of his readers'— and his own—comfortable Western perspectives.

Unlike Farmer, Nichols feels no need to categorize his book as science fiction rather than fantasy, and so he offers no explanation, magical or pseudorational, for the coexistence of Alvarez, Blake, and Kerouac in a single context; he simply lets the pleasures of recognition and the multiplication of points of view add to the fascinations of his imaginary world and the delights of his images and language. He has, in other words, recognized that to exploit the type qualities of historical personae fully, one must both abandon the mass audience and relinquish, or at least postpone for another book in another mode, the illusion of contact with that real person of whom the persona is, literally as well as etymologically, a mask. Failure to accept these limitations can only wreck the ship of fantasy on the rocky shores of history.

## Blurring the Boundaries: Postmodernist Variations

In science fiction and science fantasy, recombinant fiction is distinguished by tension between the mimetic or referential qualities of the historical figure and the fantastic effects of recombinant juxtaposition, a tension of which the writers themselves are not always aware. With the occasional exception such as Samuel S. Delany, whose interest in semiotics informs his work, writers of science fiction and fantasy are more often influenced by scientific developments than by aesthetic or philosophical theories. The majority of recombinant fiction today, however, proceeds from a complex intellectual critique of mimetic fiction; these writers seek to escape plot, character, and theme as well as time and space. Their work has been variously described as transfiction, parafiction, metafiction, superfiction, surfiction, postpostmodern fiction, and even postcontemporary fiction: a collection of labels resulting, it seems, from critics' and writers' inability to agree about that troublesome category, the "postmodern." In his vituperative attack upon postmodern art, Charles Newman has called the concept a "terminological fiction" (16); Christine Brooke-Rose considers it "self-cancelling . . . lazy, inadequate" (10); and Ihab Hassan sees the term as having "changed from awkward neologism to derelict cliche without ever attaining the dignity of concept" ("Wars" 48). Yet though definitions of postmodernism "multiply according to the canon chosen" (Bradbury 323), that much-debated term still seems the simplest way to identify a widely varied group of fiction writers who are recognizable as much by their associations—with the journal *boundary 2,* the magazine *Fiction,* the Swallow Press in Chicago and the independent publishing group the Fiction Collective—as by their fictional practice.

Their literary pedigree can be traced to Stein and Beckett in prose and William Carlos Williams in poetry, their theoretical basis to the importation of Continental theory in the sixties. Profoundly influenced by the structuralist and poststructuralist critiques of referentiality and of identity, they have attempted to develop a fictional praxis demonstrating that critique. The starting point for some has been a scathing attack upon modernism, which they see themselves as having surpassed. Modernist "Distance, detachment, depth, essentialism, anthropomorphism, humanism, analogies, and the privileging of sight have all been anathematized. . . . Symmetry, shapeliness, and binary oppositions . . . are clearly at a discount" (Wilde 43–44). Modernist art is criticized as excessively intellectual, controlled, and hermetic. Though it insisted upon the self-sufficient qualities of the work of art, modernism remained essentially mimetic, repeating and respecting the things of the world, whether physical objects (as with the imagists) or states of mind (as with Joyce). Even Stein aimed at "exact reproduction of either an inner or an outer reality" (211), and this assumption that realities can be precisely replicated informs many modernist metaphors for artistic creation. Eliot's idea of the artist as catalyst in a chemical reaction, Hulme's "architect's curve," and Brooks's well-made urn, all conceive of the work of art as a completed object rather than an ongoing process, its sources and effects as predictable as a laboratory experiment. The precise and ordered forms that resulted were intellectually coherent even when embodying fragmentation or ambiguity, and thus, despite the modernist credo that art "should not mean but be," such works allowed readers to seek—the postmodernist would say to "impose"—controlling meanings in image or idea. The antimodernists argue that these works did not offer a real experience impinging upon or continuous with the reader's day-to-day experience: based upon an "iconic poetics of transcendence" (Spanos 38), modernist fictions could only remain separate from experience, even when expounding theories of experience or providing intense re-creations of experience, because they aimed to formulate or represent experience. Thus, an intellectual structure was imposed upon irrational and emotional experience that, according to contemporary thought, language can never adequately contain or describe.

Self-defined postmodernists make seemingly contradictory pronouncements: on the one hand, they make grand claims for the power of language to remake reality by remaking consciousness, and they aim to dissolve the dualities of life and art, objectivity and subjectivity, waking and sleeping. On the other hand, they sometimes argue against any transcendent importance for art: fiction is play, it should be fun. These two clusters of critical ideas delineate not two distinct branches of the banyan tree of postmodernism but rather two distinct moods of its practitioners, whose disdain for permanent or coherent intellectual structures is reflected in their continually revised and inconsistent aesthetic. The purpose of fiction, says one postmodernist spokesman, is to "rescue experience from history, from politics, from commerce, from theory, even from language itself—from any system, in fact, that threatens to distort, devitalize, or manipulate experience" (Sukenick, "Thirteen" 91). To the famous modernist dictum, "Only connect," Sukenick's narrator in "The Endless Short Story" responds, "the important thing is to evade connections . . . annihilate the important thing" (116). Similarly, a Guy Davenport narrator urges, "Let us desist, lest quite by accident we be so unlucky as to put these things in order" ("Field of Snow" 185). The postmodern project is thus to reveal more fully the fluid, chaotic, and indeterminate qualities of experience, through an art that erases all boundaries, dualities, fixed structures.

To some extent, such pronouncements on the purpose and method of fiction are less postmodern than post- and contra-the simplified modernism of those contemporary critics who mock or deplore experimental fiction on the grounds (rarely explicit) that a novel must have coherent characters, coherent sequence, and coherent theme, though perhaps nothing so naive as a plot. For though postmodernists find the self-contained, rationally ordered, mimetically motivated forms of modernist literature to be inadequate responses to contemporary experience, they owe a considerable debt to the formal experiments of modernism and to the modernist insistence that the work of art need not justify itself upon pragmatic or moral grounds. To see American postmodernists as having completely surpassed Joyce or Beckett is to neglect the extent to which they acknowledge, in their less combative moods, debts to symbolism and surrealism, to the undifferentiated individual psychologies of Lawrence, to the "revolution of the word" of Stein and Joyce, and to the autobiographical or mock-autobiographical works of Henry Miller, who "invented a world of his own, personages of his own, including himself" (Nin 156), and William Carlos Williams, for whom the poem was "continuous with speech, with conversation, with thought, with experience, and not a special category."

Postmodernist fiction thus differs from its modernist precedents less in specific narrative techniques (such as the "nodality" and "paratactics" that David Hayman identifies in writers from Joyce to Sollers) than in the theoretical perspectives from which it justifies such techniques. The beginnings of a conscious postmodern program in American fiction date to the late 1960s, when writers such as Derrida, Cixous, Barthes, and Kristeva became available in English. With varying degrees of rigor, American postmodernists have drawn upon poststructuralist theories of language and identity both as the basis for their technical experiments and as a frequent topic of discussion in their works (Thiher). The recombinant use of historical figures in antimimetic, nonrepresentational postmodern fictions is directly traceable to these theoretical assumptions.

The poststructuralist view of the radical contingency of language, with the correlative view that both identity and what we call reality are textual, is most broadly felt in the postmodern distrust for system of any kind. If all perception, all knowledge, all emotion and experience is mediated by distorting linguistic structures, the artist's desideratum is to convey a radically unmediated, unstructured, and decentered fictional experience that will abolish all duality, "all distinctions between the real and the imaginary, between the conscious and the subconscious, between the past and the present, between truth and untruth" and, it might be added, between self and other, writer and reader, book and life (Federman, "Surfiction" 8). As this study has emphasized, it was these dualities and the underlying empiricist respect for fact and for the concept of coherent identity that discouraged, in the realistic fiction of the past, the mixing of historical figures with more purely fictional characters. Once rigid distinctions between categories of experience, particularly between "real life" and artistic representations of it, have broken down, such mixing becomes not only allowable but inevitable.

The concept of intertextuality also helps to explain the ubiquity of historical figures, living and dead, in postmodern fiction. If all experience is textual or fictive, if history itself is a fiction and fiction is an epistemology, then historical figures are no more or less "real" than so-called fictional characters. Rejecting the formalist ideal of the book as an autonomous object, postmodernists blur the boundaries between art and life, in an attempt "to submerge the frame, to call in question the lines of demarcation, to render problematical what is, as it were, inside a text and what is outside of it" (Tanner 25). The book becomes just one more text, itself created out of other texts. The historical figure is a valuable tool in this project; because openly borrowed from the text of history, such a figure "opens the artifact, the discrete text, into the intertext" (Caramello 7). The fantastic appropriation of such figures foregrounds the reader's role as coproducer of the text and emphasizes the illusory nature of both fact and originality, working to "transfer the source of meaning from the text to the reader's reading of it" (Craige 56). The reader thus becomes an "accomplice" (Federman "What Are" 25) to the subversive activity of decentering and deconstructing the official fictions that falsify experience, disguise power, and construct false consciousness. As Jerome Klinkowitz argues, this form of "participatory reading" is far more radical than the imaginative participation in the traditional fictional world (*Life of Fiction* 4).

The recognizable public figure is extremely useful for this process, because so clearly a part of the world that the reader shares with the writer. In realistic fiction, a character's name provides the scaffolding to which are added the informative details by which the writer builds a character; though, of course, readers do participate in this process of building, they are able to maintain an illusion of passivity in the author's hands. But the name of a historical figure is a capsule characterization, a self encoded on microchip that releases a full picture when plugged into the reader's mind and so jumps the gap between fiction and life, writer and reader. As in Gide's use of Alfred Jarry in *The Counterfeiters,* this practice can "fuse levels or modes of reality by bringing together their representatives in a single action" (Spencer 60). Of *Blind Date* Jerzy Kosinski remarks,

> The inclusion of "real life" characters . . . makes the novel in my eyes more, not less imaginative and perhaps less "subjective." In any case, these "real life" heroes are no more or less real than the novel's other characters. . . . They all inhabit together the imaginative space of the novel that, by its nature, abolishes the ranking of "real-unreal."
>
> The so-called "historical figures"—Lindbergh, Monod, the Manson killers—influence the way we perceive ourselves in a society, our moral and ethical values, our concept of justice, our fear of evil. And don't they influence us pretty much the same way fictional characters do?
>
> Whatever the reader "recognizes" in the act of reading the novel belongs, by virtue of his imagination, to *him*, not the author. By its very nature language fictionalizes our "real" experience. To me, "recognition" by the reader—the semi-conscious power of projection into another time, place, and identity—is fiction's foremost principle.

Kosinski, like his peers, is determined to involve the reader directly, to implicate the reader by blurring the lines between fiction and life: "You are actually creating the situation when you are reading about it; in a way you are staging it as an event of your own life" (Cahill 149). In his novels, historical figures appear and disappear exactly as do the fictional characters with whom they are on intimate terms; the one significant distinction is that the fictional characters often go unnamed, being identified by occupation ("a typist from the office") or by some physical characteristic, if at all. Like historical figures, these anonymous fictional characters encourage participatory reading, for readers may visualize in Kosinski's vague typist one from their own experience. Kosinski claims a kind of truth for his works, insisting that his novels are "sociologically" accurate, that even the most bizarre and brutal events or situations in the books exist in every American city. But this insistence is in some ways as much a pose as his enigmatic public persona; through carefully orchestrated lies—or, to use a kinder term, fictions—about similarities between his own experiences and those of his violent, amoral protagonists, he fuels speculation about the extent to which he may have participated in the horrifying events he portrays (Klinkowitz, "Betrayed"). Thus Kosinski's own life has become a work of fiction inseparable from his writings, in response to which "the perceiver/experiencer takes on the difficult role of mediator/shaper" (Hayman 7). It is fitting that Kosinski has himself become a character in other people's fictions; Jerry Bumpus's "K" imagines Kosinski's getting the better of the Manson murderers at the famous party that Kosinski himself has fictionalized.

The combination of recognizable historical figures with relatively undefined fictional ones is common in postmodern fiction. The postmodern character is less a continuing unified identity than a locus for a set of actions, with a chaotic inner life presented not as a consciousness that remains *one* through time but as a continually changing interrelationship between the conscious and unconscious functions of the mind and the worlds apprehended by and created by that mind. Thus, characters may be named after the author, or be nameless, or bear several different names. Fanny Howe's *Holy Smoke* opens with the heroine's statement "Last night I dreamed I had a name. It was Anon" (1). This anonymous heroine is married to a man, repeatedly "found dead," variously named J, Jimmy, James, and Jaime. Such play with the hollowness of all names, which can be so easily interchanged or discarded, questions the concept of identity itself. Though postmodern protagonists are not uncommonly named after their authors, these writers reject the solipsism of fiction that simply re-creates the novelist's own experience. Naming characters after themselves and their friends, they deliberately encourage the naive assumption that events in a novel "really happened." They then upset this assumption by entangling their characters in increasingly wild and impossible adventures or by directly commenting on the action in such a way as to establish separation from the narrative, as by openly wondering what the "autobiographical" protagonist will do next.

Distortions and recombinations of recognizable historical figures operate in much the same way. In the last section of Ronald Sukenick's *98.6*, which takes place in an imaginary ideal state, Robert Kennedy is president, Golda Meir is a kind "Tante Goldie," and the State of Israel is a peaceable union of Israelis and Palestinians, in which the weather is always perfect, automobiles have been banned, and—truly a novelist's paradise—"Artists are recognized as the creators not only of esthetic works but of reality itself" (172). Though this Robert Kennedy serves as an idealized representative of certain political values, he could never be mistaken for the real Kennedy: he surfs wearing red earmuffs.

When prefabricated characterizations are revised, when expectations are reversed, the historical figure facilitates a "satirical attack upon the reader for coming already prepared for and with a set of automatic feelings" (Lee 350). Fanny Howe's lonesome heroine, in search of a kidnapped daughter named

Pepsi, frequently talks to her statue of the Virgin Mary, a sort of tutelary spirit who shows up at crucial moments with wry advice such as "Sneak and you shall find" and "Blessed is the Fruit of the Loom." Such upsets can provide wonderful opportunities for humor, as when Robert Mayer in *Superfolks* makes Holden Caulfield into a New Rochelle proctologist and marries Gloria Steinem to Kojak. In Alan Siegler's *Comrades*, Marx and Engels attend a convention of the Internationale at a Basle asylum, where all the inmates are ardent, well-read Marxists; Marx later goes to India "to study the ground of Being" and after his death is made into the household god Marx-ji by the Indian masses. Keith Abbot's Ernest Hemingway lives in a wigwam atop the Coit Tower in San Francisco, where his Indian wife stuffs and mounts the books he has harpooned in bookstores around town. Other distortions are more nightmarish than comic, as in Robert Coover's *Charlie in the House of Rue*, where a Chaplinesque tramp's slapstick routines become surreal and grotesque; people and objects change in his hands as he struggles to save a beautiful lady in white from hanging but is prevented by that dream-familiar inability to move and by malicious automatons not unlike the rather mechanical characters in a real Chaplin movie. At the book's end, a terrified, exhausted Charlie asks "What kind of place is this? Who took the light away? And why is everybody laughing?" (44).

The purely random use of historical figures with no discernible meaning in the narrative, as when the actor Walter Brennan briefly appears in Jonathan Baumbach's *Reruns*, helps to suppress our impulse to systematize or "totalize" what goes on in the book. Any attempt to create an overarching meaning, to treat the historical figures as allegorical or typical, is quickly frustrated and we can do nothing but float in the language. Gilbert Sorrentino's *Flawless Play Restored: The Masque of Fungo* offers a particularly hilarious demonstration of such randomized recombination. The masque opens at a "major-league ball park, the home of a team of disconcerting ineptitude," whose members are represented as the "nine elements of Ugliness. There are the pitcher, DULLNESS, the catcher, MURKI-NESS, the first baseman, UNHAPPINESS, the third baseman, IMMODERATION, the shortstop, HOMELINESS, the left fielder, WORTHLESSNESS, the center fielder, IMPERFECTION, and the right fielder, DISHARMONY." This mixture of sports concretion and classical abstraction encapsulates Sorrentino's whole procedure, seemingly meaningful but as arbitrary as any game. The "plot" centers around the poor performance of Foots Fungo, whose low batting average has, like Oedipus' crimes, produced a universe of frustration, illness, unhappiness, and depravity in characters including both historical figures—"JAMES JOYCE, a grocer's assistant" and the "MARQUIS DE SADE, a disturbed nobleman who cannot relate"—and the stock characters of sentimental fiction, such as "PADDY DOWN KILLARNEY, a thick Irish cop," "'POP' HEART, wily editor of the Belleville Vetch," and the Saroyanesque "romantic loser" Jim Jam, who gazes down foggy deserted streets, leans against lampposts, and drinks gin late at night in deserted waterfront bars.

After much inspired nonsense signifying nothing, Foots is granted a vision: a MINUSCULE FIGURE OF TY COBB appears with the advice "Keep your eye everlastingly on the ball." Home runs fly, the team is transformed into the elements of Beauty, and all the misfits in the crowd are redeemed: fever blisters are cured, antisocial tendencies evaporate, printers' ink again "courses proudly" through the old veins of Pop Heart, the Marquis de Sade decides he prefers baseball to beatings, James Joyce pledges devout belief in "Dublin and the Sultan of Turkey," Susan B. Anthony puts on a corset and declares, "A woman's place is in her stays," and shuffling Old Joe "turns into a People and puts the torch to De Camptown Racetrack." Sorrentino's mock-allegorical scenes and songs, incorporating all the elaborate machinery of an Inigo Jones production, are drawn as much from Busby Berkeley musicals as from Jonsonian masques. He has described his writing as an "attempt to destroy metaphor, simile, and allegory" (Klinkowitz 9); the only real meaning of these characters is what the language gives them. Nor does the masque itself have meaning; it is simply a "play," a game with the pictures in our heads, seeking only to delight with its exuberant variety.

Whether comic or sobering, such recombinant appropriation of historical figures emphasizes the "made-up" character of the work, its hypothetical or tentative nature, which is also foregrounded by the metafictional techniques of postmodernism. If both reader and writer conceive of the writer as "Someone sitting there writing the page . . . the writer is clearly at liberty to use whatever material comes into his head as he is writing"; by breaking the illusion that the fiction is a self-generated reflection of reality, the writer undercuts the validity of any statements the book may seem to make. The novel then becomes an "experience to respond to, not a puzzle to figure out" or a truth to adopt (Sukenick, "Thirteen" 96); any new vision it offers, any new world it conjures up, will always self-destruct.

The imagination that feeds these fictions, then, is a promiscuous one, recombining empirical data, including historical figures, from the "real" world with dreams, fantasies, and nightmares from the realm of the unconscious. Traditional fiction includes those same dreams, fantasies, and nightmares only in disguised forms and has tended carefully to separate the dreamworld from the conscious world, developing characters through public forms of expression such as dress, conversation, action, and environment and through representations of conscious thought. The unconscious, because it cannot be fixed or defined, has often been excluded; Christopher Gillie's discussion of character in the realistic novel goes so far as to argue, "To express the unconscious in a personality is usually to infringe social reality" and thus inappropriate to a genre he sees as essentially and most successfully concerned with the individual in a social context (141). But according to postmodern thought, the unconscious is *more* essential than the conscious, because it cannot be disguised or dissimulated and because in the unconscious the "misleading" factors of age, nationality, background, education, and social status disappear, and "personality traits merge" (Nin 66–67).

This extension of fiction to the realm of the unconscious, particularly the modality of the dream, is another contributing factor to the antirealist use of historical figures. Postmodernists use dreams as a metaphor for fictional creation, as a structuring principle, and as an epistemological device. Like the surrealist Alfred Jarry, who tried to make his life a "sustained hallucination," they bring to waking life the "unrestricted intuitions of time and space" and the "aura of ritual and the supernatural" that we experience in dreams (Shattuck 35), and they exploit the ability of dreams to give to ordinary experience extraordinary qualities, to manipulate time and space, and to create experience that is "many-sided and virtually inexhaustible in its potentiality for relationships, none of which are mutually exclusive" (Spencer xviii). The modality of the dream combines unconscious motives with conscious experience to produce a new experience, an expansion of reality.

As a mode of presentation, the dream is peculiarly appropriate to the postmodern desire to destroy system and structure, for there places, people, and objects from many different times and contexts may come together, entirely unrestricted by time and space, possibility and probability, or by the logic that controls conscious thought. Like dreams, many postmodern fictions have only the thinnest causal sequence and flow from episode to episode with little logical progression, changing locales and even epochs without transition or explanation—and here Woolf's *Orlando* is a forerunner. They are often organized as a series of vivid fragments, any of which may stand alone as description, speculation, or meditation and is likely to relate only impressionistically to surrounding segments.

Dreaming has, of course, long been regarded as a source of knowledge and power. The ancient Iroquois thought dreams to be expressions of the soul's desires, which if denied would endanger the dreamer and the community, and they devoted a significant portion of their cultural life to interpreting and acting out dreams (Diamond). To Carlos Castaneda's Don Juan, "controlled dreaming" could change physical reality (Noel). Although contemporary writers would not describe the power of dreams so literally, they do say that dreams—and fiction as a form of dreaming—change reality by changing the perceptions of which our reality is constructed. Proceeding, as Jung advised, "from the dream outward" (Nin 6), breaking down the duality of consciousness and unconsciousness, they incorporate their own dreams and fantasies into the art just as they would any other data: that is, "not as a subject matter but as an element of composition" (Sukenick, "Thirteen" 95).

This dream modality is part and parcel of both the breakdown of the traditional character and the legitimation of the historical character. The definable self has been eliminated, since "in the interaction of mind and world, both mind and world are new in every moment" (Craige 58). The postmodernists tend to avoid character development "for its own sake" (Spencer xx), having lost interest or faith in character as a stable entity that develops through time. If character is a fiction, if true subjectivity is improvisatory "permanent escapade" (Cixous 387), then a name identifies nothing more than a legal entity, and the name of a historical figure or the image that name evokes *is* that person no more than the arrangement of dots on a television screen is the face it approximates. One of Sukenick's characters, a woman who has posed for pornographic pictures, is unembarrassed by their circulation:

"The photograph isn't me. What do I care who looks at it?" (*uP* 185). With a similar sense of distinction between image or name and self, postmodernists allow real people to wander in and out of their fictions as they wander in and out of our dreams, simplified and bearing no necessary resemblance to their originals. They may undergo a metamorphosis from next-door neighbor to television star, or look like the real person whose name they bear but somehow not be that person, or bear the name of one person and the recognizable history of another. Such characters are often explicable only through exclusively personal associations, which the writer would hope are tied into the collective, the impersonal unconscious, but which in any case are legitimate material for the recombinant processes of the writer's imagination as it remakes the world. Historical figures thus become "instruments of signification (as Lévi-Strauss would say) rather than . . . objects interesting in themselves" (Craige 112). In Max Apple's *The Oranging of America,* for example, the question is "not so much of Howard Johnson's reality as it is of our perception of that reality and of the reality of the world we have made for ourselves . . . we acknowledge the authenticity of the mythmaking process even as we interrogate the myth itself" (Wilde 165).

Since the boundary between conscious and unconscious reality is tied to that between the perceiving self and the world perceived, the postmodern deconstruction of character entails the deconstruction of fact and of factually based history. The view that facts are created by historians through the process of selection and arrangement is hardly dependent upon those contemporary theorists who have completed the process undertaken by Collingwood and carried forth by Hayden White's analyses of the "tropes" of historical representation. But the practice of simultaneously "using concrete facts and questioning their reality status" (Hornung 57) results finally in a complete rejection of the category of fact. Philip Stevick has termed such fiction "mock-fact": it "pretends to make statements of fact about the historical and verifiable world, yet contrives to make them in such a way as to make clear to the reader that the statements in no way assert anything about the world at all" (*Pleasures* 103). The fiction histories of Doctorow and Reed analyze and revise history; recombinant fiction completely dismantles it. The historical figure has served as an important tool in this "decreation of history," which Richard Martin identifies as the aspect of postmodernist fiction that "most clearly enables us to define the boundaries which set it off against the fictions of modernism or of realism" (14).

## Kathy Acker's Plagiarized Self

The works of the punk novelist Kathy Acker demonstrate in particularly challenging form the complex relationships of the historical figure to postmodern concepts of text, of identity, and of the authorial self. Her very titles exhibit her ambiguous identity and author/ity: *The Childlike Life of the Black Tarantula, by the Black Tarantula; Great Expectations; The Adult Life of Toulouse Lautrec by Henri Toulouse Lautrec; My Death My Life by Pier Paolo Pasolini; Don Quixote, which was a dream.* One can see in Acker's semantic and stylistic crudeness, in her pastiche appropriations of famous literary texts, and in her outrageous manipulations of historical and literary figures the attempt simultaneously to deconstruct the tyrannical structures of official culture and to plagiarize an identity, constructing a self from salvaged fragments of those very structures she has dismantled.

Acker's habit of disclaiming authorship by attributing authorship to her titular subject has the effect of placing the entire work in quotation marks and thus creating an invincibly ironic "as-if" that crucially skews the reader's attempt to interpret, logically or emotionally, the extreme states of mind the book represents. The covers of any book are, in a sense, quotation marks, delineating the boundaries between what someone—traditionally, the author—"said" and a larger context, a world, in which that statement is made and has meaning. But mimetic fiction encourages us to experience the book as both a world in itself and a pure representation of "the" world rather than as a controvertible statement about an idiosyncratic experience. Acker's authorial impersonations emphasize the radical derivativeness of all texts, their mediated, unreliable, and quite probably falsified status, and remind us that the reader who expects to encounter in a book some reality, or even some great soul, will always be made a fool. The "author" of these novels is a part of the title, a part of what's been made up; where then is the "real" Acker? And is the entire narrative to be read as parody?

Acker's technique of quotation and cross-quotation equally forbids us to identify with, merge into, her fictional characters. What are we to make of a female narrator named "Henri Toulouse Lautrec" who recounts the life story of her brother "Vincent Van Gogh" while searching through Paris with "Hercule Poirot" for clues to the murder of, among others, "Melvyn Freilicher," a real person documentably alive in the "real" world of documentation? What of the whore Giannina's infatuation with the American poet "Ron Silliman" and her erotic reminiscences of him? This undifferentiated use of figures from history, from literature, and from contemporary literary circles merges all realms of language in which meanings reside and thus destroys meanings by destroying the contexts that focus them. Brought into forced conjunction, these irreconcilable contexts split open and spill their constituent parts into a formless intertext.

Despite the seemingly illimitable license of Acker's pornographic imagination, one senses always a "holding back" in her habit of quotation and plagiarism, an unwillingness to own—in the sense either of possession or of admission—her work. Think, for instance, of Toulouse Lautrec's bedtime story, a perfect imitation (or theft?) of the confessions magazine genre, in which a girl is raped by her crazed Vietnam veteran brother; or of the long section evoking and parodying the sentimentality of movie magazines as it traces a touching love affair between James Dean and a prepubescent Janis Joplin. When the rape victim finds a man kind enough to help her recover from her trauma—"with the help of the man I love, I have become at last a real woman" (*TL* 83)—or when Jimmy and Janis find true love, Acker only provisionally admits to her narrative a sweetness and innocence that she would not, it seems, acknowledge as one of her own voices. The narrator's judgment that the confessions story is "trash" (*TL* 84) is superfluous, for stylistic parody combined with patently ludicrous premises has already judged or placed in quotation marks the longings and sadnesses expressed in those stories. Of course, the book as a whole is similarly bracketed. But Acker uses such double-distancing much less often where the narrative speaks for the enraged, offensive, almost obscenely needy personae that seem closer to Acker's own public persona as former actress in live sex shows, queen of punk, the libidinous Kathy who "Goes to Haiti" in another of her works.

Yet even these marginally coherent personae are engaged in a terrified flight from identity; "if I don't keep throwing myself into the unknown, I'll die," says Giannina (*TL* 45). Such death is preferred, even required, by "the Boss" that rules this cybernetic wasteland; at one point Don Quixote decides to throw herself out a window, so that "The Boss'll begin to recognize and respect me. Once I'm dead, I'll be someone" (*DQ* 122). Only a fixed or "dead" self is recognizable; only a recognizable self is useful, locatable, controllable in the world of work and wages. The alternative is to have no identity, to be no one, at which point one can "be—whoever I want. I can do anything I can be anyone one day and the next day do be anyone else, even the same one" (*DQ* 158). This state is simultaneously exhilarating and frightening, for it implies a radical isolation from others, a refusal of the human contact that affirms finitude or boundary. "Without the touch of another human, I'm nothing," says Don Quixote. "For, being untouched, I can do (be) anything (one) and so, am nothing" (*DQ* 161). Complete lack of definition is nothingness; it is also perfect potentiality, complete freedom to redefine, to experiment, to live in that "permanent escapade" of Cixous's phrase. The Acker protagonist, then, embarks upon an anxious search for balance between the isolate nothingness of no identity and the death of fixed identity. The ideal (if such a term makes sense in this context) seems to be that goal expressed by Acker's version of Wedekind's Lulu: "Now I must find others who are, like me, pirates journeying from place to place, who knowing only change and the true responsibilities that come from such knowing sing to and with each other" (*DQ* 97). Impinging upon and shaping this quest are the vectors of gender, culture, and politics, represented here by characters plagiarized from literary and historical texts.

Particularly intriguing is Acker's play with gender in the naming of certain of her narrators and in passages such as the long "Heterosexuality" section of *Don Quixote*. In transforming herself, equating herself with the male figures of Toulouse Lautrec, Pasolini, and Don Quixote, Acker might seem to reject the female self to which she is born. But what becomes explicit is that this renaming of female experience operates to validate it. In the "womb of art," Don Quixote comments, the male artist sees all women as either pirates or slaves (*DQ* 93), either dangerous brigands or loathesome victims; Acker redefines, even conflates, female sexual adventurism and female vulnerability by attributing these qualities to admired male figures. The historical Toulouse Lautrec is in our minds more genius than monster, though his crippled body made the latter definition dominate his own sense of self. We see him as bold, smiling, gregarious: vibrant as the dancers and racehorses that he loved to paint. Acker makes him a woman, whose self-hatred echoes the sense of woman as monster that has led

Acker's work to be described as "abusive" to women (Hoffman). This Toulouse Lautrec is a site of deprivation, of ravenous hunger; so deformed that only money will buy her either sex or love, she narrates her self-abasing yearnings in painful detail. That the character is female makes it possible for us to believe this unqualified vulnerability; that the character is Toulouse Lautrec makes it impossible for us to dismiss the pain as female hysteria; thus female pain, legitimized by the still-male locus of the name, is transformed from a merely pathetic and rather embarrassing phenomenon to one of gravity, to be pitied and seriously examined. Simultaneously, other valorized male referents are given degrading female associations: Paul Gauguin is the local cleaning woman, Rousseau and Seurat are teachers who train whores. Proper noun and pronoun conflict, the devalued female pronoun pointing to a valorized referent that remains male in our minds, and so the characterization annuls both grammar—that formalization of difference—and gender.

The "Heterosexuality" section of *Don Quixote* employs this pronoun play in a more emphatic way, as the girl (boy) De Franville and the boy (girl) Villebranche, with their semipalindromic names, reverse each other's gender confusions and finally mirror each other. De Franville is biologically male but has erased his sexual self, refusing to become a male like his brutal father; the result is "more than androgynous: he had to erase loving, sexuality, and identity" (*DQ* 129). Villebranche is biologically female but "didn't look or act like a woman because, she had been so rejected as a woman, she had flagellated herself into being someone she wasn't. . . . Even though she had to be a boy because there was nothing else she could be, she wasn't a boy" (*DQ* 130). References to each are doubly gendered (he/she, hers/his) until only the most attentive—or gender-anxious—reader can retain a clear gender image for either character. The feminized man and the masculinized woman are both "spoken" by Villebranche, who takes on a male voice when recounting/inventing De Franville's perspective on their encounter. Quotation marks proliferate in this multiply framed narration: the narrator of Don Quixote's story narrates Villebranche's narration of De Franville's narration. And invisible quotation marks hover over those portions of Villebranche's life story that repeat well-known passages from *Jane Eyre*. To complicate matters further, there are suggestions that the dog Villebranche may be Don Quixote's self or sexuality (*DQ* 126). The alternation of voices between Don Quixote and dog, and then between boy (girl) and girl (boy), physically resembles dialogue but has the effect of an obsessive monologue by a single narrator who could be male or female, human or "doggish." Finally the two figures are nothing more than alternative sexual identities that the student of sexuality has plagiarized from the cultural textbook, creating himself/ herself as "male" or "female" in opposition to the biological script to which he/she was born.

The title character Don Quixote is similarly mutable in gender, a woman who becomes a knight on a noble quest to "love someone other than herself" and thus to right all wrongs. "She decided that since she was setting out on the greatest adventure any person could take, that of the Holy Grail, she ought to have a name (identity). She had to name herself" (*DQ* 9). Naming herself for a man, becoming a man, is the only way she can become a knight, since knights are by definition male. A female warrior remains defined by her gender; despite her armor, her weapons, her intrepidity, Jeanne d'Arc remained the "Maid" of Orleans. So in order for the nobility of this woman's quest and the dangers of her ordeals to be esteemed, she/they must be seen as male. Once again through grammatical terrorism, the clash of pronoun and proper noun, Acker effects a revaluation of female experience. A botched abortion and its medical complications, unrequited love and its psychological horrors, become knightly battles that the female warrior meets unafraid. Searching for love and

marriage, tackling "giants"—men—with courage, she is "inexhaustible indefatigable—a true knight" (*DQ* 23). But Don Quixote's knightly or male qualities cut her off from the love she
seeks. To become a man's love object, she must relinquish
her subjectivity. Told by the "handsome man" that she must
"Either become normal, that is anonymous, or die" (*DQ* 33),
she accepts the loss of her self-given name, the loss of her self-
given identity, and thus the loss of life. Preparing to enter the
anonymity of normality, a kind of death, she writes a will that
concludes, "I was wrong to be right, to write, to be a knight"
(DQ 36): wrong to write down or name herself, wrong to
presume to do battle with her experience. The result is the
echoing silence of a textual world created through what Hassan calls "the languages of omission, ambiguity, games, and
numbers . . . the language of silence [that] conjoins the need
both of autodestruction and self-transcendence." It is the language of "a consciousness spinning loose of history, trying to
twist free of words and things" (*Dismemberment* 12, 247). Those
words and things that propose to represent history are painful
constraints upon consciousness, particularly upon the female
consciousness alienated from a male language and from that
history in which to be female is "To be a bitch" (*DQ* 29).

The "Second Part of Don Quixote" is subtitled, "BEING
DEAD, DON QUIXOTE COULD NO LONGER SPEAK.
BEING BORN INTO AND PART OF A MALE WORLD,
SHE HAD NO SPEECH OF HER OWN. ALL SHE COULD
DO WAS READ MALE TEXTS WHICH WEREN'T
HERS." The loss of speech is the beginning of reading; the
now-dead knight must construct a female self out of preexistent texts. A series of famous literary works are plagiarized,
paraphrased, rewritten, as the only way of talking about Don
Quixote's condition as woman "born into and part of a male
world." In an essay titled "Imagination as Plagiarism," Raymond Federman has argued that "imagination does not invent
the SOMETHING NEW . . . but merely imitates, copies, re-

peats, proliferates—plagiarizes in other words—what has always been there" (565). Such a plagiarizing or re-imagining imagination is original only in its omissions and inaccuracies, the absences surrounding its inclusions, the forgetfulness around its remembering, the seams where plagiarized texts come together and redefine each other. "What has always been there" becomes visible in this process of selective, disruptive repetition.

It is with historical and literary characters that these seams of conjunction become most visible in fiction. The specific language of a plagiarized source might or might not be recognizable; the characters who inhabit it are always attributable and thus patently stolen. Of her plagiarism, Acker has said, "by taking these texts and just putting them there as simply as I can, and not making anything of them, not saying anything, not doing anything, I'm doing something that . . . really feels good and has joy in it" (*Straits* interview). But the tactic can never be so simple; it is impossible to "take" a text and not make anything of it, not say anything, not do anything. Surely it is no accident that Don Quixote's reading list includes Emily Bronte, who complexly renders female madness and desire and the punishment for those transgressions; *Paradise Lost,* that mythological justification for the ways of man to woman; *Romeo and Juliet,* which dignifies the equation of death and love. Surely it is not by accident that this narrative about language and gender conflates Wedekind's femme fatale Lulu with Shaw's Eliza Doolittle, whose "depressing and disgusting" (*DQ* 78) speech is eradicated by the man who shapes her to his desires and to his own language. Like the stylistic parodies and authorial impersonations of *Toulouse Lautrec,* this plagiarism of literary selves (no more fictional or textual than are the earlier historical figures) again suspends the meaning of Acker's narrative, placing quotation marks around these melodramatic expressions of sorrow, madness, degradation.

Acker also practices plagiaristic rewriting upon the texts of history, for Thomas Hobbes appears as "the Angel of Death," "woofing" to an equally canine Richard Nixon about how nasty, brutish, and short is a dog's life. It is 1967, but Richard Nixon is president nevertheless; in a remark that explains remarkably little, the narrator explains, "this is about Nixon because it all occurred in the past" (*DQ* 109). History as an organized and organizing structure has evaporated, leaving only fictions (*DQ* 27). Once again Acker's language literalizes her analogies; each political figure is transformed into a dog, an "it" that "barks" or "woofs" its opinions. Kissinger, for instance, "In order to get the Nobel Peace Prize . . . barked an order to Morris to woof negotiations secretly with the foreign minister of Biafra" (*DQ* 106). The effect is ludicrous, particularly in passages from Hobbes where the disjunction between elevated diction and canine referent cancels the sober respect normally accorded to official discourse, philosophical or political.

Such distortions and misrepresentations of historical and literary figures are, like distortions of grammar, necessary to the postmodern project. Says Don Quixote to the dogs who howl around her, "I write words to you whom I don't and can't know, to you who will always be other than and alien to me. These words sit on the edges of meanings and aren't properly grammatical. For when there is no country, no community, the speaker's unsure of which language to use, how to speak, if it's possible to speak" (*DQ* 191). Yet this place on the edges of grammar is also the place of safety from the cruelties of the world. The neglected child Villebranche, reading *Jane Eyre* on a windowseat enclosed by curtains (like the one where Jane Eyre herself reads), enters a "world which didn't contain parents. . . . Here, when I read, my own world and the book's world meet. Since there's no room for anything else, I'm safe." The meaning of the book is "always distant from me," and so the frightened child finds a realm of freedom and security there "at the edges of meaning" (*DQ* 143).

Acker's fictions are themselves located at the edges of meaning, the edges of grammar, the edges of gender: a place where the emptiness and the fullness of the undefined personality— of "no-thing-ness"—coexist in a vertigo of antireferential reference. Just as her character the Black Tarantula copies favorite pornography books in order to "become the main person in each of them," Acker dismembers and recombines literary and historical selves in a frantic effort to define, however temporarily or conditionally, a functioning self. Nothing is finally delineated but "the nonpresence at the center of the work of art" (Federman, "Imagination" 573), the writing creature doomed to repetition and replication, and so the next novel "by Kathy Acker" seems likely to be pseudonymous again, as indeed any fiction—any self—is pseudonymous in the postmodern crisis of identity.

In the speculative and postmodern fictions described, historical figures are cut loose from history and allowed to float free in the timeless, limitless realm of "mental space." Watching their encounters with other creatures of the imagination, we see how easily the characters of truth can mingle with the characters of fiction, how closely they resemble each other. And so we must also see that the truths we believe we can know about real people are themselves fictions, constructs of language, simplifications of the marvelous complexities of human identity. That warm, breathing human being to whom a particular name was attached is no more adequately represented by the sober documentations and analyses of biography or history than by a fictional fantasia. In these recombinant fictions, the juxtaposition of historical figures with figures from other historical eras or other levels of reality dissolves our structures of knowledge and systems of thought. The historical figure, which served as a truth claim in early fiction, here serves as a kind of "falsity claim": for its own reality, for the reality of the narrative in which it is evoked, and for the reader's reality as well. We are all historical figures, as misrepresented in the fictions we make up about ourselves as in the plots written by others that we sometimes inhabit so uncomfortably and as marvelous in our dislocations and re-combinations as any Greek goddess having lunch with Susan B. Anthony at a mountain pass in Nepal.

# 5

## Lies, Libel, and
## the Truth of Fiction

WRITERS WHO NO longer accept accuracy as an obligation or even as a virtue, who see history and character as fictions, quite easily put aside the old aesthetic objections to historical figures in fiction. But other objections, legal and humanitarian, arise when a writer uses a *living* person as a fictional character; this situation puts to the most extreme test the claims that fact, history, and character do not exist. Even though the same theories that justify naming a character Abraham Lincoln or Henry Ford can justify naming a character Richard Nixon, few authors have had the courage—or the bad taste, depending on one's point of view—to present an unfavorable characterization of a living person, and those who have done so have been accused of exploitation, inhumanity, even vampirism, by the friends and sometimes also the enemies of their subjects. The use of a living person intensifies a central ethical question of fiction: to what extent may a writer legitimately use another person for fictional ends, possibly exposing that person to unwanted attention, ridicule, or contempt? And the practice also raises the legal question of whether, and to what extent, a work of fiction can be termed libelous. Through the masking tactics of changed names and circumstances, most novelists have managed to evade both of these questions. But in recent years, the increasing importance of nonfiction elements in serious fiction has again brought them to the fore.

According to one authority on civil law, "A great deal of the law of defamation makes no sense" (Prosser 737), and perhaps nowhere is this more true than in its application to fiction. For that law has accreted like a coral reef from the dessicated skeletons of thousands of legal cases, most of which concern nonfiction or journalism. Novels charged as libelous have generally been squeezed into a Procrustean bed of precedents based on genres with very different methods and effects, even though both legal and literary commentators have argued that fiction should be treated differently than accounts that present themselves as factual. The history of libel cases involving fiction, except for those cases in which novelists have sued each other or, like Fenimore Cooper, have sued a critic, is generally a history of unknown works by unknown writers, perhaps because the talents of more skillful writers can turn even an unflattering portrayal into a sort of distinction, perhaps because better writers more completely integrate their original materials, perhaps simply because their fame makes them less vulnerable. For whatever reasons, only a handful of cases have dealt directly with the unique qualities of fictional truth as it might constitute the "falsity" demanded by most definitions of libel. But the threat of libel prosecution still produces a peculiar form of writer's cramp for those novelists who want to tell certain kinds of truth. This chapter first provides a detailed survey of libel law as it applies to fiction; with this legal background in mind, I will then consider how our legal system might approach one of the most notorious uses of a real person in contemporary fiction: Robert Coover's treatment of Richard Nixon in *A Public Burning*.

## Fiction and the Law

Literary depictions of living people have always come under
legal restraints, particularly when the writer has actually
named names. The first Roman legal records, the Twelve
Tables, invoked the death penalty for only two practices, one
of which was "chanting an evil charm" against a specific individual; Rome's first epic poet, Naevius, was exiled for satirizing
a powerful family by name; and in Horace's time, "the poet
who named his victim ran a grave risk and was always liable
to be taken before the pretor" (R. Elliott, 120, 125). But before
Gutenberg, slander—spoken defamation—was a much more
common charge than libel, its written counterpart. The
church's domination of letters through the Middle Ages and
later the strict governmental control over who could publish
and what could be published significantly reduced the possibilities for libelous publications. In early English law, defamation
was seen less as a crime against an individual than as a breach
of the peace, tending to incite discord and disrespect for authority. As such, defamation of a public official or church
official was a more serious offense than defamation of a private
individual and was punished with much more regularity.
Cheek branding, ear amputation and banishment were the
fate of three Puritans convicted of "seditious, schismatical, and
libellous books" criticizing religious officials in 1637 (Lawhorne
5). Aphra Behn was arrested for a brief, uncomplimentary
remark about the king's rebellious son in one of her epilogues.
But the perpetrators of the scurrilous verse attacks that were
the ammunition in the Restoration's rowdy version of literary
criticism seemed untouched by the law, and their victims had
no other recourse than retaliation in kind or self-defense in
angry prefaces, prologues, and letters. By 1728, when Pope
was writing his *Dunciad*, the law afforded some protections for
literary lampoons, but public opinion was not so forgiving; his

friends lamented his choosing such a low form in which to exercise his high talents. Pope's twofold defense appealed to classical precedents, arguing that his victims deserved this chastisement either because they were such bad writers or because they had attacked him first. In this he echoes Boileau, who defended himself against similar charges by listing examples of particular satire from Lucillius, Juvenal, Horace, and every other major classical satirist and argued, "without any prejudice either to our Conscience or the Government, one may think bad Verses bad Verses, and have full right to be tir'd with reading a silly Book" (40). But the voices raised in defense of the practice, such as that of Walter Harte, who compared Pope's satire to the "Wrath of Jove long delayed" (37), were outnumbered by those who decried it as petty malice and cruelty.

Writers bold enough to criticize the ruling party found that these royal or ecclesiastical victims had considerably more powerful weapons than rhymed couplets with which to retaliate. At this time, the fact that a publication was true did not constitute a defense. In fact, the operative principle was "the greater the truth, the greater the libel," since a true statement would damage a person's reputation more than a false one. American courts broke with this British principle in 1735, when the newspaperman John Peter Zenger was acquitted by a democratic-minded jury favoring the use of truth to oppose arbitrary authority. Since then, American courts have reduced the scope of defamation law in order to protect the constitutional right to free speech. As a result, successful prosecutions for libel are fairly uncommon. Suits against novelists are particularly rare, since people depicted in already published novels would only "call attention to their fictional selves" by suing (Mitgang, "Gwen Davis" 15). Of all defamation suits brought, approximately three-fourths are dismissed on grounds of insufficient evidence before ever going to trial. And though many juries—in recent media cases, about four of five—decide in favor of the plaintiff, higher courts very often reduce the damages awarded or entirely overturn the convictions (Kaufman 27). A study of three hundred libel cases brought to trial between 1977 and 1980 showed that plaintiffs won "only 5 percent of the suits that went through trial and appeal procedures" ("Study Discounts" 12).

Despite the relative rarity of successful prosecutions, the exorbitant legal costs, sometimes running into the millions, of the appeals procedure can make even an unsuccessful suit ruinous to a defendant and burdensome to a publisher. As a result, even the remote threat of a libel suit can kill a book's chances of publication, despite the fact that most publishers shield themselves by stipulating in contracts for novels that the publishers may not be held liable for any damage suits resulting from publication (Pace, "Authors' Groups" 19). Though most publishers carry libel insurance for themselves and for magazine or newspaper writers, fiction writers have rarely been extended such protection; the presumption is that only the writer knows to what extent a fictional depiction might be libelous and so only the writer is responsible. Despite the prevalence of the publisher's self-protection clause, writers were shocked when Doubleday sued the novelist Gwen Davis for $138,000 in legal costs and damages resulting from a successful libel suit against the novelist and the publisher. Doubleday and Davis later settled out of court. But the resultant uproar encouraged Viking Press to break with tradition and offer free liability insurance to its fiction writers, agreeing to pay all but one thousand dollars of the twenty-five thousand dollar deductible written into the policy (McDowell, "Viking" 17). If other publishers follow suit, libel insurance for novelists could become as common and as necessary as malpractice insurance for doctors. For, like medicine, the law is an inexact science. And until the courts develop a coherent definition of what constitutes defamation in fiction, writers and publishers will always be in doubt as to just how far a novel can go.

The actual definition of defamation and its "elements," that is, those facts a plaintiff must establish in order to prove that defamation has occurred, is deceptively simple. Defamation is any public expression, written or spoken, painted or filmed, that tends to "diminish the esteem, respect, goodwill, or confidence in which the plaintiff is held" (Prosser 739). Libel is written defamation; slander is spoken. The plaintiff must show that the statement in question is false; that it is defamatory; that it is "of and concerning" the plaintiff; that it is unprivileged, that is, not serving the public interest in some direct or indirect way specified by the law; and that it is actionable, either because it makes a charge considered libelous per se, such as accusing the person of having committed a serious crime, or because it caused pecuniary harm to the plaintiff. But the actual law of defamation, as continually revised and reinterpreted by countless judicial decisions, is a labyrinthine entity varying from state to state, community to community, even year to year, for each of the elements of the offense is exceedingly complex in its applications to specific cases, differing with such considerations as the "identity of the plaintiff, the identity of the defendant, the character of the allegedly defamatory statement, and the jurisdiction whose law applies" (Sack 39), as well as the current standards of just what sort of statement is defamatory. For example, in 1952, to say falsely that someone was a socialist would certainly be held defamatory; today, the same statement might be considered defamatory in some settings and not so in others.

Applying the law becomes even more complicated in cases involving fiction because of the many different ways in which fiction writers appropriate and modify the identities of actual people. These methods fall into several broad categories, each of which is open to prosecution for libel: the traditional realistic novel, whose characters are often composites or versions of people the author has known but are not intended to be recognized as such; the roman à clef, offering thinly disguised characters based quite directly and openly on real people; and the speculative and fantasy fiction, sometimes called "faction," which treats actual people under their own names in clearly fictional ways. The struggles of the courts to evaluate these different forms of fiction in terms of the elements of defamation raise fascinating literary as well as legal questions, particularly in regard to the elements of reference, falsity, and privilege: how does fiction "refer to" the factual world? what constitutes "truth" in fiction? and what good reasons could justify libelous fictions?

The law, a profoundly relativistic tool, does not assume that absolute truth exists or that words are "about" reality in any simple way. So, in order to establish that a fictional character is "of and concerning" a real person, it is necessary to show not that the character is absolutely identical to the real-life model but that the shape of the literary person is congruent enough to the real human being in its broad outlines—such as name, appearance, occupation, age, or history—that readers would not only recognize the similarity of the two figures but would assume that the character represents the real person. After establishing this congruence, the prosecution must also, in most states, establish that the fiction differs significantly enough in shading or detail that it is not, in its defamatory portions, congruent to truth. Each part of this comparison-contrast exercise rests upon accumulated similarities rather than absolute identity.

First, the fiction must refer to the actual plaintiff; only the person defamed may sue, and this means that depictions of people no longer living, as in Doctorow's *Ragtime*, are not actionable, unless the depiction reflects directly upon a living person. For example, parents may not sue an author for depicting their child as a criminal, but they may sue an author for writing that the child had been illegitimate, for this charge would reflect directly on the parents themselves. Groups may not sue for a defamatory depiction of one member of the group, though a member of a relatively small group may be able to bring personal suit on the basis of a defamatory reference to the whole group (Sack 117). Any entity capable of having a reputation—corporations, schools, unions, think tanks—may sue for attacks on that reputation (though such impersonal entities may not sue for invasion of privacy, a tort that concerns hurt feelings; the courts have determined that corporations do not have feelings).

But in what sense is a fictional character "of and concerning" its real-life correlative? Fiction writers themselves tend to argue that the congruence with real life is inevitable but irrelevant, because the fictional context will automatically transform any real-life material; Bernard Malamud, for example, protesting one judgment against a novelist, remarked, "it is the nature of imaginative fiction that any human being residing in a fictive work is not in essence a biographical entity" (Pace, "Authors' Groups"). Rarely does a writer reproduce in absolute detail the history, appearance, and behavior of a real person, but equally rarely does a writer create a character entirely without resemblance to some real person. The establishment of substantial similarity between the fictional person and the plaintiff has traditionally been the major point of difference between libel cases involving fiction and those involving nonfiction. As in so many legal questions, this one tends to be answered by an appeal to common sense: would a reasonable third person, knowing or knowing of the plaintiff, "have no difficulty linking the two"? (McDowell, "State Court" 20).

The traditional disclaimer, "Any similarity between the characters in this book and real people, living or dead, is purely coincidental," is considered irrelevant to the question of a linkage between a fictional person and an enraged real person. Equally irrelevant are purely cosmetic disguises such as minor name changes: "Cornigan" for "Corrigan" in one important case. On the other hand, the use of a person's name is not, in and of itself, adequate to establish reference in the absence of other significant similarities. Though there have been cases in which an entirely accidental "reference" to a real person, in which a genuinely fictional character happens to resemble a real person in name and other characteristics, has been ruled libelous, more recent judgments have reversed these precedents. Where a work is "both fictional and intended to be such, courts have increasingly refused to rule in favor of plaintiffs bearing the same name as that of the fictional character" (Silver 1078).

To decide whether a book is "both fictional and intended to be such" (is it possible for a book to be fictional *without* being intended as such?), courts have focused upon the extent to which the original person or entity has been disguised, assuming that where the disguise is thin, recognition was intended. The authors of one recent novel fended off a threatened libel suit by changing the names and locations of the liberal think tanks the novel had depicted as Soviet fronts: the "Institute for Progressive Reform," allegedly based on the Institute for Policy Studies (IPS), became the "Foundation for Progressive Reform"; the "Multinational Institute," based on IPS's European branch, the Transnational Institute, became the "Third World Exchange." After the name changes were made, the director of IPS said, "I think we've now established that the book is just a novel, and this claim that it's some kind of truth is just a fantasy" (McDowell, "Changes" 44). Though the authors had said that the institutions were fictional "composites," the close similarities between the names of the real organizations and the original fictional names indicated that the authors had intended readers to make a very specific and literal connection, just as Philip Roth's "Tricky Dixon" and Ishmael Reed's "Noxon D Awful" were clearly intended to refer to Richard Nixon.

But even more genuine attempts to "fictionalize" have been

held libelous on the basis of whatever a particular jury in a particular place at a particular time has judged as "excessive" resemblance between fiction and reality. The best-known recent case against a novelist has been *Bindrim v. Mitchell*. Dr. Paul Bindrim, a California therapist known as the "father of the nude marathon," sued Gwen Davis Mitchell, the author of a novel about the "human potential movement" called *Touching*, on the grounds that a "reasonable third person reading the book would understand the book's crude, aggressive, and unprofessional fictional character to be, in actual fact, the plaintiff acting as described" (McGill 1, 8). The author and publisher maintained that the character, named Dr. Simon Herford, was fictional; that, in any case, "Dr. Bindrim was a public figure who came under the permissible rules of publication without liability . . . and that there was no knowledge of or reckless disregard of truth or falsity in the book" (Mitgang, "Gwen Davis"). The jury disagreed, awarding Bindrim twenty-five thousand dollars in damages from the author and fifty thousand dollars from the publisher. The Burger Supreme Court, which is generally understood to have "backtracked somewhat in the area of protection against libel" suits, declined to review the case (Pace, "New Dispute").

The irony of Bindrim's arguing, for the purpose of defending his reputation, that a reasonable person would recognize Bindrim himself in a portrayal of a crude, aggressive, and unprofessional therapist points up the paradoxical tasks of the prosecution in such cases: establishing that the depiction is both true enough to be a recognizable reference to the plaintiff and false enough to constitute defamation. In a similar case with a different outcome, Robert Tine was sued by his former lover, Lisa Springer, for his depiction of a fictional Lisa Blake. The New York Appeals Court overturned the original ruling, which favored Lisa Springer; the judges argued that although the depiction was indeed defamatory, the differences in "last names, occupations, addresses, and life styles" were significant enough that the depiction was not "of and concerning" the plaintiff. The dissenting judge, a highly respected jurist in the area of defamation, argued, the "dissimilarities which the court stresses . . . are the very basis for the allegation of defamation" (McDowell, "State Court" III:20). In other words, the court had essentially ruled that the knowing and defamatory falsehoods involved were so false and so defamatory that no one would believe them. The evolution of this case illustrates a very common sequence: a jury, sympathizing with the honest distress and outrage of a person who feels she has been traduced and reacting against the defamatory depiction itself, finds in favor of the plaintiff; a high court then overturns the jury decision, giving less weight to the emotions involved and more to the strict legal principles that, to protect free speech and free writing, set up so many obstacles to the plaintiff that the attempt to establish one element of the case may essentially disprove another.

When argued in court, the question of referentiality is generally treated as a question of the author's intention that the fictional character be understood as a realistic portrayal of a real person. In realistic fiction, significant similarity is assumed to indicate that the book is not really fiction but an "ill-concealed attempt to evade the laws of libel by 'passing off' truth in an alleged fiction" (Silver 1069). Oddly enough, then, a writer who attempts to "Tell all the truth, but tell it slant," in a disguised version of real-life experience, may be more liable to prosecution than a writer who tells open, outrageous lies about a real person—so long as they are clearly lies. One of the largest libel awards ever overturned in this country was in the case against the author Philip Cioffari and *Penthouse* magazine, which had published a clearly fantastic short story entitled "Miss Wyoming Saves the World." The fictional Miss Wyoming, a baton twirler named Charlene, was an "insecure woman of little orthodox talent who relies upon her extraordinary sexual powers to win the attention of the pageant judges."

Kimerli Jayne Pring, a former Miss Wyoming who had twirled a baton as her beauty-contest talent, sued for defamation. The author claimed that his character was "entirely a product of his imagination"; further, he and *Penthouse* argued that "because of the fantastic nature of Mr. Cioffari's story, a 'reasonable person' would not understand it as being factual, or about real people." According to Pring's lawyer, Cioffari had attended the Miss America pageant in which she had competed; Kimerli Pring shared at least fifteen characteristics besides baton twirling with the fictional Charlene; and a great number of people, perhaps not very reasonable ones, had harassed her after the story appeared, with phone calls, notes left on her car, and abusive approaches on the street. The Wyoming jury decided that *Penthouse* had acted with "knowledge of falsity or reckless disregard for the truth," even though the story did not claim to be true, and Pring was initially awarded twenty-six million dollars from *Penthouse* and thirty-five thousand dollars from Cioffari (McGill 1, 8). But on appeal, Cioffari's arguments prevailed. The U.S. Court of Appeals in Denver ruled two to one that the story, though "gross, unpleasant, and crude," was a "complete fantasy" that could not refer to a living person. The dissenting judge disagreed that the story was "pure fantasy protected by the First Amendment since the story contained both fact and fiction" (Blair 41).

As a context for the Cioffari decision, we might compare another form of knowing falsehood: the *National Enquirer*. This popular newspaper is in fact a form of fiction. Former writers for the magazine have told that many of its items are simply invented; others are rumors reported at face value; others are based on "recycled" facts, taken out of their original contexts and given entirely new, invariably scandalous, meanings. Yet because its victims are public figures, who are considered by the law to have forfeited some of their protection against defamation and invasion of privacy, the magazine had escaped litigation until the comedian Carol Burnett brought her suit, the first ever, against the *Enquirer*. She was able to establish that the magazine was guilty of "actual malice": that is, that the editors had had good reason to believe that the item they were about to print was not true, and was awarded $1.6 million. The one real difference between the *Enquirer*'s fact-fiction mix and that of fantasy fiction manipulating the images of famous people, is that the *Enquirer* claims to be factually true, pretends to refer to the real person in a literal way, whereas the writers of "faction" will generally say that they are referring not to the real person but to the person's mythic self or persona, which is not at all congruent with the real self.

Now, even a mildly sophisticated reader knows that the *Enquirer* is not factual, just as any sophisticated reader knows that symbolic or allegorical use of the name and image of a famous person does not constitute a literal reference to that person. But to an unsophisticated audience, the effect of such knowing falsehoods is identical whether the publication purports to be factual or fictional. Many readers of fiction, and not only naive ones, assume that every fictional mother is at least partially a depiction of the author's mother and that narrators, particularly first-person narrators, speak directly for the author. Ideally, the legal determination of whether or not a story would damage a person's reputation should be based on its probable impact on those who are likely to read it; under this principle, the fictional Miss Wyoming did indeed refer to Kimerli Pring, since a good number of actual readers of *Penthouse* understood it as so referring, or at least preferred to believe that the fictional smoke must come from some real-life fire. If this ideal actually prevailed, the very same story could be judged defamatory if appearing to the notoriously gullible readership of the *National Enquirer* and not defamatory if appearing as a short story in a literary magazine, whose readers presumably would have the critical sophistication necessary to recognize fantasy or allegory. But in reality, some cases are decided on the "average reader" principle and others on the contradictory "reasonable man" principle, all of which leaves publishers and writers understandably nervous.

The element of falsity, like the element of referentiality, becomes at once perfectly simple and troublesomely ambiguous with these fictions that clearly refer to a recognizable person but, equally clearly, are not literally true. In most jurisdictions, a true statement, no matter how damaging, does not constitute defamation, though it may constitute invasion of privacy. But establishing the essential truth or falsity of a fictional depiction requires shifts of logic and definition that would do Lewis Carroll proud. For on the one hand, every fiction is by definition false, in the simplest sense of the word; but on the other hand, fiction writers often claim that they truthfully represent the world as they see it, though that representation may appear in hyperbolic, symbolic, surrealistic, or allegorical terms. As one judge remarked, "[there are] many truths, important to society, which are not susceptible of that full, direct, and positive evidence, which alone can be exhibited before a court and jury" (Silver 1069 n.). In the service of such truths, an author may choose to use knowing and obvious factual falsehoods. When Dante placed prominent Italians in his fictional inferno, he was not, of course, claiming that they actually inhabited a particular circle of a real physical place but rather was placing them in the metaphoric equivalent of a real spiritual state. To ask whether it is true that Vitaliano belongs in that particular circle of hell makes no sense, for degrees of good and evil are not, finally, questions of fact or truth. They are questions of opinion.

The law has not yet developed an explicit principle for treating such knowing falsehoods, but a close parallel exists in the common law treatments of humor. Ridicule, like much fantasy fiction, "differs from other modes of libel in its clear signal that the matter described is not, and often cannot be, true" (Silver 1093). The question of "reckless disregard for truth" does not apply to such cases, and ridicule is generally awarded more leeway than factual statements, at least if the humorous intention is obvious. The methods of humor—exaggeration, name-calling, irony, or simple nonsense—are considered to exist outside the realm of truth and falsity. At least one recent decision in a defamation suit recognized that imaginative art inhabits the same limbo. The New York painter Paul George had exhibited a work called "The Mugging of the Muse," which depicted two men, dressed as thugs and wearing masks recognizable in the New York art community as the faces of the painters Jacob Silberman and Anthony Siani, mugging a female figure identified as "The Muse of Art." The case went to trial and George was ordered to pay each man thirty thousand dollars in damages. But the New York Appeals Court overturned this decision on the grounds that the painting was "obviously allegorical and symbolic," expressing the opinion that Silberman and Siani were "destructive of art" but obviously not claiming that the two men were actually back-alley criminals. The ACLU's case for George had argued that a painting "cannot be libelous because it is based on the artist's imagination and not truth or falsehood" ("Appeals Court" 80). The arguments in this case would transfer well to cases involving obviously allegorical or symbolic fiction. In fact, Judge Learned Hand once opined that clearly false verbal depictions should be allowed *more* leeway than similar visual depictions, since the visual depiction would be more striking and thus more damaging to its subject's reputation (Silver 1083). Like George's painting, political cartoons have long been considered as expressions of opinion and therefore protected by the constitution, for "Under the First Amendment there is no such thing as a false idea" or a false opinion (*Gertz v. Robert Welch*). If fiction too is seen as an expression of opinion, it should be equally protected.

No right is absolute, and so no infringement of a right is always a crime. Under common law, one may always commit a crime in order to prevent a greater crime from being committed. With the same underlying logic, American courts have long recognized that the society's interest is served by broad freedoms that can bring harm to individual members of the society. The constitutional principle that free speech and a free press are necessary to a free society means that people have the right, in certain circumstances, to make defamatory statements. Such "privileged" communications are exempt, to a greater or lesser degree, from the laws against harming the reputation of another. Legislators, governmental officials, and participants in judicial proceedings hold an "absolute" privilege, an immunity to prosecution for statements made while performing official duties. We all hold a "conditional" privilege covering defamatory statements made on certain occasions, such as to protect one's own or the public's interest, if the statement be "made in good faith, without 'malice' in its common law sense" (Sack 267).

One of the most important applications of this conditional privilege is that of "fair comment" upon the performance and character of public officials. In the landmark case of *The New York Times v. Sullivan* in 1964, the Supreme Court dramatically extended this common law privilege by giving it a constitutional basis. Before the Sullivan ruling, courts had disagreed as to whether the privilege extended to misstatements of fact as well as to statements of opinion; most had held that such misstatements were not privileged, on the basis that "while men in public life must expect to be subjected to public comment, opinion, and criticism, they were not to be made the victims of misrepresentation as to the facts without redress, lest desirable candidates be deterred from seeking office, and the public interest suffer" (Prosser 819–20). The Sullivan decision reversed this precedent, holding that even false statements of fact were privileged if made without "knowledge of falsity or reckless disregard of the truth." Three of the justices went even further, saying that the privilege should be absolute even when the defamers "maliciously speak falsely and know that they are disseminating untruth" (Morris 11). As Justice Brennan's much-quoted opinion for the majority states, the case was seen "against the background of a profound national commitment to the principle that debate on public issues should be uninhibited, robust, and wide-open," and were newspapers required to be absolutely certain of the truth of every statement they published, unpleasant truths would be less likely to come to light. Later decisions extended the *Times* privilege to invasion of privacy questions and to public figures other than public officials, even to some people who involuntarily had become of interest to the public.

The effect of the *New York Times* decision was not, as many people believe, to deny public officials and public figures any recourse when they are defamed. But it did significantly increase the burden of proof upon a public figure plaintiff, who now must not only prove that the statement in question is false but must show with "convincing clarity" that the defendants were guilty of "actual malice," meaning that they knew or had good reason to suspect the falsity of the item before they printed it. Simple negligence, the failure to check out the item carefully, does not constitute "actual malice." Strictly speaking, this decision could only make things more difficult for novelists, since fiction is unquestionably a form of knowing falsehood. But in effect, the *Times* case and subsequent decisions have provided a more liberal climate for fictional treatments of public figures and may be partially responsible for the increase in such treatments in the last two decades, if only because many writers erroneously believe that public figures are now fair game. This decision, affirming so dramatically the importance of free comment upon public officials, has paved the way for commentary that is imaginative rather than expository, dramatic rather than analytic. The question of how the *Times* decision might apply to open fictional treatments of public officials remains unresolved at this point. But the increasing popularity of such treatments suggests that the Supreme Court will eventually have to deal with the issue. And given the present Court's record on free speech issues, such a case could substantially restrict a fiction writer's freedom to treat living individuals.

## The Public Burning on Trial

Since it would have provided such an intriguing test case, one might almost regret that one novel was never the basis for a libel suit: Robert Coover's *The Public Burning*. This political phantasmagoria centers on the three days in 1953 before Julius and Ethel Rosenberg were executed for allegedly selling the secret of the atomic bomb to the Russians. The book names nearly every politician, jurist, and public figure involved with the case; its central consciousness is Vice President Richard Nixon. A monumental book in size and in aspiration, and monumental in its bad taste, it was excoriated for its "overwrought" tone, for being "overwritten . . . heavy-handed . . . scabrous," for the "nastiest conceivable intrusion into the selfhood of others" (Bell, Gray, G. Elliott). But it was praised, sometimes by these same critics, as brilliantly conceived, as "remarkably comprehensive and even moving," as "an extraordinary act of moral passion" (Gray, Edwards). It is, by turns, all these things, and so is not a book one can recommend without reservation. But its very excesses and oversimplifications, as well as its author's unusually explicit theory of history and character, demonstrate the philosophical justifications for a free and outrageous—perhaps libelous—fictional treatment of a living historical person, even a former president of the United States.

The novel takes place during the three days in 1953 before

Julius and Ethel Rosenberg were executed for allegedly selling the secret of the atomic bomb to the Russians; it begins with Justice William O. Douglas's issuing of a stay of execution while the rest of the Supreme Court had left for summer recess; covers the Court's immediate reconvening and the subsequent, possibly illegal, vacating of Douglas's stay; and concludes with the Friday night electrocution, here a "public burning" in Times Square, a nightmarish patriotic pageant enlisting the talents of American mythic heroes as varied as Betty Crocker, the Republican elephant, and the Marx Brothers. Each of the book's four parts is divided into seven chapters, alternately first-person interior monologues from the point of view of Vice President Richard Nixon and collages of contemporary current events, interpreted as episodes in a cosmic comic-book battle between Uncle Sam and the communist Phantom. Separating the four main sections are three "intermezzos": "The War Between the Sons of Light and the Sons of Darkness: The Vision of Dwight David Eisenhower," compiled from the president's public papers from the first half of 1953; "The Clemency Appeals: A Dramatic Dialogue by Ethel Rosenberg and Dwight Eisenhower," taken from Ethel's letters to the president and his speeches and letters about the Rosenberg case; and "Human Dignity Is Not for Sale: A Last-Act Sing Sing Opera by Julius and Ethel Rosenberg," based on the Rosenbergs' letters, with "Choral effects, courtesy of Congressional Records." In the epilogue, Nixon is buggered by Uncle Sam as the sign that he has been chosen to be one of the Incarnations of that national superhero.

The novel, clearly based on exhaustive research, is full of specific details from the trial records, from the lives of the defendants and of Nixon, and from the news of the time. But Coover offers no way to distinguish this remarkably complete information from purely imagined details, for the purpose of the book is not to convey facts but to dramatize the larger meaning of the events. One of its epigraphs is a line from

Eisenhower: "I did not come to tell you things that you know as well as I." Indeed, Coover's book, though made up of ideas, details, and events "pillaged" from history (P. Bell 68), has new things to tell: never directly answering the question of the Rosenbergs' guilt or innocence, it presents their deaths as just one part of a manic public response to the "Red Menace" and ridicules that response as an essentially primitivistic and ritualistic attempt to exorcise tribal fears. The book is not so much an attack on the errors of this particular case as an attack on the cultural myth that shaped, exaggerated, and justified those errors. In a letter, Coover has termed the book a "counter-erfiction," a "struggle with a mythologically determined world-view, which included the dogma of History." The book both ridicules and replicates the myth making that we call History.

To do this, Coover had to deal both with a public event and with a prominent public figure, for no imaginary event or person, however convincingly portrayed, could show so clearly how this myth making operates. The actual details of the case and the public statements about it are quite as fantastic as Coover's own imaginings; indeed, it is startling to read factual accounts of the case after reading the novel, for many details that seemed obviously fictional turn out to be true, such as the Jell-O box with the red stripe that allegedly served as a recognition signal between Red spies. Such details establish the general madness of the proceedings and the even greater madness of the soberness with which people responded. To point up the strangeness of these actual events, Coover pairs them with similar but more exaggerated fantasies. For example, his comic-strip battle between the Sons of Light and the Sons of Darkness is articulated quite solemnly and only slightly less extremely in Eisenhower's speeches, which describe America as God's chosen country and Communism as the AntiChrist. Such terms are familiar; we hear them in every political campaign without really listening to them. But within the fantastic context of the novel, arranged and selected for maximum effect, these familiar terms appear insane. The fact that they come from actual speeches by actual people gives the satire a sharper bite.

Paradoxically, Coover's desire to demonstrate the archetypal qualities of a historical event demanded that he treat, openly and specifically, the actual event rather than an invented case presenting the same archetypal patterns or a historical case paralleling the contemporary event, as Arthur Miller had done with "The Crucible," another work on the Red Scare. The two authors' different modes demand different methods; Miller's realistic play made its point by analogy; Coover's surrealistic novel makes its point by fusion. To show the effects that mythical thinking can have on real people and real events, Coover demonstrates the process of myth making by providing alternative mythical versions of a real event and of a real person.

In choosing a highly placed official—Nixon was actually President during much of the time when Coover was writing, and the book had been planned as an "election-year present for the incumbent" (McCaffery 59)—Coover may have been simply taking the opportunity to bait a widely disliked politician, as Philip Roth did less directly in *Our Gang*. And, in fact, a president is, in the legal sense, a relatively safe target for satire, because almost anything said or done by a president of the United States can reasonably be considered a matter of legitimate public interest and because no president is likely to draw attention to a damaging satire by suing the author. Still, though no suit was ever brought against the book, its publication was significantly threatened by the fear of such suits; Coover says that it would "never have occurred" to him to change the names, but the thought occurred "to all the lawyers in the publishing industry. They wanted me to commit that 'cowardly lie' of which I was later accused" (letter).

Initially accepted by Dutton, the book spent two years in lawyer-imposed limbo before it was finally published as a Richard Seaver book by Viking. Coover seems to have been sustained through his battles over the book by his conviction that its purpose justified whatever discomfort it might cause real people. When asked whether he had had doubts about the technique, Coover answered, "I couldn't possibly have done otherwise than I did," arguing that all his material was "public data" and that he was simply "playing with" the data as one would with "any other public information." He did not feel at all troubled about his use of public figures, especially those responsible for the executions; only for the Rosenberg sons did he feel some concern, and he notes that he never used the sons' names in intimate scenes, that he treated them not as individuals but as "abstractions" (Bonetti). The elder son, he says, was "enthusiastic" about the book, the younger son less so but still "friendly." Now, all this talk about public information, data, and material does not entirely reflect the content of the book, which is less than factual in its use of facts and is often cruel in its satire—which is, in other words, likely to damage reputations in the eyes of a sizable and respectable group of reasonable people. But Coover voices two legitimate legal defenses against a libel charge: the truth of the utterance and the right to fair comment upon a public official, especially a culpable one, on a matter of public interest. In addition, the novel itself presents a philosophical justification for the technique: it denies the very possibility of damaging a public figure through satire, on the grounds that the public reputation and the public persona are fictions with no real connection to the actual person.

Wishing to battle a particular worldview, Coover appropriated one of the creators and creations of that worldview. His summary treatment of a well-known public figure was a clear attack on History in a way no treatment of a purely fictional character, or even of a character based on and named after an obscure historical figure, could be. A name change would have contradicted the book's thesis that a name and the image we attach to that name have no necessary connection with reality, just as an event and our understanding of it have no necessary connection with what really happened, if anything "really" happened. Coover does not believe that the use of a real name obligates the writer to tell the truth. True, there is some element of accusatory "naming" in the novel, a version of the tribal magic in which violation of a person's name destroys the person: all the members of Congress are named, all the jurors and witnesses and judges and justices. But Coover's primary target is less these people than the "public fairytale" in which they took part. To attach a man's name "to a sin and print it" is a "magical disturbance of History. It is a holy act and an act of defilement at the same time" (194–95). Coover offers an imaginary history and an imaginary Nixon to displace and discredit the official history and person, which he sees as no less fictional than his novel. To Coover, the journalist and the novelist both produce myths, both conjure and exorcise with language, but where the journalist, believing objectivity is possible, attempts to suppress the magical powers of language, the novelist consciously uses those powers for the same sorts of conjuration and exorcism the journalist performs unconsciously. Public figures are the actors, priests, and sometimes sacrificial victims, in rituals to which the ordinary citizen is only a spectator, and so the public figure must be explicitly included in any thorough replication of the process.

Benjamin Demott has argued that novelists such as Coover choose historical subjects in order to focus the "reader's eye" on "creative energy reshaping common experience, common consciousness, common sense in language," and he finds "nothing political" about the process (99). Coover does focus attention on his own imaginative construct, his own reconstruction of a political event, rather than on the facts of the event, but to say that this is not political is to perpetuate one of the very views that the book subverts: that politics and aesthetics can be separated. Here, politics is indistinguishable from religion, and history indistinguishable from imagination; the identity of modes that we consider distinct is precisely the point of the novel. Coover's purpose is to make real his own myth and to make mythical the official reality.

Even granting the usefulness of a public figure for these purposes, one might still question why Coover chose Nixon, who, though an accomplished Red-baiter, was never directly involved in the Rosenberg case. A safer and more obvious choice might have been Joseph McCarthy, who contributed so much to the hysteria that led to the death sentence for a crime usually punished less severely. The least charitable explanations of Coover's choice come from people such as George F. Will, who felt that Coover was simply indulging his personal animosity toward Nixon in a "literature of hate." But the choice had other justifications. Like McCarthy, Nixon used anticommunist sentiment to build his career, and his position as vice president gave anticommunism a credibility that no senator could have given it. The fictional Nixon feels himself to be somehow the "author" of the trial, of the "*style* of the performances, as if I had through my own public appearances created the audience expectations, set the standards, keyed the rhetoric, crystallized the roles" (120). Like McCarthy, Nixon helped to create the myth of the Red Menace, but unlike McCarthy he was never discredited for his part in that myth. He went on to be elected president and reelected; something in the man appealed to a significant segment of the American public. As such, he provides an intriguing puzzle: to understand him might be to understand the Red Scare itself.

And Nixon's personal qualities made him the ideal narrative voice for Coover, who had wanted "someone who lived inside the mythology . . . yet not quite in the center." Wanting a character through whom he could "reach skeptical conclusions," Coover valued Nixon's self-consciousness, his analytical approach to problems, and his suspiciousness; wanting a "clown" to provide relief from the "series of circus acts" that were the original concept for the novel, he valued Nixon's "talent for making a fool of himself" (McCaffery, "Robert Coover" 58,59). The character named Richard Nixon finally has many uses in *The Public Burning*: he is the reader's source, sometimes reliable, sometimes not, of all information about the Rosenbergs; he serves as a representative American psyche (sometimes a representative American boob); and he shows how the creation of a simplified public face can victimize a real and complex person. The book is not about Richard Nixon, though he takes up so many of its pages. It is finally about the American habit of mixing ideology with entertainment and about the fabrication of history, themes that Coover sees as justifying his satiric portrayal of a living person. Coover's skepticism about the whole idea of history is based on several distinct views that are fully developed in the novel: that what we know of history is distorted by media that see the world through the lens of ideology; that people who believe in history (particularly in specific doctrines of purpose) tend to act out roles appropriate to their scripts of historical meaning; and that historical interpretations are myths created to serve the same primitive needs served by ancient religions.

## History as Myth, Character as Role

Coover devotes two full chapters to the role of the media in creating myth, each chapter treating one institution of the American media: *The New York Times* and *Time* magazine, the "Nation's Poet Laureate." Despite their different methods— the *Times*' inclusiveness, monumental size, and sober mien, and *Time*'s compression, brevity, and razzle-dazzle style—both feed the tribal fears that Coover sees as the cause of the Burning, though neither can actually create or suppress these subconscious urges. *The New York Times* is depicted as a Stonehenge-like monument, "great slabs of stone, lead, and zinc" (188) among which pilgrim-commuters wander in a religious trance, seeking not knowledge but revelation. The *Times* is "essentially tactile, not cognitive, a confrontation of life with life" (190), less a source of information than a communion service. It provides an illusion of design and of purpose through its random juxtaposition of items that ironically comment on or complement each other: "The news that 905 MORE CAPTIVES / ESCAPE FROM CAMP is paired with an ad for UNITED HUNTS: *Send them off to camp looking their nicest . . .*" (190). Its conglomeration of the tragic and the trivial makes the *Times* unassimilable. Its attempt at objectivity becomes its own defeat, for "objectivity is in spite of itself a willful program for the stacking of perceptions; facts emerge not from life but from revelation, gnarled as always by ancient disharmonies and charged with libidinous energy. Conscious or not, *The New York Times* statuary functions as a charter of moral and social order, a political force-field maker, defining meaningful actions merely by showing them" (191). Moreover, the human habit of perceiving connections between contiguous items, even where no necessary connections exist, defeats the intention to present a series of discrete small truths. And the formalization of today's truth out of the flux of events provides a false sense of control and order that allows people to escape confusion; reading about what has been selected as yesterday's news, people can ignore events happening around them that have not yet become officially real through appearance in the news. By ritual repetition of meaningless names and numbers—deaths, births, weddings, robberies, polls—the *Times* provides a comfortable sense of events captured and subdued, quite unlike the novelist's presentation of the same events in all their wild improbability.

The *Times* comforts by dulling, paralyzing; *Time* does so by intepreting all events in the same energetic way and from the perspective of the same comfortable ideology. In this novel, *Time* is a character, not a magazine; "he" speaks in free verse throughout the book and meditates on truth and history and his role in America through a whole chapter. Says *Time*, "Raw data is paralyzing, a nightmare. . . . Poetry is the art of subordinating facts to the imagination, of giving them shape and visibility, keeping them *personal*. It is, as Mother Luce has said, 'fakery in allegiance to the truth.' . . . *only* through the frankly biased and distorting lens of art is any real grasp of the facts—not to mention Ultimate Truth—even remotely possible" (320). Except for the reference to Ultimate Truth, this statement could describe Coover's own understanding of facts and art. But *Time* fails to grasp the truth because he views all events in light of the mythology of American greatness and methodology of "human drama"; his simplified ideology cannot tolerate ambiguity. So the truth for *Time* depends upon his ability to comprehend: if events overwhelm him, "he will belittle them" (329). *Time* speaks for a communal mind equally incapable of tolerating ambiguities; indeed, his remarks are often prefaced by the grammatically odd phrase "Time say," suggesting that *Time* is not, ultimately, "he" or "it" but I or you or we. *Time*'s eye for the dramatic situation leads him to present the Rosenbergs as characters that fit the prevailing myth: they are agents of the Phantom, embodiments of the evil of communism, ready made scapegoats for a nation frightened of itself. The secret of *Time*'s success is that he too believes the myth.

History, for Coover, is not the objective and rational product of scientific examination of facts but a myth, or a set of myths, sometimes mutually exclusive, produced as a means of dealing with primitive fears and desires. In his understanding of the Rosenberg executions as a ritual of purification, Coover echoes the analyses of several European critics at the time. The U.S. correspondent for *Le Monde* called the execution a "ritual murder" and the Rosenbergs the "expiatory victims of the cold war"; in the Parisian daily *Liberation*, Jean-Paul Sartre wrote, "you have quite simply tried to halt the progress of science by human sacrifice. Magic, witch hunts, auto-da-fes" are the responses of a country terrified by the shadow of its own technological power, demonstrated so awesomely at Hiroshima (quoted in Schneir 241, 254). To erase collective guilt for unleashing this terrible power, say these critics, America projected that guilt onto the two who had supposedly stolen the "secret"—not a secret at all, according to most atomic scientists—and given it into the hands of the communist Antichrist. By punishing so severely the alleged act of espionage, the country transferred its guilt and fear after Hiroshima onto the Phantom of communism and his minions. The danger then would seem to be from the outside instead of from the nation's own rampant scientism.

Coover dramatizes this understanding of the trial in a form peculiarly American: a ritual and a Hollywood spectacle, a sacramental entertainment. His Americans respond to fear and confusion in two ways: they explain away all ambiguity by falling back on their mythological worldview, which couches in religious terms an understanding of life drawn from Western movies and superhero comic strips, and they release their tension through laughter, belittling those things their dogma cannot explain. They serve an elaborate primitive religion Coover never names but that could be called Americanism; despite a Judeo-Christian vocabulary, it is essentially pagan. Its chief deity, of course, is Uncle Sam, who leads the Sons of Light in battle against the Sons of Darkness, the followers of the rival deity the Phantom. If these sound like comic-book characters (and indeed, Uncle Sam leads a Legion of Superheroes), it is no accident, for Coover sees the cold war mentality as no less simplistic than the formulas of comic books.

Uncle Sam works directly in the world, performing miracles, and also works indirectly through his Incarnations, the presidents. Nixon, hoping to be chosen for this distinction, imagines the Incarnation as a surrender to divine power: he hopes "to be possessed by Uncle Sam, be used by him, moved by him . . . to feel his presence pushing out from behind my features, distorting them, printing them on the blank face of the world"

(261). Uncle Sam "shazamms" himself into his chosen representative when there is difficult work to be done. The Rosenbergs, he says, have undergone a different kind of possession and so must be executed under the rule that "any man who is dominated by demonic spirits to the extent that he gives voice to apostasy" (3) must suffer the fate of sorcerers and wizards: burning.

The religion has a sort of Virgin Mary in the Statue of Liberty, "full of grace and reinforced copper" (319); it has its holy texts, the "Book of Study" (legal precedents) and the "Covenant" (the Constitution); the executions are held at Times Square, "an American holy place long associated with festivals of rebirth" (4). John Foster Dulles is a "Christian missionary" and Nixon the "lay evangelist and cleanser of the temple" (105). Nixon comes to think of the Burning Trees golf course as "Burning Bush" because it is there that he hears, through Ike, the counsel of the deity, who advises him on "statecraft and incarnation theory, rules for the Community of God, the meaning of the sacred in modern society and the source of the Phantom's magical strength, the uses of rhetoric and ritual, and the hierology of free enterprise, football, revival meetings, five-card stud, motion pictures, war, and the sales pitch" (83). Even the marriage boom of the fifties is a religious phenomenon, a "nationwide ritual of sanctification," part of Uncle Sam's "in-depth campaign to reaffirm the social order in the face of the Phantom's disruptions" (225). In its all-inclusiveness, this imagined sacred life resembles Ishmael Reed's conspiracy theory of history in *Mumbo Jumbo*, and like Reed, Coover intends to discredit the ruling History and the whole idea of reliable history. His depiction of real people, real events, as all illustrating one fantastic theory is no crazier, he would say, than interpretation of all world events in light of a single simplistic interpretation of Good (us) versus Bad (them).

With all American political activity only a modern form of

primitive religion, the execution becomes a ritual casting out of witches or scapegoats in response to the presence of evil in the community. Though we might imagine electrocution as only a stronger form of the buzz we get from a malfunctioning electrical appliance, it is indeed a burning, for it kills by raising the body temperature to such a degree that smoke curls from the skull of the victim and the smell of cooked flesh is said to fill the room. Like the ancient fire festivals, this execution took place near the summer solstice, June 18. Like ancient sacrifices, it occurred in response to evils of unknown origin and power: in olden times, a plague or a drought; in modern times, our own bomb and its passage into the hands of our enemies. Uncle Sam describes the execution as a "consecration, a new charter of the moral and social order of the Western World. . . . We're goin' up there to *wash our feet*, son!" (91). This "fierce public exorcism" will "flush the Phantom from his underground cells" (4) and provide ritual release to the communicants who are suffering from free-floating anxiety, hatred, and fear.

The devotees of this religion are a hundred million common folk, who kneel, pray, cry, and praise in unison and who are all present as one audience at the sentencing, at the altars of the media, and at the great Hollywood spectacle of the public burning. They speak a psalmic lingo that is sometimes matched and sometimes undercut by Uncle Sam's divine utterances. The sentencing scene, for example, is antiphonal, the nation intoning communal responses such as "Wickedness must be humbled and left without remnant!" to Judge Kaufman's speech (24). When the death sentence is pronounced, Uncle Sam says, "'Those who have cast their lot with me shall come to dominion! Those who have cast it with the Phantom shall get their ass stacked!' And then the people say: 'Bless Uncle Sam and all his unerring works!'" (25). The people share nightmares, confusion at the communist challenge to

the American sense of superiority, and a childlike faith in
Uncle Sam. During the "Phantom's Hour," after Justice Douglas has stayed the execution, the

children of Uncle Sam, slipping uneasily into their beds, are beset
with nightmare visions of Soviet tanks in Berlin, dead brothers lying
scattered across the cold wastes of Korea, spreading pornography
and creeping socialism, Phantomized black and yellow people rising
up in Africa and Asia . . . and the Rosenbergs, grown monstrous,
octopuslike as Irving Saypol the federal prosecutor depicted them,
breaking out of their cells, smashing down the walls of Sing Sing with
their tentacles, and descending upon the city like the Beast from
20,000 fathoms. (107)

Coover here fights reductivism with reductivism; if communists are cold-blooded godless murderous monsters, then anti-
communists are simpleminded primitives. If Communists are
Moscow's robots, without individuality or free will, then "the
people" are Uncle Sam's infants, crying in their sleep over
imaginary bogeymen. His simplification of a hundred million
individuals into one communal mind is just a larger version of
his simplification of the real Richard Nixon into the "Richard
Nixon" of the novel.

Coover's novel seeks both to demonstrate and to explain
that what we call history—or truth—is not a compilation of
facts but a juggling, an arrangement, even a defiance of facts,
to serve a "public fairytale" (letter). Governments have always
known the flexibility of facts; when Nixon tries to discuss
seriously the merits of the courtroom testimony, Uncle Sam
tells him he is being a fool: "hell, *all* courtroom testimony
about the past is ipso facto and teetotaciously a baldface lie.
. . . Like history itself . . . the fatal slantindicular futility of
Fact!" (86). Facts not only can be manipulated but are inherently futile and false; any testimony about the past is a lie
because nothing anyone can remember about the past is equal

to the totality of the past. Even honest attempts to tell the truth will fail, because all knowledge is incomplete, all perceptions slanted. And even if we could know "what really happened," we would only know events that were shaped by specific perceptions, sometimes irrational, sometimes subconscious, of History itself.

For when people begin to think historically, they shape their actions to suit their theories. If the theory is warped (and what theory is not, to some degree?), so will the actions be warped. Throughout this novel, Nixon and others comment on the Rosenbergs' staginess. Nixon, himself a prisoner of a role that warps his true self, suspects the Rosenbergs of also playing a role: "we all seemed moreover to be aware of just what we were doing and at the same time of our inability, committed as we were to some higher purpose, some larger script as it were, to do otherwise" (117). Throughout his ruminations on the case, Nixon returns almost obsessively to the plays in which he had acted as a student and in which Ethel had acted during her brief amateur career (including, ironically, one in which she played the sister of a man condemned to death). To Nixon, the whole trial and execution are an enormous drama, "a morality play for our time" (120), serving the ritualistic needs that drama first arose to fulfill. "It was," he says, "as though we'd all been given parts to play decades ago, and were still acting them out" (361).

In fact, many observers who believed the Rosenbergs guilty saw their steadfast denials of guilt as an act inspired by fanatical devotion to communism, even though a confession would almost certainly have brought a reduced sentence (a telephone line to the White House was kept open until the very moment of execution, to allow for presidential clemency in the case of a last-minute confession). These observers thought the Rosenbergs were willing martyrs for their cause, allowing the drama of their situation to draw attention to their criticisms of the United States' system of justice. In this view, every statement, every plea, including the couple's letters to each other and their children's appearances at rallies, was part of a unified propaganda campaign directed by Moscow.

Coover sees the dramatized qualities of the Rosenbergs' actions in a less simplistic light. Guilty or innocent, these two had been turned into symbols, "linked . . . to archetypes" (212), and could not escape that link, could not act naturally, if any action of a condemned person can be termed "natural." Coover's Nixon, an astute critic of literary style and tone, senses a false note in the death house letters, "the almost total absence in them of concrete reality, of real-life involvement— it was all hyperbole, indignation, political cliche, abstraction" (305). Nixon sees these as "letters mailed to the world" (313), not genuine expressions of love between a husband and wife. Though Nixon's perceptions are not always reliable, in this case they have validity. The letters written after the sentencing do seem intended for public consumption. Perhaps this is why Ethel's letters to Julius lessened in 1952 and nearly ceased in 1953: the sense of public statement that had dominated their private letters from the time they had begun to be published as part of the clemency campaign must have come to seem unbearably inadequate and unnatural, particularly because expressions of hope must have felt more and more useless as the legal process dragged on, appeal after appeal was denied, and the executions approached. Any actor tires of a role to which the audience does not respond; Ethel's role as courageous and hopeful idealist, believer in American justice and in the American people's kind hearts, met with little applause among people who could have helped her. She played her part to the end, in all matters purely public, but perhaps could not sustain the fiction in letters to her husband and fellow prisoner.

To Coover, the Rosenbergs themselves believed in the mythology that killed them: with their lawyer, who insisted on playing fair; with their consistently high-minded public statements; with their refusals to make a confession; they upheld the ideal that in America, justice would prevail. Thus even the victims of the historical dogma participated in it. The myth created by the primitive needs for ritual and for sacrifice is sustained, says Coover, by the media and reinforced by the actions of the principal actors in the drama. With all these forces shaping "fact," how can even an approximate historical truth be found? Coover's Nixon attempts to make sense of the morass of contradictory facts but finally surrenders to the myth.

## The Public Character: Coover's Nixon

Coover's theory of history as a myth created by the interaction of private and public forces parallels his theory of character as a role created by the interplay of private memory and public relationships. This theory implies more than simple role playing, for even while Coover's Nixon is aware of acting a part, he is influenced by memories and unconscious desires. Yet character is not simply a sum of memories, a totality of experiences, for any life will have a surprising number of coincidental similarities with any other. Nixon is constantly noticing parallels between himself and others, particularly the Rosenbergs. He feels, for example, that similar desires "to reach the heart of things, to participate deeply in life" (128) led him to the vice presidency and the Rosenbergs to their political activities. Both his father and Julius' father had failed in business. Both he and Julius had been active in church youth organizations, and each had contemplated a religious career. Each had had serious illnesses at about the same age and near-fatal accidents. Similarly, both he and Ethel were

second children in our families, we both had an older brother, younger brothers, both had old-fashioned kitchen-bound mothers and hard-working failure fathers, were both shy and often poor in health, both preferred to be by ourselves, both found escape in books and schoolwork and music, both were honor students, activists and organizers, loved rhetoric and drama, worked hard for our parents, had few friends, never dated much and mated late. (313–14)

Nixon and Eisenhower "both came from small towns out west and families of brothers, both dreamed of becoming railroad engineers or seeking adventure in Latin America, both loved football, suffered from nervous stomachs, became military officers, played poker, and had had genuine Horatio Alger careers" (258). Puzzled by what produces the differences between people with such similar backgrounds, Nixon finally attributes the differences to simple luck or strength of will. What he does not realize is that the similarities are not really significant; the experiences he shares with Ike and the Rosenbergs are shared by thousands or millions of people from that generation.

Nixon seems to have appealed to American voters because he was himself of middle American stock, and Coover characterizes him as a man with a very ordinary, even banal, consciousness, despite his unusual ambitions. He comes from a small town, an ordinary family; he acts in high school plays, sits on the bench in high school football; he goes to an undistinguished college, belongs to an unknown fraternity (in fact, one he himself founded), lives in a dorm, works out at the gym. Only his indefatigable powers of work set him apart from the others, get him elected to college office, and make him the winner of debates. He falls in love with girls who do not love him and remembers breaking up with his first love as a major trauma; he looks back on his whole youth with uncritical self-adoration, considers reusing a speech from his high school speech class, measures world events against the "stomach-churning excitement of a school football game, a piano recital, dance date" (146). He sees his smallest triumphs as evidence of major talent, maintaining adolescent fantasies of infinite potential: "I might have been another Jack Benny" (173); "I might have been a great jazz pianist" (177); "if I'd had time for theology, I might have revolutionized the goddamn field" (366).

Like many ordinary Americans, Nixon takes pride in the most uneducated of tastes in art, architecture, food: "I did a lot of the cooking, whipping up terrific suppers of canned chili, spaghetti, pork and beans, soup . . . a western with mayonnaise. Jell-O with bananas and whipped cream . . . history will show I was one of the few Americans of my time who really knew how to eat" (141). He shares the national stereotypes of Jews and blacks and the national fear of foreigners, of "irrepressible unAmerican accents, the sour babble of steerage passengers and backpack peddlers" (128). Most of all, he truly believes in the American dream, as he says, "because I have seen it come true in my own life" (295). Despite his political cynicism and his belief, "Deviousness wins votes" (33), he is a genuine believer in the moral superiority of America and in the threat of communism. And he is one of several people who rush to pull the switch again when Ethel Rosenberg survives her first electrocution. As Hannah Arendt concluded in her analysis of nazism, evil is banal; it comes out of the limitations of ordinary people, not the malevolence of a few demonic ones. Coover emphasizes Nixon's commonness to establish him as a type who acts out the reaction of common people to uncommon situations: unable to find an answer to his questions, he falls back on the authority of Uncle Sam, who assures him that the Rosenbergs are guilty and that their death will be good for the country. Reassured, he dismisses his doubts and sleeps easy.

This Nixon is not an idiot entire, and therein lies one of the problems with the characterization. Nearly all the specific information about the Rosenbergs' past, the evidence raised against them and the trial proceedings, comes through Nixon, who shuffles through mounds of evidence trying to understand the case. He shrewdly evaluates the strengths and weaknesses of the defense and of the prosecution. He is capable of considerable sympathy and insight in his imaginative re-creation of the Rosenbergs' pasts. Though his ideas are often naive and hopelessly sentimental, his own personal history, his childhood and adolescent traumas give him the ability to sympathize with the couple. Indeed, the Nixon character often seems to be speaking for the author, particularly in his critiques of the trial and of the style of the letters. So much of Nixon's time "on stage" is spent in this kind of factual analysis that his own character is not finally the focus of interest. But neither is he a sufficiently transparent narrator to allow the Rosenbergs to become the focus. His functions as representative American and as satiric target conflict with his function as narrator. This is, of course, an excellent way to prevent readers from responding to the book as a reliable source of facts, for everything the narrator tells us, no matter how reasonable-sounding, will be undercut by his bumbling elsewhere. Yet the wealth of fact in the book prevents one from reading simply for entertainment or generalized satire; this produces a state described by Walter Knorr as an "anxiety of critical reception" (226), in which we feel that we have learned something but cannot know what we have learned, being unable to separate reliable information from unreliable. If true wisdom is knowledge of one's ignorance, then this is a book that makes one wise.

Had Nixon sued Coover for libel, his lawyers would have had little trouble establishing that this published statement would be understood by a reasonable person to refer to the real Richard Nixon. Most critics recognized a distinction between the real and the imagined Nixon, describing him as a historical character "reconstructed" as a fictional character, as a "character who couldn't be Richard Nixon and couldn't be anyone else," as a "figure called Richard Nixon" (Edwards 26, Perez 619, Demott 98). Yet they also realized, and often lamented, the obvious fact that Coover's use of Nixon's name, of intimate details of his personal life, and of his public utterances implies a degree of accuracy that the fantastic context cannot wholly belie. He *is* writing about the real Richard Nixon, using the real man's childhood, education, love life, and political career, to produce a full and convincing character not only named Richard Nixon but also representing Richard Nixon to a significant degree. Readers with some sympathy for the real Nixon found this characterization inexcusable under the name of Richard Nixon, though it might have been acceptable under another name. Paul Gray, for example, argued,

[the] portrait of an ambitious, insecure and privately obsessed public man is remarkably comprehensive and even moving. If only the character were not named Nixon, all would be well. But Coover allows no distinction between his fiction and the living man; much of the humor depends on a knowledge of the real Nixon's career. As the fictional Nixon's humiliations increase . . . what could have been an act of imagination sours into something rather less attractive than vampirism. (71)

A number of common assumptions surface here.

First, Gray assumes that by using the name, Coover is asserting that the events he portrays are true. But according to the law, no one has an exclusive right to a name; it is the name in conjunction with a recognizable portrayal of a person's individual characteristics that allows us to say that a collection of words "refers to" an individual; the name is the least important constituent in that reference. Like the primitive tribe, Gray attributes a magical power to the name, feeling that it is primarily the name and not the innumerable other verifiable details of Nixon's life (Whittier College, the Checkers speech, the way he met his wife, the plays he acted in, his brother who died in childhood) that constitutes "Nixon" and has the power to harm. Yet those details are absolutely integral to the "portrait" Gray admires.

The comparison to "vampirism" suggests that, by using the name, Coover is sucking the lifeblood from a living person in order to fuel the walking corpse of his novel, as if the novel had no life other than what it invokes by the magical incantation of the name. Even though those fictional "humiliations" are wildly imaginative, Gray denies them the status of an "act of imagination." Somehow, he feels, this character feeds off its real life model in a way qualitatively different from the way in which, say, Robert Penn Warren's Willie Stark feeds off Huey Long. But a simple change of name would be useless without accompanying changes in the character's personal circumstances. As long as people remember Nixon, a name change would fool no one, as no one was fooled by Roth's "Tricky Dixon" or Reed's "Noxon D Awful." Once people do not remember the subject, a name change becomes irrelevant, as indeed that character itself might become irrelevant to people who did not live through Vietnam and Watergate. Though Coover uses Nixon's name, one cannot say that he allows no distinction between his character and the real Nixon, for his character participates in imaginary public events that could not be literally true, even though they may be symbolically true. Coover would argue that fantasy is a realm of metaphorical, not literal reference; by eliminating any illusion of reality he also eliminates any claim to literal truth. But since the referential component of the book is so major, most juries would probably decide that much of the book is indeed "of and concerning" the real Nixon.

The question of whether or not a reasonable third person would find the book defamatory is somewhat more complex. Few readers would be comfortable with such a portrayal of themselves, under their own names, however fantastic the context. For once people have imagined us doing something embarrassing or contemptible, they have seen us doing that thing, and this makes a well-dramatized, clearly fictional fantasy about a real person more damaging in some ways than an undramatized false statement printed as fact. Any strong image has staying power, and highly ridiculous images are always strong; they remain "true" in the imagination even if they claim no truth. Such a fictional fantasy is the verbal equivalent of an optical illusion, and photographic optical illusions, even when clearly illusive, have been held defamatory. In this context, the cry that the book "accuses real people of the foulest motives and the most hideous behavior imaginable—all without the slightest basis in fact" (Podhoretz 34) is understandable, though the "hideous" behavior that Nixon is accused of in this book is usually only the commonplace vulgarities we all commit every day and is considerably less hideous than some behavior, with irrefutable basis in fact, that could be laid to the account of this particular real person. Coover does go considerably beyond satirizing Nixon as a representative American type, and his satire of Nixon's personal foibles is the least attractive aspect of the book. This Nixon can never get through a sentence without stammering. His tendency to sweat under pressure, his heavy beard, his facial expressions ("I smiled and scowled as seemed appropriate") are all relentlessly exploited. Like the man who said, "You won't have Dick Nixon to kick around any more," this one complains about being misunderstood and persecuted; he asks himself, "Why was I always the whipping boy? Who turned him against me?" (340) and whines, "I'm not hard enough for politics, I don't deserve to be President, I'm too good" (524). An egotist who likes to compare himself to Lincoln, to Teddy Roosevelt, he is so self-absorbed that he says to Ethel Rosenberg, an hour before her execution, "if you think you've suffered, just imagine how it's been for *me*!" (432). And Coover does often descend to the low humor—scatological and sexual in particular—characteristic of the most adolescent forms of revenge upon people in power; all this certainly tends to expose Nixon to "ridicule and contempt."

Yet the novel is not simply a hatchet job on a politician the author disliked. For the character named Nixon is painfully aware of his weaknesses and of people's reactions to him. He knows that he is no favorite with Ike, knows people perceive him as too slick, knows that his "stern Quaker eyes and heavy cheeks" give him an "unfortunate scowly sinister look" (46). As a politician, a successful one, he has been forced to look at himself more honestly than any ordinary person ever need do. This Nixon is finally a victim of the myth he has created about himself. He realizes that once he became a public figure, he was "no longer a free agent" (174), that to "lead a land of free-enterprise entrepreneurs was to be their communal socialized property" (262). "Richard Nixon," a person whom Richard Nixon sees as "something other than myself" (367), cannot even grow a beard if he wants to, for that would change his public face and cost him votes. Familiarity is the key for the successful public face; though any normal human being changes, the straitjacket of a public identity allows only gradual and natural changes, the kind that are not chosen. Thus, the real person and the public figure become more and more alienated from one another. Nixon speculates, "maybe the caricature came first and the face followed" (187), the actual face turning into the exaggerated and simplified public face. This Nixon must "struggle with his face" (204) when he steps outside his house after a marital tiff. He is always mugging for some nonexistent camera or for the camera that every eye becomes to the vote seeker. He takes certain poses to suggest certain qualities, constantly worries about how he appears to others, and then complains that he has no friends, that no one really knows him. It is to Ethel Rosenberg, the condemned woman, that he finally reveals his secret version of himself as a passionate, artistic, sensitive man. And he is pathetic in his self-deception even then.

This other side to the satiric character complicates the answer to the question of whether the book, taken as a whole, would "tend to diminish the esteem, respect, goodwill, or confidence in which the plaintiff is held." Though ridicule is often held to be defamatory, the determination of whether a particular instance of humor is libel or "good-natured fun" turns on whether the humor "carries a sting and causes adverse rather than sympathetic or neutral merriment" (Prosser 743). Now, many readers of *The Public Burning* commented, often with surprise, on the sympathy they felt for Coover's Nixon. Skeptic and idealist as well as clown, this character does evoke fellow feeling, to the extent that some readers who detested Nixon the politician winced at Coover's more pointed satiric jabs at the fictional Nixon. The humor, both adverse and sympathetic, may have actually rehabilitated his reputation in some quarters. Whether the book, taken as a whole, would have a defamatory effect cannot be answered with a simple yes or no.

The question of the "substantial falsity" of the book is equally difficult to answer. Coover's portrayal of Nixon has considerable basis in fact; many of the fictional Nixon's statements are exact quotations from the real Nixon. Coover describes himself as having been "locked to the television" throughout the Watergate crisis, reading everything Nixon said or wrote for the public, collecting "several thousands of lines" that "waited for their moment to enter the story." He consciously worked for a sense of Nixon's "syntactic and emotional peculiarities"—in other words, for a "true" portrayal of the real man's mind (Bonetti)—and he plausibly re-creates the secret daydreams, petty resentments, and insecurities about education and background that could have contributed to the real Nixon's Enemies List, tape recordings, suspicion of the eastern establishment, and odd public pronouncements. But this very factual basis, the familiarity of these statements and attitudes, makes the satire sometimes so cruel that even many people who personally dislike the man must hope that he did not read this book. In the fictional context, statements that seem perfectly reasonable and even likable in other contexts seem ridiculously self-indulgent. Individually, they are accurate; taken as a whole, they are sometimes misrepresentations and certainly produce the kind of humor that carries a sting.

When we move from Coover's relatively realistic psychological portrayal of a character named Richard Nixon to his fantastic portrayal of that character's romancing Ethel Rosenberg or dropping his drawers before the assembled nation in Times Square, we move to a realm more clearly false on the literal level. Here, of course, Coover was making statements he knew to be false, statements so obviously false that no one would literally believe them. Under the law, it is not necessary that readers believe a statement to be true in order that the statement be understood as defamatory. But one might argue that such extreme fantasy scenes are the fictional equivalent of the political cartoons that are, however unpleasant, an accepted part of the politician's life. As the most public figure in American life, a president has forfeited most of his protection against such portrayals, including comedy skits on television and comic imitations by Rich Little and his ilk. On the symbolic and allegorical levels, Coover's fantastic lies are merely dramatizations of the *opinion* that Richard Nixon exemplified those characteristics of the American psyche that made possible the execution of the Rosenbergs. Though the power of fiction gives Coover's metaphors the declarative effect of a statement of fact and the staying power of a strong visual image, his central idea is but one idea among others, neither true nor false, and so could be protected as a form of free speech, whatever a jury might decide about the defamatory intent or effects of the novel.

But Coover's Nixon is not a pure cartoon, as can be seen by comparison with Uncle Sam. Uncle Sam is a conglomerate of the most exaggerated aspects of America, a collage of all the people, events, words, and ideas that come out of and become part of American history and myth. Even Ethel Rosenberg, says Uncle Sam after the execution, "is a part of me now, both her and her brave engineer, just as much as Pocahantas, Billy the Kid, or Bambi" (531). Uncle Sam has emotions, rage and humor, but no personality, no motivation. He is a force, not a mind. He is a bully, a shrewd Yankee peddler, a magician who pulls doves out of his top hat, a Sut Lovingood comic rube, a Biblical prophet, a wrathful god, a superhero with massive biceps, a wizard blowing smoke rings, a testy old uncle who abuses his nieces and nephews even as he comforts them. His language splices together the locutions of the King James Bible and the crudest of provincial clichés. He delivers verses from Scripture and racist jokes with equal glibness and with no shift in tone. His speeches read like a "Beverly Hillbillies" screenplay written by James Joyce: a compendium of lines from popular songs, from religious ritual, from folk humor and folklore, abounding with puns, wordplay, and neologisms. Though Coover, enamored of his creation, makes the same jokes too often and lets the hyperbolic oratory continue too long, it is a creation of remarkable demonic energy, the best expression of the author's disgust at and fondness for his country, and the focus of some of the best scenes in the book.

The scenes with Uncle Sam have the garish coloring and crude outlines of an animated film, the same loud, frenetic jerkiness. If Coover's Nixon is a composite photograph, his Uncle Sam is a Saturday morning cartoon, who fascinates like those fast-moving and eye-catching entertainments. At its best, the character expresses in symbolic forms all the outrage that Coover feels at the rituals of Americanism, as when Uncle Sam brings a spark of atomic fire from Nevada to chase away the darkness the Phantom has dropped on Times Square:

> For a moment Uncle Sam seems to hover flickeringly above them, his craggy features lit eerily from beneath by the fiery glimmer in his cupped hands, his coattails flapping blackly behind him—and then he plummets down upon them like a falling star! . . . When they open their eyes again, it is to see their Star-Spangled Superhero standing

stark and solemn above them on the Death House stage, cradling freedom's holy light in his outstretched hands and gazing down upon them with glittering eyes sunk in deeply shadowed sockets—weird this light he holds: fierce enough to blind if stared at directly, yet casting no radiance, illuminating nothing except Uncle Sam's hands and face, as though virtually all its light were bent in upon itself. (494)

When "freedom's holy light" becomes a sort of hellfire and good old Uncle Sam a sunken-eyed devil, Coover expresses his attitude toward the myth far more effectively than in his interminable pokes at Sam's Incarnation, Richard Nixon. One could imagine the same scene with Nixon in the place of Uncle Sam or in Uncle Sam's clothes: the same gaunt face, the same unilluminating light. And such a version could have been equally effective—in making that particular point. Such a use of Nixon as pure persona would have been considerably easier, and less outrageous, than Coover's actual use of Nixon as both a central consciousness for the reader to identify with and a clown for the reader to laugh at. And a pure cartoon might also have allowed for the unified effect that critics of the novel tend to prefer.

But Coover never sought to sculpt a well-wrought urn. His own metaphor of a circus offers a better description of the book's goals: a dizzying mixture of drama, pathos, humor, and spectacle. The book is, in Northrop Frye's terminology, a Menippean satire, with all the crudeness, excess, and unevenness that form entails. With his talk of magic, of conjuring, of communal consciousness, of dream time, of struggle with myth, Coover calls up an old, old understanding of satire as a weapon, the old forms of satire based on repetition of a man's name, when words were thought to be powerful enough to stop armies, to kill. And perhaps it is to a more primitive concept of justice that we must leave Robert Coover. The ancient belief was that, if the satire was false, the poet's curse would fall upon his own head. If Coover's satire is more than spiteful baiting of a man who cannot defend himself, it will be remembered. If not, it will be forgotten: the worst punishment any novelist can endure.

Given the mass of conflicting precedents and principles that make up existing libel law, and the potentially disastrous consequences of a libel suit, whether successful or not, one must wonder a bit that any writer is so rash as to spin a fiction that might invite a suit. But the liars, libelers, and simple dreamers who take the chance feel quite justified in whatever use they make of other people's selves. Some argue that all public figures have sold their faces, voices, and histories to the devil creator of the myths that are politicians' public images. Some cite aesthetic privilege, appealing to the transforming power of art and to the artist's prerogative to mold human clay like any other. Some believe that "character" is an outmoded concept, that none of us has an essential and inviolable self that can be harmed by a literary reference. And occasionally, it must be admitted, the voodooistic appropriation of another's self is motivated by simple hatred or desire for revenge, and these fine-sounding arguments are only rationalizations after the fact. But whatever the motivation, it is impossible to produce fiction that bears no trace of the people who have entered the writer's life and field of vision, and so the courts will continue to face the problem of distinguishing between the legitimate and illegitimate truths and lies that will continue to take root in the fertile medium of fiction. One might hope that some coherent principle to distinguish fictional libel from nonfictional libel will develop. But until that happens, the cautious writer will keep an eye cocked for the policing presence of the law before playing too fast and free with a recognizable individual. This particular cop is unpredictable, sometimes jolly, sometimes cranky, and it is best not to provoke him without a good defense lawyer to take along to court.

# 6

# Conclusion

FICTION TELLS ITS truths slantwise, like any mirror. Not even the purest silver-backed crystal can give a true reflection, all mirror images being, after all, reversed, and false, as anyone knows who has idly regarded an unpleasant stranger in a store window and realized, shocked, that the stranger is one's self and then has seen the strangeness resolve itself into the self one knows from one's own mirrors. The writer has always used mirrors to create the illusions of familiarity and of strangeness, to reveal and to conceal, but has often, like the magician, hidden the mirrors that make the body float. And why not, since magic offers great pleasures? Yet there is something childish about these pleasures when unaccompanied by the adult's contrapuntal skepticism: How did he do that? How did she distract me? Where are the wires and the mirrors? And similarly the mature reader may wonder, casually or obsessively: where did the writer get this character? Who is the original, of which I see the reflection? The more we know or care about an artist's work, the more we wish to know of that person's mind, and life, and world. It is a personalized response not officially approved of these days but nevertheless much indulged in our pilgrimages to an idol's birthplace or grave, our articles sacrificed on the altars of panel discussions, our litany recitals of favorite passages, and our affectionate private references to certain writers by their first names: Emily and Walt, Charlotte, and the others who have somehow touched us, mind to mind, world without time and without history.

This communication or communion, disembodied though it be, is part of why writers write: to be heard and to be known. And equally important is the writer's desire to forge or preserve a connection with experiences that have marked him or her, with the life that slips through the fingers, and not least, with the people who people that life. Under realism, such direct connections between real people and fictional characters have been minimized, displaced, though often the writer encodes the connection in a name that half-consciously identifies a real-life original. One thinks of David Copperfield, whose initials so suggestively transpose those of his creator-original, or of James's Milly Theale, whose name so much resembles that of her original Minny Temple. Upon losing to distance, time, or death a dearly beloved or dearly despised human being, a writer seeks preservation, repossession, or resurrection through fiction. Thus even so frankly invented a portrait as Ondaatje's of Buddy Bolden, so frankly insulting a one as Coover's of Nixon, is finally commemorative, for its very existence asserts that the historical original deserves to be considered and remembered.

In the past decades, the strategies of disguise and of displacement by which authors have pretended that their characters were pure inventions—the changed faces, heights, weights, dates, and places—have fallen away, until a writer-protagonist named Elizabeth in a novel by Elizabeth Hardwick can find no answer to the accusing question "Why didn't you change your name? Then you could make up anything you like, without it seeming to be true when all of it is not" (90).

The answer to the question is probably that the writer can make up whatever she or he likes in any case, since the whole purpose of fiction is to make a kind of truth out of the "made-up." Once both writer and reader understand that all mirrors are bent, there are no necessary limitations on the representation and even misrepresentation of historical figures.

Welcome to the funhouse.

In this study, we have seen a variety of ways in which contemporary writers are making use of the historical figure, justifying free manipulation of such materials on the basis of contemporary theories of language and history. But whatever the philosophical similarities among the writers, the real-name "phenomenon" is actually several phenomena quite different in intent and effect. The writers I have discussed can be placed along a continuum, varying in their degree of reverence for and personal involvement with their historical subjects and in the degree to which they maintain a mimetic illusion when treating such subjects. Their techniques also have implications for the ultimate fate of the works they produce.

The fictional biographers belong on the least extravagant end of the continuum. While not claiming literal truth for their portraits, they present historical figures as complex, coherent individuals, whose experiences they believe they have approached through imagination and whose lives they perceive as meaningful. These historical figures are represented in the full textures of mimetic fiction, though the mimetic illusion is undercut by metafictional devices as well as by the impossibly detailed quality of the portraits themselves.

Some critics have argued that this mixed breed has neither the vitality of a mutt nor the beauty of a purebred. But though bad books of this sort are more common than good ones, as is true of any sort of book, the good ones have suffered from a casual critical neglect, a general prejudice against biographical fiction. Even in favorable reviews, the critic sometimes seems almost embarrassed to go on record as admiring a member of this untouchable literary caste. As with tokenism in employment, where a token who performs well is seen as atypical of the group, the reviewer often couches the praise in cautions against the pitfalls of the form, which this particular writer, heaven knows how, has escaped. Of *Eleanor,* for example, Saul Maloff wrote, "Rhoda Lerman risks everything as a novelist by casting the entire narrative in Eleanor's voice" (14), as if that simple choice of point of view could somehow overwhelm all a writer's skills. Fiction biographies have thus often fallen into the great black holes in our definitions of serious fiction.

Our willingness to group in the single category of "novel" such disparate books as *Wuthering Heights* and *The Sun Also Rises* shows that the category is hardly dependent upon characters' being made up or even significantly removed from the novelist's experience. Why then should the open use of historical figures seem troubling, since significant ties to real-life originals are often equally recognizable in mainstream novels in which the names have been changed? Take, for example, *Humboldt's Gift,* a roman à clef that was discussed as such from the beginning; Von Humboldt Fleischer, everyone knew, was based closely upon Bellow's old friend Delmore Schwartz, and Charlie Citrine, with his problems with alimony and past wives and his habit of obsessive talking like so many other Bellow protagonists, was a Bellow character; and most readers who had read the reviews would have been thinking, at least fitfully, of Schwartz and Bellow when reading of Humboldt and Charlie and wondering to what extent the novel was true. How different is this, in essence, from reading Lerman on Roosevelt or Ondaatje on Bolden?

The usual rejoinder is that one would not have to know about Delmore Schwartz to appreciate Bellow's Humboldt. The same is true of most fiction biographies, and this self-sufficiency becomes more and more absolute the further removed we become in time and emotion from a historical original, whether that original is named or disguised. Dickens's Skimpole is a character known by many of Dickens's contemporaries and by most students of Dickens to be a caricature of Leigh Hunt. Those contemporaries were uneasy at the effect on Hunt of being publicly satirized; we can enjoy the character without such misgivings, for Leigh Hunt exists to us almost exclusively *as* Skimpole, just as some unknown woman chatters on as Miss Bates in *Emma,* anonymous but not forgotten, wherever her grave might be. Once time has passed, the real person is displaced by the literary replica, and the work can then, perhaps only then, be judged solely as a work of fiction. Until that displacement occurs, readers will enjoy the added dimension of recognition but suffer added uneasiness, both of which disappear once that real-world link is gone.

The best of the fiction biographies are simply good novels; their effects do not depend upon the readers' knowledge of the historical characters. Writers create these historical characters on the page exactly as they would create more purely fictional characters. And so the historical component of the fiction biographies does not threaten to date them. Any work of literature becomes dated to some extent by changes in customs, values, and language: that crumbling stone of the book sculptor. Works that remain intelligible over time are those that teach us about their worlds as we read, those written commemoratively, out of love for the things of this world, written as if for posterity even when aimed at a specific contemporary audience. Who could be more topical, more dated, than Homer, with all that business about shipbuilding and all those folk heroes, possibly historical figures, for characters? Homer could have been more allusive, more cryptic; could have depended upon his audience's knowledge to fill in what the text did not tell. But he repeats his world, gives the unnecessary details, tells the story *as if* to teach even things his contemporaries would have known. We love to see the things we love repeated, and such loving redundancy in literature makes a book explain itself in such a way that it remains intelligible centuries later.

Dealing with grubby Grub Street reality instead of enduring ideality, seemingly obsessed with contemporary people and situations, the works of the first novelists were never expected to last: their subject matter was too ephemeral. But Defoe's seventeenth-century pickpocket and Smollett's eighteenth-century misanthrope still appeal to twentieth-century readers, despite dated costumes, scenery, and dialogue. Though the source of an antiquarian delight, the "facts" or time-specific aspects of mimetic fiction are eventually almost irrelevant to the essential core of such works.

This becomes less true for the fiction histories, which represent a drawing back from the historical figure, an ironic stylization in which the complexities of a well-known historical individual are simplified into the outlines of the public persona by which that individual has become known. The fiction historian depends to a greater extent than the fiction biographer on readers' expectations of the historical figures; Freud and Jung's riding through the Tunnel of Love at Coney Island is funny only to readers who know something about Freud's influence on twentieth-century views of sexuality. The fiction history, using historical figures as representatives of universal types or tendencies, focuses on the endless repetitions of history rather than on the uniqueness of any individual in history. Much of this metahistorical meaning of such novels is lost if readers cannot understand the writers' ironic inversions of factual history. But most fiction histories continue to offer a plenitude of self-explanatory mimetic detail and thus allow a broad variety of readers to participate to some extent in the fictional experience. Thus, both fiction biographies and fiction histories remain within the tradition of the novel as usually defined, if we include writers before Defoe in that tradition.

But recombinant fictions find their roots in forms older than the novel, in Dryden's and Pope's and Boileau's satires on literary idiocy, and even further back in the satires of primitive tribes for whom words were weapons. Their allusive, shorthand references to historical figures will make them ultimately unintelligible, the inescapable fate of any highly allusive art. Four hundred years ago, poets made use of classical gods and goddesses, characters without character development, functioning as coded idea symbols, automatic response producers. Today those classical allusions, meaningless to most readers, have been replaced by the politicians and film stars of the new pantheon, who inhabit the public consciousness as myths not much different from those of classical Greece. The homage paid at Elvis Presley's grave shows his followers' devotion to an idea based only loosely on the paunchy pill-popper who is buried there. Such contemporary myths serve the same function in recombinant fiction as the classical myths have done for literature in the past, though we may scorn the icons of our own scruffy age and maintain a nostalgia for those of an ancient age, probably equally scruffy.

But these contemporary allusions can never form a language of symbolic references comparable to the classical, which by various accidents of history lasted for centuries and informed whole literary traditions. Our own culture's myths are unlikely to find institutional reinforcement of the kind resulting from the peculiar marriage of Christianity and paganism, from the church's control of education, and from the standard requirement of Latin and Greek that eventually led those well-educated Christian boys to read pagan epics and the anything-but-pious verses of Ovid. Because allusive art relies upon reader participation and recognition of very specific current references and depends more on manipulation of images in the readers' minds than on creation of images, it is planned for obsolescence. Jokes, juxtapositions, and allusions lose their force when they must be explained by footnotes, and so the best of the recombinant works may join the *Tale of a Tub* or the *Dunciad* in respectable obscurity: offering some pleasures still accessible, but such a preponderance of those that must be explained that the full pleasure will be available only to scholars. However much we admire the wit, the poetic energy, the animus of a work such as the *Dunciad*, it is only by an extraordinary effort of imagination that we can approximate the experience of its first readers. To us, Theobald and Cibber are only names, not living creatures, not even human creatures except in the most abstract way, and the poem's value lies not in what it does to them but in its independent, nonreferential status as the opposite of dullness. To Pope's audience, the poem's primary effect and function were contemporary: a revenge of genius upon known, named fools. For us, that dimension is gone.

The writers of recombinant fiction are fully aware that their fiction depends upon undependable, volatile connections between their own and their readers' experiences; they know that their art will self-destruct and they fully accept that fact. Believing that fiction is a part of experience, not apart from it, and that experience is ephemeral, they believe that literature must be equally ephemeral. Any attempt to fix that flow of experience is doomed; the real goal of a writer is not contact with some hypothetical posterity but an intense, brief connection with readers now, hoping to tap strong responses by calling up the powerful associations of very specific names and images. The general condition of the literary life also contributes to this suspicion of the idea of deathless prose. The world's uncertainty, the plethora of words in the world, and the pluralism of styles and viewpoints make it impossible for any sane writer to speak with the resounding assurance of a prophet. One response is to substitute allusion for explanation, fast connection for slow development, a brief place in experience for a chance in the rigged lottery of history. As with the ephemeral pleasures of good conversation, most of these fictions will be heard once and then forgotten. Ephemeral, yes; but perhaps certain aesthetic pleasures and certain lessons can only be contemporary and specific and, like most things in the world, must pass.

Ironically, anything appearing novel—as opposed to simply original—in a novel tends to be castigated as mere novelty. A better word might be *noveltry*, since by trying new things the novel only lives up to its name, as the devil lives up to his through deviltry. The noveltry of the real-name phenomenon has sometimes been understood as merely a gimmick to cash in on the current popularity of nonfiction. This economic *ad hominem* does not hold, for writers pandering to a popular audience would not choose such obscure subjects as a tenth-century saint or a jazz musician known only to the dedicated jazz buff, and would not so often exclude themselves from a mass audience by their dense, poetic language; complex structures; and frank experimentation. Even if some do begin writing with phantom dollar signs blurring their vision, the good ones are lured by their own talent away from *People* magazine gossip and back into the funhouse that the profitable readership finds weird or dull. Still, the general climate of interest in nonfiction *has* probably fed the trend, by making the old disguises seem outworn. Economic factors, public preferences, and publishing practices have always influenced what writers write, from the illuminated manuscripts of the church-dominated Middle Ages, to the courtly and elegant art of the aristocracy-dominated Renaissance, to the serialized novels of the middle class-dominated nineteenth century, to the fragmentary, fact-oriented art of our own media-dominated century. The talented writer can always navigate with and tack against the prevailing winds, charting courses no more constricted than the passable straits of traditional forms like the sonnet or the five-act play.

The fiction biographer, the fiction historian, and the writer of recombinant fiction, whose techniques and effects are in many ways so different, are unified by their common loss of faith that fiction and reality are separate realms. This sense that history and identity are verbal constructs, necessarily removed from the "real thing," has freed many writers to do new things within familiar modes. Realistic novelists use real people realistically, satirists use them satirically, postmodernists use them deconstructively; like all things outside or inside the writer's imagination, a historical figure can provide suitable material for any style or mode. Impatient with traditional pretense, because unashamed of partial truth, these writers owe no allegiance to the bogeys of accuracy and objectivity; as a result, they can find no reason *not* to use historical figures, whether their focus is personal psychology, cultural or national identity, historical cyclicity, epistemology, ontology, religion, art, saints, witches, criminals, or clowns.

And only the names have not been changed.

# Works Cited
# Index

# Works Cited

Abbott, Keith. *Rhino Ritz: An American Mystery*. Berkeley: Blue Wind Press, 1979.

Acker, Kathy. *The Adult Life of Toulouse Lautrec By Henri Toulouse Lautrec*. 6 vols. New York: TVRT Press, 1975.

————. *The Childlike Life of the Black Tarantula, by the Black Tarantula*. New York: TVRT Press, 1975.

————. *Don Quixote: Which Was a Dream*. New York: Grove Press, 1986.

————. *Great Expectations*. New York: Grove Press, 1983.

————. *My Death, My Life, by Pier Paolo Pasolini*. London: Pan, 1984.

————. Interview. *Straits* (Summer 1985). Quoted in *Contemporary Authors*. Vol. 122. Detroit: Gale Research Company, 1988. 16–17.

Adams, Timothy Dow. "Obscuring the Muse: The Mock-Autobiographies of Ronald Sukenick." *Critique* 20 (August 1978): 27–39.

Ahern, Tom. *A Movie Starring the Late Cary Grant and an As-Yet Unsigned Actress* and *VERDIS: "A Gorgeous Gallery of Galatial Synecdoches."* The Treacle Story Series 1. Philadelphia and Providence: Treacle Press, 1976.

Aiken, Joan. "Identifying the Past: Reflections of an Historical Novelist." *Encounter* 64.5 (May 1985): 37–43.

Akin, William E. "Toward an Impressionistic History: Pitfalls and Possibilities in William Styron's Meditation on History." *American Quarterly* 21 (Winter 1969): 805–12.

Aldridge, John W. *The American Novel and the Way We Live Now*. New York and Oxford: Oxford University Press, 1983.

Alter, Robert. "History and Imagination in the Nineteenth-Century Novel." *Georgia Review* 29 (1975): 42–60.

————. "Mimesis and the Motive for Fiction." *TriQuarterly* 42 (1978): 228–49.

————. "The New American Novel." *Commentary* 60 (November 1975): 44–51.

Ambler, Madge. "Ishmael Reed: Whose Radio Broke Down?" *Negro American Literary Forum* 6 (1972): 125–31.

Amis, Kingsley. "Real and Made-Up People." *Times Literary Supplement* 27 July 1973: 847–48.

Anderson, Jervis. "Styron and His Black Critics." *Dissent* 16 (Mar.–Apr. 1969): 157–66.

Anderson, Poul. *A Midsummer Tempest.* New York: Tom Doherty, 1984.

"Appeals Court Upsets Verdict That a Painting Was Libelous." *New York Times* 12 Dec. 1982: 80.

Aptheker, Herbert. "A Note on the History." *Nation* 16 (Oct. 1967): 375–76.

Aristotle. *Poetics.* Trans. Ludovico Castelvetro. In *Critical Theory Before Plato.* Ed. Hazard Adams. New York: Harcourt Brace Jovanovich, 1971. 146–53.

Ashley, Robert Paul, and Edwin M. Moseley, eds. *Elizabethan Fiction.* New York: Holt, Rinehart and Winston, 1953.

Babitz, Eve. *Slow Days, Fast Company: The World, The Flesh, and L.A.* New York: Alfred A. Knopf, 1977.

Baker, Houston A., Jr. *"The Last Days of Louisiana Red." Black World* 24.6 (1900): 51–52, 89.

Balch, Emily Greene, ed. *Occupied Haiti.* New York: Writers Publishing Co., 1927.

de Balzac, Honoré. Preface. *La Comedie Humaine.* Philadelphia: George Barrie & Sons, 1895.

Banks, Russell. *Searching for Survivors.* New York: Fiction Collective, 1975.

Bannister, Mark. *Privileged Mortals: The French Heroic Novel, 1630–1680.* Oxford: Oxford University Press, 1983.

Barnes, Julian. *Flaubert's Parrot.* New York: Alfred A. Knopf, 1985.

Baumbach, Jonathan. *Reruns.* New York: Fiction Collective, 1974.

Baumgarten, Murray. "From Realism to Expressionism: Toward a History of the Novel." *New Literary History* 6 (1975): 415–27.

Bayer, William. *Visions of Isabelle.* New York: Delacorte Press, 1976.

Bayley, John. "Character and Consciousness." *New Literary History* 5 (1974): 225–35.

Beerbohm, Max. *The Bodley Head Max Beerbohm*. Ed. David Cecil. London: Bodley Head, 1970.

Behm, Marc. *The Queen of the Night*. Boston: Houghton Mifflin, 1977.

Behn, Aphra. *Love-Letters Between a Nobleman and His Sister*, Part I. 1683. In *The Novel in Letters: Epistolary Fiction in the Early English Novel, 1678–1740*. Ed. Natascha Wurzbach. Coral Gables, Fla.: University of Miami Press, 1969, 199–282.

Bell, Gene H. "Fantasy, History, and the New Fiction." *Commonweal* 103 (5 Nov. 1976): 718–23.

Bell, Pearl K. "Coover's Revisionist Fantasy." *Commentary* 64 (October 1977): 67–69.

Bellamy, Joe David, ed. *The New Fiction: Interviews with Innovative American Writers*. Urbana, Chicago, and London: University of Illinois Press, 1974.

Berger, Morroe. *Real and Imagined Worlds: The Novel and Social Science*. Cambridge: Harvard University Press, 1977.

Bermann, Sandra. Introduction. *On the Historical Novel (Del romanzo storico)*. By Allesandro Manzoni. Trans. Sandra Bermann. Lincoln and London: University of Nebraska Press, 1984.

Betsky, Celia. *Review of The Public Burning. Commonweal* 104 (28 Oct. 1977): 693–96.

Bindrim v. Mitchell, 92 Cal. App. 3d 61, 155 Cal. Rptr. 29 (5 Med. L. Rep. 1113), *cert denied*, 100 S. Ct. 490. 1979.

Blair, William G. "Libel Lawyer Says Penthouse Ruling Aids Writers." *New York Times* 7 Nov. l982: 41.

Boccaccio, Giovanni. *Boccaccio on Poetry: Being the Preface and the Fourteenth and Fifteenth Books of Boccaccio's Genealogia Deorum Gentilium*. Trans. Charles G. Osgood. New York: Bobbs-Merrill, 1930.

Boileau. "A Discourse of Satires Arraigning Persons by Name." Augustan Reprint Society Publication 132. Los Angeles: University of California Press, 1968.

Bonetti, Kaye. "An Interview with Robert Coover." Columbia, Mo.: American Audio Prose Library (cassette), 1980.

Bradbury, Malcolm. "Modernism/Postmodernism." In *Innovation/Renovation: New Perspectives in the Humanities*. Ed. Ihab Hassan and Sally Hassan. Madison: University of Wisconsin Press, 1983. 291–310.

Bradford, Gamaliel. *Biography and the Human Heart*. Boston and New York: Houghton Mifflin, 1932.

Brooke-Rose, Christine. "Eximplosions." *Genre* 14.6 (1981): 9–21.

Brophy, Brigid. *The Adventures of God in His Search for the Black Girl.* Boston and Toronto: Little, Brown & Co., 1974.

Bryant, Jerry H. "Who? Jes Grew? Like Topsy? No, Not Like Topsy." *Nation* 222 (25 Sept. 1972): 245–247.

Buechner, Frederick. *Godric.* New York: Atheneum, 1980.

Bumpus, Jerry. "K." In *Heroes and Villains.* New York: Fiction Collective, 1986. 62–92.

Busch, Frederick. *The Mutual Friend.* New York: Harper and Row, 1978.

Cahill, Daniel J. "On E. L. Doctorow." *Fiction International* 4/5 (1975): 132–33.

———. "An Interview with Jerzy Kosinski on Blind Date." *Contemporary Literature* 19 (1978): 133–42.

Campbell, Lily B. *Shakespeare's "Histories": Mirrors of Elizabethan Policy.* San Marino, Calif.: Huntingdon Library, 1947.

Cantor, Jay. *The Death of Che Guevara.* New York: Alfred A. Knopf, 1983.

Capouya, Emile. "Epic for an Unlikely Century." *Nation* 230 (7 June 1980): 697–98.

Caramello, Charles. *Silverless Mirrors: Book, Self, and Postmodern Fiction.* Tallahassee: University Presses of Florida, 1983.

Carr, Edward Hallett. *What Is History?* London: Macmillan; New York: St. Martin's Press, 1961.

Carrard, Philippe. "Historical Narrative and Testimonial Function." Unpublished paper, 1985.

Casciato, Arthur D., and James L. W. West, III. "William Styron and *The Southampton Insurrection.*" *American Literature* 52.4 (1981): 564–77.

Charyn, Jerome. *The Franklin Scare.* New York: Arbor House, 1977.

Cixous, Helene. "The Character of 'Character.'" Trans. Keith Cohen. *New Literary History* 5 (1974): 383–402.

Clarke, John Henrik, ed. *William Styron's "Nat Turner": Ten Black Writers Respond.* Boston: Beacon Press, 1968.

Clemons, Walter. "Houdini, Meet Ferdinand." *Newsweek* 14 July 1975: 73–76.

———. "Shock Treatment." Review of *The Public Burning. Newsweek* 8 Aug. 1977: 75–76.

Clifford, James. " 'Hanging Up Looking Glasses at Odd Corners': Ethnobiographical Prospects." In *Studies in Biography.* Ed. Daniel Aaron. Cambridge and London: Harvard University Press, 1978. 41–56.

Coleridge, Samuel Taylor. Lecture 3 of "A Course of Lectures." *The Complete Works of Samuel Taylor Coleridge.* Ed. W. G. T. Shedd. New York: Harper & Bros., 1884. 4: 250.

Coles, Robert. "Arguments: The Turner Thesis." *Partisan Review* 35 (Summer 1968): 412–14.

Cook, Monte. "Who Inhabits Riverworld?" In *Philosophers Look at Science Fiction.* Ed. Nicholas D. Smith. Chicago: Nelson-Hall, 1982. 97–104.

Coover, Robert. *Charlie in the House of Rue.* Lincoln, Mass.: Penmaen Press, 1980.

————. Letter to Naomi Jacobs. 12 December 1981.

————. *The Public Burning.* New York: Viking, 1977.

Core, George. "*The Confessions of Nat Turner* and the Burden of the Past." In *The Achievement of William Styron.* Ed. Robert K. Morris and Irving Malin. Athens: University of Georgia Press, 1975, 1981. 206–22.

Corrigan v. Bobbs-Merrill, 228 N.Y. 58, 126 N.E. 260. 1920.

Couturier, Maurice, ed. *Representation and Performance in Postmodern Fiction.* Montpellier, Vt.: Delta, 1982.

Cowley, Malcolm. *A Second Flowering: Works and Days of the Lost Generation.* New York: Viking, 1973.

Craig, John. *Craig's Rules of Historical Evidence.* 1699. History and Theory: Studies in the Philosophy of History 4. 'S-Gravenhage: Mouton, 1964.

Craige, Betty Jean. *Literary Relativity: An Essay on Twentieth-Century Narrative.* Lewisburg, Pa.: Bucknell University Press, 1982.

Crittenden, Charles. "Fictional Characters and Logical Completeness." *Poetics* 11.4–6 (Dec. 1982): 331–44.

Davenport, Guy. *Eclogues: Ten Stories by Guy Davenport.* Berkeley, Calif.: North Point Press, 1981.

Davis, Lennard J. *Factual Fictions: The Origins of the English Novel.* New York: Columbia University Press, 1983.

Day, Robert Adams. *Told in Letters: Epistolary Fiction Before Richardson.* Ann Arbor: University of Michigan Press, 1966.

Defoe, Daniel. Preface. *Moll Flanders.* 1722. New York: New American Library, 1964.

————. Preface. *Robinson Crusoe.* 1719. New York: New American Library, 1960.

DeJean, Joan E. *Libertine Strategies: Freedom and the Novel in Seventeenth-Century France.* Columbus: Ohio State University Press, 1981.

Demott, Benjamin. "History & lit." *Atlantic Monthly* 240 (Nov. 1977): 98–101.

Diamond, Edwin. *The Science of Dreams.* Garden City, N. Y.: Doubleday, 1962.

Dickens, Charles. Preface to *Barnaby Rudge.* 1841. Vol. 6 of *The Works of Charles Dickens.* New York: Bigelow, Brown and Co., n.d.

Dickstein, Morris. "Black Humor and History: Fiction in the Sixties." *Partisan Review* 43 (1976): 185–211.

Doctorow, E. L. *Billy Bathgate.* New York: Random House, 1989.

——. *Drinks Before Dinner.* New York: Random House, 1978.

——. "False Documents." *American Review* 26 (1977): 215–32.

——. *Loon Lake.* New York: Random House, 1979.

——. *Ragtime.* New York: Random House, 1975.

Duffy, Maureen. "Commentary: Of Loyalty, Money, and Power." *Times Literary Supplement* 27 July 1984: 843.

Edel, Leon. *Literary Biography.* Toronto: University of Toronto Press, 1957.

Edwards, Thomas R. Review of *The Public Burning. New York Times Book Review* 14 Aug. 1977: 9, 26.

Elkin, Stanley. "Representation and Performance." In *Representation and Performance in Postmodern Fiction.* Ed. Maurice Couturier. Montpelier, Vt.: Delta, 1982. 181–91.

Elliott, George P. "Fiction and Anti-Fiction." *American Scholar* 47 (1978): 398–406.

Elliott, Robert C. *The Power of Satire: Magic, Ritual, Art.* Princeton, N. J.: Princeton University Press, 1960.

Emblidge, David. "Marching Backward into the Future: Progress as Illusion in Doctorow's Novels." *Southwest Review* 62 (1977): 397–409.

Farmer, Philip José. *The Dark Design.* New York: G. P. Putnam's Sons, 1977.

——. *The Fabulous Riverboat.* Introduction by Richard Gid Powers. Comments by author. Boston: Gregg Press, 1980. Rpt. New York: Putnam, 1971.

——. *The Magic Labyrinth.* New York: G. P. Putnam's Sons, 1980.

——. *To Your Scattered Bodies Go.* New York: G. P. Putnam's Sons, 1971.

Federman, Raymond. "Imagination as Plagiarism [an unfinished paper]." *New Literary History* 7 (1976): 563–78.

——. "Surfiction—Four Propositions in the Form of an Introduction." *Surfiction: Fiction Now . . . and Tomorrow.* Chicago: Swallow Press, 1975.

——. "What Are Experimental Novels and Why Are There So Many Left Unread?" *Genre* 14.1 (1981): 23–32.

Fielding, Henry. *Joseph Andrews.* 1742. New York: Holt, Rinehart & Winston, 1948.

———. *The Life of Mr. Jonathan Wild the Great.* 1743. Ed. David Nokes. Harmondsworth and New York: Penguin, 1982.

Fischer, David Hackett. "The Braided Narrative: Substance and Form in Social History." In *The Literature of Fact.* Ed. Angus Fletcher. New York: Columbia University Press. 1976. 109–33.

Fleishman, Avrom. *The English Historical Novel: Walter Scott to Virginia Woolf.* Baltimore: Johns Hopkins University Press, 1971.

Fletcher, Angus, ed. *The Literature of Fact.* New York: Columbia University Press, 1976.

Flippo, Chet. "An Interview with Tom Wolfe." *Rolling Stone* 21 Aug. 1980: 31–37.

Foley, Barbara. "From *U.S.A.* to *Ragtime:* Notes on the Forms of Historical Consciousness in Modern Fiction." *American Literature* 50 (1978): 85–105.

———. *Telling the Truth: The Theory and Practice of Documentary Fiction.* Ithaca: Cornell University Press, 1986.

Frazer, Sir James George. *The New Golden Bough.* Ed. Theodor H. Gaster. New York: S. G. Phillips, 1959.

Friedman, Alan. "Mumbo Jumbo." *New York Times Book Review* 6 August 1972: 1, 22.

Friedman, Melvin J. *"The Confessions of Nat Turner:* The Convergence of 'Nonfiction Novel' and 'Meditation on History.'" *Journal of Popular Culture* 1 (Fall 1967): 166–74.

Friedman, Melvin J., and Irving Malin, eds. *William Styron's The Confessions of Nat Turner: A Critical Handbook.* Belmont, Calif.: Wadsworth, 1970.

Frye, Northrop. *Anatomy of Criticism.* Princeton, N.J.: Princeton University Press, 1957.

Gardiner, Judith Kegan. "Aphra Behn: Sexuality and Self-Respect." *Women's Studies* 7 (1980): 67–78.

Gaudin, Colette. "Marguerite Yourcenar's Prefaces: Genesis as Self-Effacement." *Studies in Twentieth-Century Literature* 10.1 (Fall 1985): 31–55.

Gavin, Thomas. *Kingkill.* New York: Random House, 1977.

Gertz v. Robert Welch, 418 U.S. 323. 1974.

Gillie, Christopher. *Character in English Literature.* London: Chatto & Windus, 1967.

Gittings, Robert. *The Nature of Biography.* Seattle: University of Washington Press, 1978.

Goreau, Angeline. *Reconstructing Aphra: A Social Biography of Aphra Behn*. Garden City, N. Y.: Dial Press, 1980.

————. *The Whole Duty of a Woman: Female Writers in Seventeenth Century England*. Garden City, N. Y.: Dial Press, 1984.

Gray, Paul. "Uncle Sam Takes on the Phantom." *Time* 8 Aug. 1977: 70–71.

Grayson, Richard. *With Hitler in New York and Other Stories*. New York: Taplinger, 1979.

Guerard, Albert J. "Notes on the Rhetoric of Anti-Realist Fiction." *TriQuarterly* 30 (1966): 3–50.

Guetti, Barbara Jones. "'Travesty' and 'Usurpation' in Mme de Lafayette's Historical Fiction." *Yale French Studies* 69 (1985): 211–21.

Gussow, Mel. "Novelist Syncopates History in 'Ragtime.'" *New York Times* 11 July 1975: 12.

Hardwick, Elizabeth. *Sleepless Nights*. New York: Random House, 1980.

Harpham, Geoffrey Galt. "E. L. Doctorow and the Technology of Narrative." *PMLA* 100.1 (Jan. 1985): 81–95.

Harte, Walter. "An Essay on Satire, Particularly on the Dunciad." 1730. Augustan Reprint Society Publication 132. Los Angeles: University of California Press, 1968.

Harvey, W. J. *Character and the Novel*. Ithaca: Cornell University Press, 1965.

Hassan, Ihab. *The Dismemberment of Orpheus*. New York: Oxford University Press, 1971.

————, and Sally Hassan, eds. *Innovation/Renovation: New Perspectives in the Humanities*. Madison: University of Wisconsin Press, 1983.

————. *Paracriticisms: Seven Speculations of the Times*. Urbana, Chicago, and London: University of Illinois Press, 1975.

————. "Wars of Desire, Politics of the Word." In *Representation and Performance in Postmodern Fiction*. Ed. Maurice Couturier. Montpelier, Vt.: Delta, 1982. 47–55.

Hayman, David. *Re-Forming the Narrative: Toward a Mechanics of Modernist Fiction*. Ithaca: Cornell University Press, 1987.

Higginson, Thomas Wentworth. "Nat Turner's Insurrection." *Atlantic Monthly* August 1861: 173–87.

Hoffman, Roy. Review of *Blood and Guts in High School*, by Kathy Acker. *New York Times Book Review* 23 Dec. 1984: 16.

Holden, Alan. "Styron's Slave: *The Confessions of Nat Turner*." *South Atlantic Quarterly* 68 (Spring 1969): 167–80.

Honan, Park. "The Theory of Biography." *Novel* 13 (Fall 1979): 109–20.

Hornung, Alfred. "Recollection and Imagination in Postmodern Fiction." In *Representation and Performance in Postmodern Fiction.* Ed. Maurice Couturier. Montpelier, Vt.: Delta, 1982. 57–70.

Howe, Fanny. *Holy Smoke.* New York: Fiction Collective, 1979.

James, Henry. *The Art of the Novel.* 1907. New York: Charles Scribner's Sons, 1934.

Judovitz, Ealia. "The Aesthetics of Implausibility": *La Princesse de Clèves. Modern Language Notes* 99.5 (1984): 1037–56.

Kaiser, Ernest. "The Failure of William Styron." In *William Styron's "Nat Turner": Ten Black Writers Respond.* Ed. John Henrik Clarke. Boston: Beacon Press, 1968. 52–65.

Kaplan, Justin. "The 'Real Life.'" In *Studies in Biography.* Ed. Daniel Aaron. Cambridge and London: Harvard University Press, 1978. 1–8.

Kaufman, Irving R. "The Media and Juries." *New York Times* 4 Nov. 1982: 27.

Kelly, Gary. "'Intrigue' and 'Gallantry': The Seventeenth-Century French *Nouvelle* and the 'Novels' of Aphra Behn." *Revue de Litterature Comparee* 218.2 (1981): 184–94.

Kelsey, Carl. "The American Intervention in Haiti and the Dominican Republic." *Annals of the American Academy of Political and Social Science* 100 (1922): 113–202.

Kendall, Paul Murray. *The Art of Biography.* New York: Norton, 1965.

Keneally, Thomas. *Gossip from the Forest.* New York and London: Harcourt Brace Jovanovich, 1975.

Kernan, Alvin B. *The Plot of Satire.* New Haven and London: Yale University Press, 1965.

Klinkowitz, Jerome. "Betrayed by Jerzy Kosinski." In *Literary Subversions: New American Fiction and the Practice of Criticism.* Carbondale and Edwardsville: Southern Illinois University Press, 1985. 127–48.

_____."An Interview with Jerzy Kosinski." In *The New Fiction.* Ed. Joe David Bellamy. Urbana, Chicago, and London: University of Illinois Press, 1974. 142–68.

_____. *The Life of Fiction.* Urbana, Chicago, and London: University of Illinois Press, 1977.

Knorr, Walter L. "Doctorow and Kleist: 'Kohlhaas' in *Ragtime." Modern Fiction Studies* 22 (1976): 224–27.

Kosinski, Jerzy. "An Interview with Jerzy Kosinski on *Blind Date*." Interview by Daniel J. Cahill. *Contemporary Literature* 19 (1978): 133–42.

Kostelanetz, Richard. "New Fiction in America." In *Surfiction: Fiction Now . . . and Tomorrow*. Ed. Raymond Federman. Chicago: Swallow Press, 1975. 85–100.

Kramer, Hilton. "Political Romance." *Commentary* 60 (Oct. 1975): 76–80.

La Fayette, Marie Madeleine de. *La Princesse de Clèves*. 1679.

Langdale, Cheri Davis. "Aphra Behn and Sexual Politics: A Dramatist's Discourse with Her Audience." In *Drama, Sex and Politics*. Ed. James Redmond. Cambridge: Cambridge University Press, 1985. 109–28.

Lash, Joseph. *Eleanor and Franklin*. New York: Norton, 1971.

Lawhorne, Clifton O. *Defamation and Public Officials: The Evolving Law of Libel*. Carbondale and Edwardsville: Southern Illinois University Press, 1971.

Le Clair, Thomas. Review of *The Public Burning*. *New Republic* 17 Sept. 1977: 37–38.

Lee, L. L. "What's New in Fiction, If It's Possible?" *Style* 9 (1975): 335–52.

Lee, Sophia. *The Recess or A Tale of Other Times*. 1783–85. 3 vols. New York: Arno Press—McGrath Publishing Co., 1972.

Lerman, Rhoda. *Eleanor: A Novel*. New York: Holt, Rinehart & Winston, 1979.

———. "The Novel as Alembic." Unpublished paper, [1980].

Letson, Russell. "The Faces of a Thousand Heroes: Philip Jose Farmer." *Science Fiction Studies* 4 (1977): 35–41.

———. "The Worlds of Philip Jose Farmer." *Extrapolation* 18 (1977): 124–30.

Lewis, R. W. B., and C. Van Woodward. "Slavery in the First Person: Interview with William Styron." *Yale Alumni Magazine* Nov. 1967: 33–39.

Lindquist, Carol A. "Aphra Behn and the First Epistolary Novel in English." *Publications of the Arkansas Philological Association* 3.2 (Winter 1976): 29–33.

Lubarsky, Jared. "History and the Forms of Fiction: An Interview with E. L. Doctorow." *Eigo Seinen* 124 (1978): 150–52.

Lucianus Samotensis. *The Dialogues of Lucian*. Trans. William Tooke. Ed. and introduction by N. N. Penzer. London: Navarre Society, n.d.

Lukàcs, Georg. *The Historical Novel*. 1937. Trans. Hannah Mitchell and Stanley Mitchell. Rpt. London: Merlin Press, 1962. Atlantic Highlands, N. J.: Humanities Press, 1978.

Lyons, John D. "Narrative, Interpretation and Paradox: *La Princesse de Clèves.*" *Romanic Review* 72.4 (1981): 383–400.

Lyotard, Jean-Francois. "Answering the Question: What is Postmodernism?" Trans. Regis Durand. In *Innovation/Renovation: New Perspectives in the Humanities.* Ed. Ihab Hassan and Sally Hassan. Madison: University of Wisconsin Press, 1983. 329–41.

Mabillon, Jean. *De Re Diplomatica.* Paris: L. Billaine, 1681.

Mackey, Nathaniel. "Ishmael Reed and the Black Aesthetic." *CLA Journal* 21 (1978): 355–66.

Mailer, Norman. *The Armies of the Night: History as a Novel, the Novel as History.* New York: New American Library, 1968.

Malin, Irving. "Nat's Confessions." *Denver Quarterly* 2.4 (Winter 1968): 92–96.

Maloff, Saul. "History Used and Abused." *New York Times Book Review* 20 May 1979: 14, 42.

Manzoni, Allesandro. *On the Historical Novel. (Del romanzo storico.)* Trans. and introduction Sandra Bermann. Lincoln and London: University of Nebraska Press, 1984.

Marquis, Donald. *In Search of Buddy Bolden: First Man of Jazz.* Baton Rouge and London: Louisiana State University Press, 1978.

Martin, Jay. "The Deaths of the Novelists, the Lives of the Biographers." *Humanities in Society* 3.4 (1980): 361–75.

Martin, Richard. "Clio Bemused: The Uses of History in Contemporary American Fiction." *Sub-Stance* 27 (1980): 13–24.

Mayer, Robert. *Superfolks.* New York: Dial Press, 1977.

McCaffery, Larry. "Literary Disruptions: Fiction in a 'Post-Contemporary' Age." *Boundary 2* 5.1 (Fall 1976): 137–50.

———. "The Magic of Fiction-Making." *Fiction International* 4/5 (1975): 147–53.

———. "Robert Coover on His Own and Other Fictions: An Interview." *Genre* 14.1 (Spring 1981): 45–63.

McDowell, Edwin. "Viking Giving Writers Free Liability Insurance." *New York Times* 21 Jan. 1982, sec. 3: 17.

———. "Changes Made in Novel After Suit is Threatened." *New York Times* 10 May 1981: 44.

———. "State Court Dismisses Libel Suit Over Novel." *New York Times* 16 Dec. 1982, sec. 3: 20.

McGill, Douglas C. "Writer's Plight: A Libel Suit." *New York Times* 19 July 1981, sec. 11: 1.

McKeon, Michael. "The Origins of the English Novel." *Modern Philology* 82.1 (Aug. 1984): 76–86.

――――. *The Origins of the English Novel, 1600–1740*. Baltimore: Johns Hopkins University Press, 1987.

Melville, Herman. *Israel Potter: His Fifty Years of Exile*. 1855. London, Bombay, and Sydney: Constable and Company, 1923.

Mendelson, Edward. "Authorized Biography and Its Discontents." In *Studies in Biography*. Ed. Daniel Aaron. Cambridge and London: Harvard University Press, 1978. 9–26.

Mesnard, Christine. "De l'histoire à la géologie: Le Temps yourcenarian au passé." *Licorne* 7 (1983): 187–95.

Miller, J. Hillis. "Narrative and History." *English Literary History* 41 (1974): 455–73.

Mish, Charles. "English Short Fiction in the Seventeenth Century." *Studies in Short Fiction* 6 (1969): 233–330.

Mitgang, Herbert. "Gwen Davis to Appeal First-Amendment Libel Case." *New York Times* 15 Aug. 1979, sec. 3: 15.

――――. "Publishers Expect Libel Decisions to Have 'Chilling' Repercussions." *New York Times* 9 Dec. l979: 30.

Molinaro, Ursule. *The Autobiography of Cassandra, Princess and Prophetess of Troy*. Lynnville, Tenn.: Archer Editions Press, 1979.

Moore, Ann M. "Temporal Structure and Reader Response in *La Princesse de Clèves*." *French Review* 56.4 (Mar. 1983): 563–71.

Morgan, Fidelis. *A Woman of No Character: An Autobiography of Mrs. Manley*. London and Boston: Faber & Faber, 1986.

Morgan, Speer. *Belle Starr*. Boston: Little, Brown & Co., 1979.

――――. Interview with Kaye Bonetti. Columbia, Mo.: American Audio Prose Library (cassette), 1981.

Morris, Clarence. *Modern Defamation Law*. Philadelphia: American Law Institute—American Bar Association Committee on Continuing Professional Education, 1978.

Morris, Robert K., and Irving Malin, eds. *The Achievement of William Styron: Revised Edition*. Athens: University of Georgia Press, 1975, 1981.

Myers, John Myers. *Silverlock*. 1949. Dutton. New York: Ace, 1984.

Mylne, Vivienne. "Changing Attitudes Towards Truth in Fiction." *Renaissance and Modern Studies* 7 (1963): 53–77.

Nashe, Thomas. *The Unfortunate Traveller*. 1594. In *Elizabethan Fiction*. Ed. Robert Paul Ashley and Edwin M. Moseley. New York: Holt, Rinehart and Winston, 1953. 199–308.

Nelson, William. *Fact or Fiction: The Dilemma of the Renaissance Story-teller.* Cambridge: Harvard University Press, 1973.

Newman, Charles. *The Post-Modern Aura: The Act of Fiction in an Age of Inflation.* Evanston, Ill.: Northwestern University Press, 1985.

*The New York Times, Inc., v. Sullivan.* 376 U.S. 254, 281. 1964.

Nichols, Robert. *Daily Lives in Nghsi-Altai.* New York: New Directions, 1977–79. *Book I: Arrival* (1977). *Book II: Garh City* (1978). *Book III: The Harditts in Sawna* (1979). *Book IV: Exile* (1979).

Nin, Anais. *The Novel of the Future.* New York: Macmillan; London: Collier-Macmillan, 1968.

Nizer, Louis. *The Implosion Conspiracy.* Garden City, N.Y.: Doubleday, 1973. Greenwich, Conn.: Fawcett Crest, 1974.

Noel, Daniel C. "Tales of Fictive Power: Dreaming and Imagination in Ronald Sukenick's Postmodern Fiction." *Boundary 2* 5 (1976): 117–35.

O'Brien, John. "An Interview with Ishmael Reed." In *The New Fiction.* Ed. Joe David Bellamy. Urbana, Chicago, and London: University of Illinois Press, 1974. 130–41.

Ondaatje, Michael. *The Collected Works of Billy the Kid: Left-Handed Poems.* Toronto: Anansi, 1970.

———. *Coming Through Slaughter.* New York: Norton, 1976.

Pace, Eric. "Authors' Groups Criticize Suit By Doubleday Against Writer." *New York Times* 1 March 1980: 19.

———. "New Dispute is Stirred by Doubleday-Davis Suit." *New York Times* 26 February 1980, sec. 3: 9.

———. "Publishing Leader Sees Problems in Davis Case." *New York Times* 27 February 1980, sec. 3: 19.

Palmer, Richard. "Postmodernity and Hermeneutics." *Boundary 2* 5 (1976): 363–93.

Perez, Gilbert. "Narrative Voices." *Hudson Review* 30 (1977–78): 607–20.

Plimpton, George. "A Shared Ordeal: Interview with William Styron." In *William Styron's The Confessions of Nat Turner: A Critical Handbook.* Ed. Melvin J. Friedman and Irving Malin. Belmont, Cal: Wadsworth, 1970. 36–42.

Podhoretz, Norman. "Uncle Sam and the Phantom." *Saturday Review* 17 Sept. 1977: 27–28, 34.

Poignault, Remy. "Alchimie verbale dans *Mémoires d'Hadrien* de Marguerite Yourcenar." *Bulletin de L'Association Guillaume Budé* 3 (1984): 295–321.

Ponicsan, Darryl. *Tom Mix Died for Your Sins*. New York: Delacorte Press, 1975.

Powers, Richard. *Three Farmers on Their Way to a Dance*. New York: McGraw-Hill, 1987. Rpt. New York: William Morrow, 1985.

Powers, Richard Gid. Introduction. *The Fabulous Riverboat*. By Philip Jose Farmer. New York: G. P. Putnam's Son's, 1971. v-xvi.

Prose, Francine. *Marie Laveau*. New York: G. P. Putnam's Sons, 1977.

Prosser, William L. *Handbook of the Law of Torts*. 4th ed. St. Paul, Minn.: West Publishing Co., 1971.

Quaintance, Richard E. "French Sources of the Restoration 'Imperfect Enjoyment' Poem." *Philological Quarterly* 42 (1963): 190–99.

Redgrove, H. Stanley. *Alchemy, Ancient and Modern*. Chicago: Ares, 1980.

Redmond, James, ed. *Drama, Sex and Politics*. Cambridge: Cambridge University Press, 1985.

Reed, Ishmael. *Flight to Canada*. New York: Random House, 1976.

———. *Mumbo Jumbo*. Garden City, N. Y.: Doubleday, 1972.

———. *Shrovetide in Old New Orleans*. Garden City, N. Y.: Doubleday, 1978.

Robertson, Mary F. "Hystery, Herstory, History: 'Imagining the Real' in Thomas's *The White Hotel*." *Contemporary Literature* 25.4 (1984): 452–77.

Rogers, Pat. *Hacks and Dunces: Pope, Swift and Grub Street*. London and New York: Methuen, 1980.

Rogers, Robert W. *The Major Satires of Alexander Pope*. Illinois Studies in Language and Literature 40. Urbana: University of Illinois Press, 1955.

Rose, Phyllis. "Biography as Fiction." *Tri-Quarterly* 55.3 (Fall 1982): 111–24.

Rosenberg, Brian. "George Eliot and the Victorian 'Historical Imagination.'" *Victorian Newsletter* 61 (Spring 1982): 1–5.

Roth, Philip. *The Ghost Writer*. New York: Farrar, Straus and Giroux, 1979.

Rottensteiner, Franz. "Playing Around With Creation: Philip José Farmer." *Science Fiction Studies* 1 (Fall 1973): 94–98.

Rubin, Louis D., Jr. "William Styron and Human Bondage: *The Confessions of Nat Turner*." *Hollins Critic* (Dec. 1967): 1–12.

Ryf, Robert S. "Character and Imagination in the Experimental Novel." *Modern Fiction Studies* 20 (1974–75): 317–27.

Sack, Robert D. *Libel, Slander, and Related Problems*. New York: Practicing Law Institute, 1980.

Sale, Roger. "From Ragtime to Riches." *New York Review of Books* 7 Aug. 1975: 21–22.

Salzman, Paul. *English Prose Fiction, 1558–1700: A Critical History*. New York: Oxford University Press, 1985.

Schneir, Walter, and Miriam Schneir. *Invitation to an Inquest: Reopening the Rosenberg "Atom Spy" Case*. Garden City, N. Y.: Doubleday, 1965; Baltimore: Penguin Books, 1973.

Scobie, Stephen. "Coming Through Slaughter: Fictional Magnets and Spider's Webbs." *Essays on Canadian Writing* 12 (Fall 1978): 5–23.

Shattuck, Roger. *The Banquet Years: The Origins of the Avant Garde in France, 1885 to World War I*. 1955. Rev. ed. New York: Vintage, 1968.

Shaw, Harry E. *The Forms of Historical Fiction: Sir Walter Scott and His Successors*. Ithaca and London: Cornell University Press, 1983.

Sheed, Wilfrid. "The Slave Who Became a Man." *New York Times* 8 Oct. 1967: 1–3.

Siegler, Alan. *Comrades*. New York: St. Martin's Press, 1976.

Silver, Isidore. "Libel, The 'Higher Truths' of Art, and the First Amendment." *University of Pennsylvania Law Review* 126.5 (1978): 1065–98.

Smollett, Tobias. Preface to *The Adventures of Roderick Random*. 1748. New York: New American Library, 1964.

Sokolov, Raymond A. "Into the Mind of Nat Turner." *Newsweek* 16 Oct. 1967: 65–69.

Solecki, Sam. "Dementia Praecox, Paranoid Type." *Canadian Forum* 56 (Dec.–June 1976–77): 46–47.

———. "Making and Destroying: Michael Ondaatje's *Coming Through Slaughter* and Extremist Art." *Essays on Canadian Writing* 12 (Fall 1978): 24–47.

Sorrentino, Gilbert. *Flawless Play Restored: The Masque of Fungo*. Los Angeles: Black Sparrow Press, 1974.

Spanos, William V. *Repetitions: The Postmodern Occasion in Literature and Culture*. Baton Rouge and London: Louisiana State University Press, 1987.

Spencer, Sharon. *Space, Time and Structure in the Modern Novel*. New York: New York University Press, 1971.

Spengemann, William C. "The Earliest American Novel: Aphra Behn's *Oroonoko*." *Nineteenth Century Fiction* 38.4 (1984): 381–414.

222
Works Cited

Stade, George. "Ragtime." *New York Times Book Review* 6 July 1975: 1–2.

Starr, William T. "Historical Figures in French Literature: A Brief Bibliography." *French Literature Series* 8 (1981): 130–46.

Stegner, Wallace. *The Spectator Bird.* Garden City, N. Y.: Doubleday, 1976.

Stein, Gertrude. *The Autobiography of Alice B. Toklas.* New York: Vintage, 1933.

Steinberg, Cobbett. "History and the Novel: Doctorow's *Ragtime.*" *Denver Quarterly* 10.4 (1976): 125–30.

Stephanson, Raymond. "The Epistemological Challenge of Nashe's *Unfortunate Traveller.*" *Studies in English Literature* 23.1 (1983): 21–36.

Stevick, Philip. "Lies, Fictions, and Mock-Facts." *Western Humanities Review* 30 (1976): 1–12.

Stoehr, Taylor. "Mapping Utopia in Nghsi-Altai." *Chronicle of Higher Education* 17 (16 Oct. 1978): R17.

Stoppard, Tom. Interview conducted by Nancy Shields Hardin. *Contemporary Literature* 22.2 (Spring 1981): 153–66.

Strine, Mary S. "*The Confessions of Nat Turner:* Styron's 'Meditation on History' as Rhetorical Act." In *The Achievement of William Styron: Revised Edition.* Ed. Robert K. Morris and Irving Malin. Athens: University of Georgia Press, 1975, 1981. 237–68.

Strout, Cushing. "Historicizing Fiction and Fictionalizing History: The Case of E. L. Doctorow." *Prospects* 5 (1980): 423–37.

"Study Discounts Fears About Libel Decisions." *New York Times* 27 Sept. 1981: 12.

Styron, William. *The Confessions of Nat Turner.* 1967. New York: Signet, 1968.

———. *Sophie's Choice.* New York: Random House, 1979.

———. "This Quiet Dust." *Harper's* April 1965: 135–46.

———. "Truth and Nat Turner: An Exchange: William Styron Replies." *Nation* 206 (22 Apr. 1968): 544–47.

Sukenick, Ronald. "The Death of the Novel." In *The Death of the Novel and Other Stories.* New York: Dial Press, 1969. 41–102.

———. "Fiction in the Seventies: Ten Digressions on Ten Digressions." *Studies in American Fiction* 5 (1977): 99–108.

———. "The New Tradition in Fiction." In *Surfiction: Fiction Now . . . and Tomorrow.* Ed. Raymond Federman. Chicago: Swallow Press, 1975. 35–45.

———. *98.6.* New York: Fiction Collective, 1975.

———. "Thirteen Digressions." *Partisan Review* 43 (1976): 90–101.

_____. "Twelve Digressions Toward a Study of Composition." *New Literary History* 6 (1974–1975): 429–37.

_____. *UP*. New York: Dial Press, 1968.

_____. "Upward and Juanward: The Possible Dream." *Village Voice* 25 Jan. 1973: 30.

Suvin, Darko. *Metamorphoses of Science Fiction*. New Haven and London: Yale University Press, 1979.

Swanson, Roy Arthur. "William Styron's Clown Show." In *William Styron's The Confessions of Nat Turner: A Critical Handbook*. Ed. Melvin J. Friedman and Irving Malin. Belmont, Calif.: Wadsworth, 1970. 149–64.

Taliaferro, Frances. "History Enhanced." *Harpers* 258 June 1979: 94–98.

Tanner, Tony. "Frames and Sentences." In *Representation and Performance in Postmodern Fiction*. Ed. Maurice Couturier. Montpellier, Vt.: Delta, 1982. 21–31.

Thackeray, William Makepeace. *The History of Henry Esmond, Esquire*. 1852. New York: Modern Library, n.d.

Thelwell, Michael. *The Harder They Come*. New York: Grove Press, 1980.

_____. "Arguments: The Turner Thesis." *Partisan Review* 35 (Summer 1968): 403–12.

Thiher, Alan. *Words in Reflection: Modern Language Theory and Postmodern Fiction*. Chicago: University of Chicago Press, 1984.

Tobin, Pat. "From Doctorow to Coover: Modernist History and Postmodernist Comedy." Unpublished paper, 1985.

Tonelli, Franco. "Machiavelli's *Mandragola* and the Signs of Power." In *Drama, Sex and Politics*. Ed. James Redmond. Cambridge: Cambridge University Press, 1985. 35–54.

Turner, Joseph W. "The Kinds of Historical Fiction: An Essay in Definition and Methodology." *Genre* 12 (Fall 1979): 333–55.

Tweet, Ronald D. "Philip Jose Farmer, 1918– ." In *Science Fiction Writers: Critical Studies of the Major Authors from the Early Nineteenth Century to the Present Day*. Ed. Everett Franklin Bleiler. New York: Scribner's, 1982. 369–75.

Uya, Okon E. "Race, Ideology and Scholarship in the United States: William Styron's *Nat Turner* and Its Critics." *American Studies International* 15.2 (Winter 1976): 63–81.

Vance, Jane Gentry. "Mary Lee Settle's *The Beulah Quintet*: History Interpreted, History Created." *Southern Literary Journal* 17.1 (Fall 1984): 40–53.

Vonnegut, Kurt, Jr. *Mother Night*. New York: Avon, 1967.

Watkins, Floyd C. "*The Confessions of Nat Turner:* History and Imagination." In *In Time and Place: Some Origins of American Fiction*. Athens: University of Georgia Press, 1977. 51–70.

Watson-Williams, Helen. "Hadrian's Story Recalled." *Modern Fiction Studies* 23.2 (Oct. 1984): 35–48.

Weber, Ronald. *The Literature of Fact: Literary Nonfiction in American Writing*. Athens: Ohio University Press, 1980.

Weimann, Robert. "*Fabula* and *Historica*: The Crisis of the 'Universall Consideration' in *The Unfortunate Traveller*." *Representations* 8 (Fall 1984): 14–29.

Weinstein, Mark A. "The Creative Imagination in Fiction and History." *Genre* 9 (1976): 263–77.

West, Paul. "Sheer Fiction: Mind and the Fabulist's Mirage." *New Literary History* 7 (1975–76): 549–61.

White, Curtis. "A Literature in Opposition: Reconstructing the Future, Part I." *American Book Review* 9.2 (Mar.–Apr. 1987): 3–4.

White, Edmund. "A Fantasia on Black Suffering." *Nation* 18 Sept. 1976: 247–49.

White, Hayden. *Metahistory: The Historical Imagination in Nineteenth Century Europe*. Baltimore: Johns Hopkins University Press, 1973.

――――. *Tropics of Discourse: Essays in Cultural Criticism*. Baltimore and London: Johns Hopkins University Press, 1978.

――――. "The Value of Narrativity in the Representation of Reality." *Critical Inquiry* 7 (1980): 5–27.

White, John. "The Novelist as Historian: William Styron and American Negro Slavery." *Journal of American Studies* 4 (Feb. 1970): 233–45.

Wilde, Alan. *Horizons of Assent: Modernism, Postmodernism, and the Ironic Imagination*. Baltimore and London: Johns Hopkins University Press, 1981.

Wilder, Thornton. *The Ides of March*. New York and London: Harper & Brothers, 1948.

Witemeyer, Hugh. "George Eliot's *Romola* and Bulwer Lytton's *Rienzi*." *Studies in the Novel* 15.1 (Spring 1983): 62–73.

Witten, Mark. "Billy, Buddy, and Michael." *Books in Canada* 9 (June–July 1977): 9–13.

Woolf, Virginia. "The Art of Biography," and "The New Biography." In *Collected Essays*. Vol. 4. New York: Harcourt, Brace & World, 1967. 221–28, 229–35.

Wright, Thomas F. Introduction. *Rhetoric and the Pursuit of Truth*:

*Language Change in the Seventeenth and Eighteenth Centuries*. Los Angeles: William Andrews Clark Memorial Library, University of California, 1985.

Young-Bruehl, Elisabeth. "The Writing of Biography." *Partisan Review* 5.3 (1983): 413–27.

Yourcenar, Marguerite. *Mémoires d'Hadrien*. Paris: Librairie Plon, 1958.

Zavarzadeh, Mas'ud. *The Mythopoeic Reality: The Postwar American Nonfiction Novel*. Urbana, Chicago, and London: University of Illinois Press, 1976.

# Index

*Abba Abba* (Burgess), xiv
Abbott, Keith, xviii, 132
Absolute privilege, 164
Accuracy: in biography, 25–
  26; and cyclical view of
  history, 3; in depictions of historical figures, xvii, 16; in
  fiction biography, 33, 42; in
  fiction history, 69; in
  historical novel, 70–71; and
  mimetic illusion, 19–20; in
  nonfiction novel, xv-xvi; in
  seventeenth-century fiction,
  6, 8. *See also* Fact-fiction
  mix; Facts; Objectivity;
  Truth
Acker, Kathy, 138–147; *The
  Adult Life of Toulouse Lautrec*,
  139–142, 145; *Don Quixote*,
  140–146
Actual malice, 161, 165
*The Adult Life of Toulouse Lautrec*
  (Acker), 139–142, 145
"The Adventures of God in
  Search of the Black Girl" (Brophy), 109

*The Adventures of Robinson
  Crusoe* (Defoe), 15
*Agnes de Castro* (Behn), 11
Alchemy, 47–48, 51
Allegory, 6–7, 14, 106, 109–
  111, 133–134
Allusion, 201–202
Alternative histories, 113
Alvarez, Santiago: as fictional
  character, 119, 121
Anachronism: xx, 69, 74–75,
  103; in *Flight to Canada*, 99–
  101; in *Mumbo Jumbo*, 94, 96–
  98; in *Ragtime*, 86–87
Anderson, Poul, 112
Antihistory. *See* Fiction history
Apple, Max, 137
Aptheker, Herbert, 36
Aristotle, 2
*Armies of the Night* (Mailer), xv
*Artamène, ou Le Grand Cyrus*
  (Scudéry), 7
Aulnoy, Marie-Catherine Ju-
  melle de Berneville, comtesse
  d', 8
Autobiography, 9, 10

NAOMI JACOBS is Associate Professor of English at the University of Maine, where she teaches British and American fiction. In addition to her work on history and fiction, she has published essays on pedagogy, utopian literature, and the Brontë sisters. Her current project is a book on gender and narrative technique in the works of the Brontës.